Range War

Books by J.L. Crafts

Will Toal Novels
RailRoaded
Silver City Reckoning
Clear Cut Justice
Range War

Coming Soon!
Will Toal Novels
Tahoe Destiny
Break Out

**For more information
visit:** www.SpeakingVolumes.us

Range War

J.L. Crafts

SPEAKING VOLUMES, LLC
NAPLES, FLORIDA
2024

Range War

Copyright © 2024 by J.L. Crafts

All rights reserved. No part of this book may be reproduced or transmitted in any form or by any means without written permission.

ISBN 979-8-89022-191-9

This book and all those in this series are
dedicated to William Jeffrey Crafts
October 28, 2003 to December 2, 2020.

Discerning readers of western history will undoubtedly find the story within somewhat familiar. I freely acknowledge the circumstances and many of the events in this episode of the Will Toal saga were patterned after those which transpired during the Johnson County, Wyoming, Range War in the 1880's. Even the most unappealing events described herein did take place. The Range War to which I refer was not one of the high points of western lore.

Nevertheless, while I have lifted and moved those events and individuals from Wyoming to a setting in Nevada, the story is mine and pure fiction. For further delineation of what is historical and what is not, please refer to my Fact From Fiction section at the back of the book.

J.L. Crafts

Open Range:

"...all unenclosed land outside of cities and towns upon which cattle, sheep or other domestic animals by custom, license, lease, or permit are grazed or permitted to roam."

Nevada Statute, NRS 568.355 (1983)

Chapter One

Spring 1878
Toal Ranch—Jack's Valley, Nevada

The noon sky was tall. Not a cloud to be seen. The unlimited blue stretched from horizon to horizon. The winds normally racing down the upright wall of the Sierra Mountains at the border of Will Toal's spread were calm today. Only a light breeze strummed the new growth grasslands back and forth as if strings on a guitar. He could almost hear the movement of the waist-high verdant green threads. It was a kind of music for him. Those grasses fed his herd of steers. The sale of those steers fed his family. It was a good song.

Will hesitated, stood for a moment, and looked over the top of his ranch house. The gray granite walls of the Sierras soared just off the border of his property. Snow caps of the purest white covered the crests. That snow was a good sign. It had been a while since the snowpack had been so thick. Will found himself looking up at the mountains daily. They were more than a landmark. They were the foundation of his immediate world. The stone walls created a barrier, a mighty palisade on one side of his ranch. Weather came from over their peaks. Seeing dark clouds as they floated over the mountain tops, one could almost tell when a storm would hit. The snow melt would supply a flow of water here below. It was if life could be predicted with a look at the Sierras.

Will moved up to the house and under the ramada. He dropped heavily onto a rocker he had made himself. The covered porch faced east, away from the normal onslaught of winds that crusaded down the cold heights of the Sierras. Those winds invariably headed east sucked by the hot expanse of the desert. The winds were relentless, the only drawback to this spot he called home.

His simple four-room house provided the best windbreak on the flat expanse of his three thousand deeded acres. He had originally intended to travel to California and ranch there. But he stopped here along with his friends and experienced cowhands, Raul Medina, and his son Juan. They had come from the baked plains of New Mexico and stopped here in what the locals called Jack's Valley. They stopped because they had never seen grasses so lush. The snowpack of the Sierras provided a steady yearlong melt, filling the Carson River and hundreds of unnamed brooks and creeks lining his grazing land like veins in a human. Those paths of water crossed his grasses in all manner of direction and size. The snowmelt succored the pastures just like blood to the body.

That was, except the last couple of years. The snowpack had been light two years ago and almost non-existent a year prior. It left everything east of the Sierras in a severe drought last summer. The lack of water had been tough on the herds all through Nevada. Some ranchers lost as much as forty percent of their stock. The Carson River had dried up. The creeks and watery veins on his property became dust. Will had convinced his fellow ranchers here in the south of Carson Valley to move to his second ranch higher in the Sierras along the Truckee River. While the flow out of the Truckee was far below normal, it kept the combined herds alive. The move proved to be a good one. The members of the Carson Valley Cattlemen's Association survived with only a nominal loss of stock. Thankfully, this winter saw a heavy snowfall. The Carson and Will's creeks had returned to normal. Maybe he had been lucky. But luck usually followed good decisions like a brand-new foal to a mare. It just happened as a consequence rather than intention.

But the ranches to the north of Reno had not fared as well. The ranchers in the upper reaches of Nevada turned their herds out on open ranges, public land upon which grazing claims had been filed. North of Reno, the open spaces were more barren, harder for cattle to find forage. Even though the snow melt was better this year, the ranchers on the north range were still having trouble replenishing the losses from the last two years. Will was lucky to be here. That luck just followed a good decision as to where he had decided to set up his homestead.

"Aren't you supposed to be working?"

The voice came from inside the front door to the home. It was his wife, Beth.

"Thought I'd take a break 'cause I was up most of the night working the heifers. Several needed help calving and I'm feeling a bit slow today."

"Must be nice to be the honcho. I guess you can take a break any time you feel *slow*." Beth exited the door with a towel between her hands and a large grin on her face.

Will could hear the good-natured sarcasm. The two of them did this regularly. He usually lost the battle of words in their frisky banter. Beth was much better at it. But he loved to try and throw her off guard. Tired as he was, he decided to play along. He reached his hands up behind his neck, lacing his fingers together in an exaggerated posture of repose.

"I just thought I'd come by and see if I might convince my bride to hunker down for some love and affection."

"In the middle of the day?"

"It's afternoon."

"You men are all alike. A one-track mind."

"Actually, we have more than one, but not much more. We are just like a simple two-track wagon road headed forward on the fertile plains of life."

"While your poetry is becoming mildly better, it is still short of sweeping me off my feet. Simple wagon my foot. I know what one of your tracks might be, it's the base one that leads to reproduction. What's the second?"

"Food, then love and affection. Men are simple to understand."

"I'll agree that men are simple, alright. Then, am I to understand I rank somewhere behind food?"

"That's most men. I would personally rank love and affection far ahead of food."

"Your wit is definitely becoming quicker. I suspect that answer came on the fly. I cannot imagine you had planned this conversation out. You male Neanderthals usually just barge in dragging your knuckles looking for what you call 'love and affection'."

"You know, a man goes out of his way to express his deep-felt feelings and is met with continual comparison to cave men."

"Now I'm even more impressed. You apparently know what a Neanderthal is. I'm shocked." Beth shot this last barb with a wide grin.

"Come here." Will opened his arms in an expansive invitation to sit on his lap.

"Before I put myself in any compromised position, I have a question. Where are the boys?"

"Out working the steers, right where they should be."

"So, your nine-year-old twin sons are out doing what you should be doing."

"Perfect timing."

"Well, there might be some interest exchanging heartfelt love and affection, but it will not be done out here in public under the midday sun. You'll have to come inside, Mr. Toal."

"Mrs. Toal, I've never heard a more pleasant invitation."

Just then, a rider came into the compound bordered by the ranch house, the barn, and the bunkhouse. The horse pulled up winded, but not sweated out. The rider looked to be a young man not yet twenty.

"I have a letter for Mr. Toal. Know where I can find him?"

Will stood and stepped off the porch. "You just did."

"I was told to deliver this as quick as I could." The young man leaned down and offered the envelope to Will.

"Much appreciated. Would you like something to drink?"

"Nah, I need to get back to Carson City. I have another delivery to make before dark. Thanks for the offer."

Without any further comment, the rider pulled his reins to the side and spun his mount, heading out the same way he'd come.

Will flipped the envelope over and back just to check both sides. He strode back up to the porch and again sat in his rocker.

Intrigued, Beth asked, "Who's it from?"

"Don't know. It's just addressed to Will Toal at Toal Ranch."

Will sat and opened the letter. The script was precise, feminine. He read the quick note and dropped the letter onto his lap. He rubbed both hands up and down the sides of his face and then looked at Beth.

"It's from my sister, Ella."

"I thought you told me your family was killed during the war by Union soldiers."

"I thought they were. That's what I was told by our farm hands. When I came back home after the war the farm and house had been burned to the ground. A few of the old hands saw I had come home and told me what had happened. From what they said, I thought the whole family had been killed by Sherman's soldiers."

"Where is she?"

"North of Reno, homesteading."

"So close?"

"Says she and her husband are trying to homestead a ranch on the range north of Reno."

"Why didn't she come to see you rather than send a letter?"

"Don't know. Letter says there are ranch owners who are threatening them. She's asking for help."

Beth moved behind the rocker and standing there placed her hands on Will's shoulders. The contact had a purpose. It was a touch of closeness, of concern.

"Please take this in the right way. Can you be sure this is truly your sister? It sounds very strange to have someone send a letter out of the blue especially if she has been in the area homesteading. Why not just ride down and meet in person?"

Will shook his head. "I don't know why. But Beth, I took the family's money, father's money that was buried near Grandpa's grave. When the hands said everyone had been killed, there was nothing left. So, I took the money that my father had saved and kept out in the family cemetery. That was the money I used to buy the ranch. I took all of it. If it is Ella, then I need to help. She would be entitled to part of that money. Help is the least I can give. Probably should be more."

"So, what are you going to do?"

"Ride up, find their ranch and talk."

"Sounds like she might be in the middle of some dispute. Be careful Will."

"Plannin' on it. Maybe you should come, too."

"You sure? You don't want to see her for the first time in all these years alone?"

Will scoffed. "Not at all. If it is my sister, then I want her to know you right away. We can ride together, maybe spend a night out under the stars."

Beth grinned. "That has been known to have ramifications leading to additional children."

The exchange had lightened Will's mood. He let it show as he turned to Beth. "Wouldn't be that terrible, would it?"

"I suppose not," Beth said with a smile.

Beth then came to a stop, standing directly in front of Will. The look on her face became serious. "If I do go, how will I know if it is not your sister?"

"You'll see it in my face."

Chapter Two

Spring 1878
Ferguson Ranch—North of Reno, Nevada

The stacked stone fireplace sucked smoke upward into the dark night. Orange charcoal embers glistened beneath newer logs perched on what soon would become their own fiery bier. Angus Ferguson stared silently into the mature blaze. He sat in comfort at the center of a sprawling ranch operation he had built. His ranch house was larger than most in the district and contained more amenities. But his mood matched the scorched lumber in his fireplace. He had not spoken to his guest in over ten minutes. He did not intend to ignore. His brooding had just taken him to places away from his living room.

Ferguson was a leader of men. He had been involved in numerous civic groups. Driven and possessed of a hair-trigger temper, he often intimidated by strength of personality alone. He was currently the president of the highly influential and powerful Nevada Stock Growers Association. While a man of imposing character, Angus was also a physical force. He carried his Celtic genes in a short, but stout, frame. A barrel chest matched with overly muscled arms were supported on legs with calves as thick as most men's thighs. Shoulder-length gray hair drooped, generally unkempt. A chest-length gray beard also needed a trim. Now into his sixties, his muscle structure had not softened. Neither had his drive, until late. His force of personality had taken a large blow; his only son had been killed.

Angus sat in a high-backed leather chair facing the hearth. Carter McKinnon, another rancher in the district, sat adjacent to him, also facing the fire. Both had a healthy dram of high-class amber whiskey in hand. Both seemed content on the exterior. What could be more relaxing than an evening with a friend, sipping some of the best Kentucky whiskey in the state? Yet, Angus was anything but relaxed. He felt as if his life burned like the coals in front of him. His family was gone, all of them. Soon, he, too, would be dust. Once he passed, his ranch and everything associated with it would probably slowly burn to ruin in Nevada's incessant sun. Years of toil would be as another log feeding the fires under the high desert burn.

"Angus, I came to cheer you up. Appears I've done a poor job," said McKinnon.

"I'm sorry, Carter. I canna control my own attention at times." Angus's Scottish brogue pervaded his speech, betraying his birthplace in the Highlands. "Lately, since Dirk died, there are times my mind travels to thoughts of what would have been. I imagine what life would be like if Emma had not lost those three babies. I wonder to think how things would be if she had survived the birth of the last. And lately, I cannot stop thoughts of Dirk on that ride. I see him racing with that stick of dynamite heading for the dam in my mind's eye every day. I canna push the thoughts away."

"Dirk showed himself to be a young man of courage. We all knew he was the best one to take that ride to dynamite the Truckee Dam."

Ferguson shook his head. "It was a bad decision. I should have taken the ride myself. That boy should be alive and here now, not me.

"There was no way we could have figured that camp had a sharpshooter in it with a long-range buffalo gun. Not many could have ever taken that shot at Dirk and hit him. We knew it would be a risk. He was a remarkable young man to insist on doing it himself. You should be proud of him, Angus."

Ferguson knew that McKinnon had reached for anything that might lift his friend's mood. He knew Carter was here to talk about more serious matters, none of which would be uplifting.

"Aye, pride on one's kin comes as a father, but it doesna replace what's lost." Ferguson took another sip of the whiskey. His shoulders appeared to slump even more into the leather- covered cushion of the chair.

McKinnon did not reply.

Ferguson decided it was time to move the conversation to the business at hand.

"Carter, ye are a good friend. I apologize for my mood. I only seem to let it show to my closest of friends. You see it more as you and I go back further than any others ranching here in the district."

"You are right, Angus. We need to talk. We need to do something about the nesters."

"They are thieves. They should be strung up like any other cattle thief." Ferguson did not turn to face McKinnon with his response. He continued to stare darkly into the diminishing blaze.

McKinnon consciously worked to conceal his shock at the blunt reply. But the topic needed to be addressed so he continued. "They just keep coming. There must have been ten new homesteads in the last year. I went to Carson City and talked to the clerk in the territorial land office, a Scott Fallar, to ask how many of those grangers have filed formal homestead claims. It was less than half."

"Those people doona want to claim the land. They know we have posted grazing rights in the range. It be our land they're squatting on." Ferguson's mood only darkened.

McKinnon now turned the upper half of his body to fully face Ferguson. "Angus, I've lost over two hundred head in the last year. Do you think these ranching novices know what a maverick is, know that the newborn unmarked calf goes with its branded mother?"

"Of course, they know. Carter, do ye know what is really going on here?" As typical, in his Scottish brogue the word *do* came out sounding more like *dew*. Angus now did turn to face Carter. "They are thieves, like I said. They have no intention of stayin' on the land. They throw up a fourteen-foot by fourteen-foot dwelling in a vain attempt to appear in compliance with the Homestead Law, but their only intention is to set up a spread to steal cattle."

"That's probably why most don't even bother to file homestead claims."

"Exactly."

McKinnon turned back to the fire. "This came up at the Stock Growers board meeting last week. The men seem mad, but nothing got accomplished."

"Nae, a few dinna have the stomach to do what's needed. But most do. Ronald Tisdale, Reiker Johnson and Gentry MacDonald, they all would do what's necessary."

"Angus, what's necessary?"

"String 'em up. Simple as that. We're within the law to hang rustlers on our land. Over the years you've done it; so have I. Your men caught that group of three thieves making off with fifty of your steers two years ago. What did you do with them?"

McKinnon was not sure how to reply. "Yes, we threw ropes over tree branches for all three. But Angus, we caught them red-handed. They were trying to burn out my brand. If you catch someone red-handed, I have no problem providing the justice. But we would need proof to hang someone. You just can't ride onto some claim and string the people up."

"Aye, but we can. First, they're trespassin' unless they have a formal claim. Even then, we've won in court to throw homesteaders off our range claims. We were here first. Second, we all know they are takin' our stock. How many of these newcomers ride in driving any cattle at all?"

"I've not seen anyone drive steers onto the range."

"Then, Carter, where do you think they're gettin' their *herds*?" Ferguson did not make any attempt to limit his sarcasm. "That's our *stock*, Carter. Our *stock*."

"You are right, Angus. But wouldn't we be arrested?"

"Nae. Who are they gonna arrest? Gentry MacDonald is the Attorney General of Nevada, for goodness' sake. Ronald Tisdale is a State Senator. Reiker Johnson is the Water Commissioner. They all have ranches. They have all lost stock. You heard 'em at the board meeting."

"That doesn't mean we couldn't be arrested."

"Not by that weak-bellied sheriff in Reno. I went to Leif Svensson last year to tell him I'd lost close to one hundred head. He said it wasn't his jurisdiction. He didn't do a thing. The reason we have a problem in the first place is that there is no law to turn to."

"So, what do you think we need to do?"

While Ferguson's voice had been quite animated, his body had not moved. But he now rose from his chair and walked to the side of the hearth. He turned to face Carter. His shadow-shaded profile projected dark determination.

"Carter, I've given this a good deal of thought. First, we need to get the Stock Growers Association to agree we need legal enforcement. Second, we hire our own Range Detectives. There's a man named Frank Canton in Wyoming. I'm told he cleaned out a whole group of rustlers there. We bring him here and give him the authority to hire deputies. We can give them badges. They'll look just like U.S. marshals. We tell them to ride out and watch, look for the rustlers. When they see them, then they have our authority to administer justice there and then."

"Do you think the Stock Growers will agree?"

Ferguson looked back down into the fire. "They have to. If you add up the rustling they talked about at the last meeting, our collective loss over the last couple of years is more than twenty thousand dollars in beef. That's a lot of money, Carter. They'll agree."

"Then let's get to work. I can't afford to lose any more of my own herd. The first one we need to watch is that latest arrival, Nate Crampion. Just like you said, he arrived without any stock but now has over one hundred head. He roams the range every week. My men see him out riding all the time with those cowhands of his."

Angus agreed. "I have already hired a detective from Reno, Dale Paris, to watch this Crampion. I agree, something is not right there. Aye, we need to look at Crampion first."

Chapter Three

Spring 1878
KC Ranch—Range District North of Reno, Nevada

Dale Paris rocked evenly in his saddle as he walked his horse north, further into the open range of Washoe County. The range started some two miles north of Reno, Washoe's county seat. Passable grass rangeland followed Steamboat Creek some ten miles back up to Rattlesnake Mountain. Further east, further north, or further from the inconsistent rivers, the grasses petered out into arid landscape. When he first saw this parched area, Paris thought it must look like the surface of the moon with light and atmosphere. The visage over that vast space became desolate.

Air here had such a lack of moisture it hit hard in the back of the throat when deposited through one's nostrils. The dryness sucked out any verdant life outside, and with each breath, it tried to suck out the life of those who ventured onto this range. Grass could be found near any creek. But only a short distance away from water found the ground covered in nothing but the harshest of scrub. How cattle survived out here was beyond him.

Paris stopped his horse and leaned his elbow on the top of his saddle horn, looking north. Low-rise mountains marred the open expanse. These oversized brown mounds paled in adolescent stature when compared to the majestic Sierras just to the west. But they were tall enough to interrupt the flatland horizon.

"How different the north of Nevada is from Carson Valley to the south," he murmured. The reflection just lifted from within and became audible. He shook his head in emphasis of the thought.

Carson Valley cradled natural green pastures and regularly flowed with a myriad of small watery tributaries. Grass grew knee-high all year around. An Eden at the base of the mountains. Outside of the rivers with their narrow boundaries of attached green, there was no Eden here to the north, only a Palestine of desert.

The Sierra Mountains escaped Nevada in the distance to his left. North of Reno, the mighty heights arced slowly away from the state's border into California. The Sierras ultimately folded into the Cascades as the line of peaks headed north through Oregon to Washington. All along the eastern foot of the Sierras a strip of green grass hugged the granite walls. The snow melt gave life to the grasses at their base. But as the chain of high crests moved north of Reno, the mountains angled further west, taking their attendant lush strip of grass with them to California. East of their base, east of that narrow strip where the Sierras met the flatlands, was nothing but the Great Basin, nothing but a vast desert. The only exception was the green strips along the Truckee and the range he was headed to between Steamboat Creek and Rattlesnake Mountain.

"Thank goodness for the Truckee." Again, he spoke his thought aloud. Paris had followed the river north of Reno.

The Sierras did leave the vital Truckee River before they left for California. That lifeblood flowed east from Lake Tahoe down the slopes into Reno and then headed due north for fifteen miles dumping its volumes into the dead end of Pyramid Lake, the final deposit for the Truckee. Between the Truckee and Steamboat Creek was the best rangeland north Nevada had to offer. Not much, but the best it had. This was open range land.

"Let's go, son." Paris gently squeezed the flanks of his horse. Their walk resumed.

Compressed by his weight, his saddle uttered muted squeaks with the rhythmic motion of his mount's gait. Though not large at five-foot-six,

Paris was solid. Son of a blacksmith, he had swung many a hammer shaping hot metal in his father's shop as a boy. The hours of toil early in his life left him with an ever-thickening muscle structure as he grew into manhood. But he had departed home and family to escape further years in a blacksmith shop. He'd moved into investigation work almost a decade ago. He reveled in solving mysteries, and he'd solved many. His services were now in demand all around the new town of Reno.

As an investigator, Paris normally worked by himself. His ever-present bowler hat looked out of place here on the open range. He wore the bowler because he had thought he might sign on with the famous Pinkerton Investigation group. He'd never made that connection, but people thought because he wore the bowler, he might just be a Pinkerton. He did not disabuse those who carried the thought.

This was the world of cow hands. Washoe County was the last bastion of grass in northern Nevada before the eastern desert consumed the landscape. Washoe County contained over four million acres. About a million acres of land had been claimed as range by less than twenty ranchers. Paris had been told the acreage for some of those ranches approached the size of the entire state of Rhode Island in the east. Though vast in size, the range had limits. The grass simply could not support the same number of head per acre as in Carson Valley to the south.

Paris had heard all about the history and topography of the Washoe County range from his recent employer, Angus Ferguson. Paris found Ferguson to be a man of action. Rebuffed by local law enforcement, Ferguson hired Paris as part of his overall effort to stop the loss of stock on his ranch. Ferguson had political connections, but even with those contacts, he could not get the local sheriff to control the cattle rustling. He'd told Paris the thievery from the combined ranchers had now approached five hundred to a thousand head per year. Those stolen heads of cattle were simple profit whisked away. It had to stop. If the Reno sheriff was not going to do something, he would have to take care of the problem himself.

Paris's job was simple. Locate and identify those who were doing the stealing. Ferguson said he would have others "take care of the situation." All Paris had to do was develop evidence of how the beef was being taken, and by whom. The best part of the job was the pay. Handsome sums would be extended for every thief identified.

Up ahead, Paris saw a lonely wooden cabin. The structure couldn't be much more than fifteen feet by fifteen feet. Probably housed nothing but a single room. From the outside, it looked to have been erected by someone who did not know how to build a house. The dry, windy climate had beaten the ill-fitting slab-sided wood walls into the color of weathered gray. The stiff easterly winds would probably limit the shack's life to a matter of a few years.

Around the shack were three corrals. Five to ten horses were in one of the corrals, and cattle were in the other two. The cattle looked to be ten to twenty heifers with young calves. A saddled horse was tied to the outside of the corral nearest to the abode. Smoke rose from what looked like a tin pipe. It was probably connected to a stove inside the shack. Paris could not see a well, but there was a creek nearby. At least, whoever set this homestead up planned well enough to provide for water. There was a single tree on the windward side of the home. Maybe they hoped it would be something of a windbreak. Not another tree could be seen for miles.

A man walked out the door facing Paris. He had a rifle cradled in his forearm. Paris slowed, then stopped a good hundred yards away.

"Hallo, name's Dale Paris. Can I stop and water my horse?"

"Funny place to be riding," returned the young man. Paris thought he had to be less than thirty years old.

Paris moved his horse ever so slowly closer. He wanted to act as a neighbor passing by. "Actually, I came out to see Nate Crampion. Might you be Mr. Crampion?"

While thinking to use the neighborly approach, Paris remained on his horse. Until invited to dismount, he felt better staying high. It was not only a matter of courtesy to remain mounted until invited forward, but he also felt he held a superior position. He had already lifted the leather safety off the hammer of his handgun.

"And who is Dale Paris that wants to know?"

Paris thought the question interesting. This man must have at least a modicum of education. He decided to quit with the neighborly approach and move forward on a more professional tact.

"I work for Angus Ferguson. He's losing cattle. My job is to find out who is taking them."

"You won't find any of Ferguson's cattle here. I brought my own stock of thirty head when we came. Ferguson has already sent his thugs out here to try and intimidate. Tell him to mind his own business and leave us to ours."

Paris had no intention of leaving just yet.

"Ferguson's men say they've seen you branding stock from the open range several times this year. Branding on the open range happens once in spring. That is, unless you are taking mavericks from other men's stock."

Paris intended the comment to raise the confrontation level just a bit more. He wanted to see what this young man might be made of. Could be useful, should there be a future more serious confrontation that involved gun powder.

The young man used the barrel of his rifle to raise the front tip of his wide brimmed hat. The movement worked to display a certain sense of confidence both in his person and in the use of his firearm. Paris made a note of the impression.

"You look like someone who might be more rational than the cowhands with their leg flapping chaps. So, I'll give you a bit more information."

Paris was pleased he might be making some progress. Could lead to useful evidence.

The young man continued.

"I am Nate Crampion. Nine months ago, I homesteaded this section of one hundred sixty-five acres here on what is open range. That's all legal. I bought my own starter stock and now have almost over a hundred branded head."

A woman who Paris estimated to be at most in her mid-twenties exited the door and came to a stop about ten feet behind Crampion.

"Nate, who is this man?"

Crampion answered without turning, "He says his name's Dale Paris. He works for Ferguson, honey."

Paris nodded in the direction of the lady. "Your wife?"

"More or less. We're together. Traveled west together and set up house together."

Paris perceived that Crampion displayed an obvious affection but avoided saying anything about marriage.

The woman then spoke. "Mr. Paris, we mean to start a life here. We've been told it's legal. We've built a home as the law requires and intend to raise cattle. But this man Ferguson keeps saying he owns this land, and we have to get off. That's not what the land office in Reno says. Y'all out West here are about as neighborly as the local rattlesnakes."

The twang of the young lady's speech sounded familiar, but he could not quite place it. Paris refocused on the issues at hand.

"Have you filed a formal homestead claim?"

The man replied, "We did, but the clerk keeps telling us something is holding up the process. I suspect Ferguson is behind that, too."

Paris leaned back in his saddle. He moved his right hand away from his holster in a subtle gesture of lowering the confrontation level just a bit.

Paris then offered, "As I understand it, anyone can homestead one hundred and sixty acres of government land, but they have to file a homestead claim and see it processed to conclusion. Without that final paperwork, you could be found to be trespassing on a range claim, just like the one Angus Ferguson has on file."

"He doesn't own the land. The government does. He only *acts* like he owns it." Crampion issued this response with extra emphasis. The confrontation level just raised back up.

Paris decided to do what he could to obtain any other useful information, and then end this conversation. The ultimate proof would be what occurred when he kept an eye on Crampion's activity out on the range.

"Mind if I check the brands on your stock over there in the corral?"

Crampion chortled and shook his head in disbelief. "You all just don't give up, do you?"

"Just want to be able to tell Mr. Ferguson whether the stock in your corral carry his brand or not."

"They don't. Go ahead and look. They carry the KC brand, *my* brand. Named after my parents—Karen and Charles. Ferguson and his ranch-owning cronies get together each spring, and in a combined drunk fest, watch as their hands collect each and every head on the range on which they burn their brands. I watched last spring as several of my head were taken. I protested, but was told to back off or face consequences."

"Did you tell the sheriff in Reno?"

Crampion nodded. "I did, but while he seems a nice man, he said he had nothing to do with what happened here on government land. So, since last spring I have watched my own heifers and when they drop their calves, I take them into the remote corrals I've built out on the range and put my brand on them right away. It's the only way I can stop Ferguson from taking them next spring."

Paris had to think the story had a ring of logic. But the truth would come out in the deeds, not words. The young woman now walked up next to Crampion. Her facial structure also looked familiar. Paris decided to sidestep the brand issue for a moment.

"I can tell from your accent you might be from the South."

The young lady blushed. "I am—Georgia. My family was killed by Union soldiers towards the end of the war. Nate and I decided to head west. There was nothing left for us back home."

Paris smiled. "I have a friend in the Carson Valley who is also from Georgia. His family suffered a similar fate. His name is Will Toal."

The woman jerked her arm sideways to grab Crampion's wrist. Her other hand went directly to cover her mouth. Paris watched the reaction with interest. She seemed to recover, looked at Crampion and then back to Paris.

"Will Toal is my brother. My name is Ella Toal."

Chapter Four

Spring 1878
KC Ranch—Range District North of Reno, Nevada

Winds roared down the slopes of the Sierras carrying all manner of small particles in clouds of dust. Winds were a constant here beneath the mountains, a fact of life. Will Toal stared down at the nascent fire he had tried to start in combat with the blows. He had lost the battle. No match lasted long enough to even start the kindling he'd gathered. The same thing happened last night. In an effort to let Beth experience what he had called "the real cowboy life", he had convinced her to sleep outside with him. She agreed, but was not happy to be without fire, and was forced to tuck under blankets early just to stay warm. The local dried scrub he'd collected barely smoked before being extinguished by the ever-present gusts. Time to give up and simply pull his jacket collar higher and tighter to block the morning spring chill. If the winds were this strong here at daybreak, they were going to be a sore problem later, as they always picked up force as the day progressed.

"Time to get up." Will delivered the comment with a soft touch. He knew without the warmth of a fire his bride would not be in the best of spirits.

"Coffee made?" came the reply from under the depths of blankets.

"Nope. Can't get a fire going. Too much wind. Going to be a hard-tack and water morning."

"We should have stayed in Reno."

Will nodded his agreement. "In hindsight, I'd have to agree. Last night looked clear and beautiful. Thought the winds would die down. Guess I was wrong."

Beth rolled out of her bed. "It's been a long time since I've slept in my clothes. Seem to remember the last time we were 'out on the trail' as you men call it, we had to spend a wet night in a livery stable."

Will smiled. "At least it was dry."

"Seems you have a problem with hotels."

Will could see the smallest of wrinkles form at the edge of her mouth. He knew Beth was not as upset as she was making this out to be. He pulled her up into a firm hug. "Now, how often can you say you got a hug from your cowboy first thing in the morning out on the range?"

"Not very. If it wasn't that I am quite interested in meeting your sister, I'd wait for a hug in my warm bedroom."

Will held Beth at arm's length. "Let me get you something to eat and saddle the horses. We can get moving."

Will left Beth and headed to collect their hobbled horses. A youthful morning sun rose in the east. Completely obscured by dust, it colored the world with an ethereal orange hue. Will stood facing east at the rising orb keeping the gusts to his back. Glancing to his right, he saw that his gray mustang, Powder, was doing the same thing. Smart horse. Had to do everything you could to block the dust lifting off this dried out stretch of dirt and sand. There were winds at home, too. Same as here. But the Carson Valley, and especially his own Jack's Valley, were covered with green grass. When the winds blew at home, at least they blew clean without any dust.

He lifted his rag scarf up over his nose in an additional attempt to draw a clear breath. That battle, too, was not going well. He had decided to camp out last night rather than rent a room in Reno. As he had indicated to Beth, it had turned out to be a poor choice. The weather last night had been calm, almost serene. Mother Nature had deceived him into thinking a night out on the range would be pleasant. Turned out, they should have stayed in Reno. Another sharp blow tried to take his hat. He pulled the stampede strap tighter around his chin to keep the broad-brimmed head cover in place.

Will stood thinking of his short, but full, history. After serving as a sniper for the Confederate Army during the Civil War, Will had matriculated slowly west eventually to work cattle on a ranch in New Mexico. From there Will, along with three good friends, he headed for California. He had always enjoyed bedding down at night out in the open when he and his friends, Raul, his son Juan, and Juan's wife, Maria, had arrived in Carson Valley from New Mexico. Back in 1867, the four had nothing but their horses and the tack to ride them. That is, the horses and Will's money from his family grave. He'd used that money to buy three thousand acres and seed stock of both beef and horses. The small group had built a ranch out of nothing.

Will had been instrumental in arranging for sale of the entire Carson Valley's herds of cattle to markets in San Francisco. Along with his partner, Henry Millard, they worked to form an association of all the ranchers in Carson Valley to sell their beef through the Millard-Luce network of brokers to markets in San Francisco. The arrangement had saved the Carson Valley ranchers who were on the brink of financial ruin when the deal was made.

But building a ranch here on the border of the Great Basin came with challenges, danger. Men had come close to killing Beth. Raul had died defending Will's twin boys from kidnappers. Beth had borne not only the twin boys but also a little girl, Juliette. The thoughts ran as fast as the wind heading off into the east. Life in the war had been hard. But he'd made a pretty good go of it since it ended.

Yet, that money Will used to start his life had been family money. He'd taken it all. When he had returned from the war, farm hands that had worked for the family for years told him his family had been killed by Union Soldiers scavenging local farms for food. He assumed his mother, father and sister had all been killed. But they were wrong. How could they have been wrong? Maybe the hands weren't there when the Union soldiers rode through. How did Ella survive? He was riding north to find out. He was riding north to do what he could to relieve his now-uneasy conscience.

Will lifted the bottom of his scarf and bit down on a morsel of hard tack he'd removed from his saddle bag. He always carried some hard tack on a ride of more than an hour. Habit from the war. One never knew where the next meal might come from out in open country. He hoped Beth could handle a cold meal.

* * * * *

"Come on, Powder, time to get going. Maybe my sister has a place where we can get out of the wind."

Will saddled both horses and they mounted. He hunched forward to angle the brim of his hat down, attempting to block the dust. Beth did the same. He did not have to touch Powder with his spurs. The horse was well-trained. All he had to do was increase the pressure of his lower legs and lean back in the saddle. The animal knew the day's trip had started, and it was time to move. The big mustang walked out heading north.

The sun rose higher, and the chill eased. Pale rays the color of creamy butter could now be seen above the dust clouds. The color made him think of his hunger. The pair rode close to the Truckee River as it headed toward Pyramid Lake. The letter from his sister said to ride for four miles north of Reno along the Truckee, and then head west. The grasses were better near the river. Less debris flew through the air near the water's edge. That was where Will kept Powder walking.

"Not far now, boy. Should be there within the hour."

"I assume you are talking to your horse."

Will looked at Beth. "I do suppose I have a habit of talking to Powder as if he can carry on a conversation. There are times I really think he answers."

"I was hoping you were not referring to *me* as 'boy'."

"Naw, I just slipped into the pattern Powder and I use out on the trail. We sort of talk a bit."

A wide grin now spread across Beth's face. "Even when you have the chance to talk to your wife?"

Caught off guard without a good ready-made answer, Will responded, "He doesn't ask a lot of questions."

"And I do?"

"Only good ones."

"You won't dodge your present dilemma that easy, cowboy."

Will leaned far forward, low, over Powder's neck as if to whisper into his ear. Speaking intentionally loud enough for Beth to hear, he said, "Sorry big fella, guess you and I have to go silent when the missus is present." Will did his best to match Beth's earlier grin to make sure she knew the entire show was delivered in a lighthearted spirit.

The horse dipped his head. More than likely, the movement was in reaction to the unsuspected closeness of his rider's head to his own. Will took it another way.

"See, he answered."

Beth shook her head. "Cowboys."

* * * * *

Will and Beth had left the river as Ella's letter instructed. Two hours of riding drew them out into a flat plane. Up ahead, Will saw a single-room dwelling standing near the only tree in sight. A simple lean-to large enough for maybe three horses stood off to the left of the main structure. It had been placed just under the tree no doubt to provide shelter for saddled horses to keep out of the wind. Other than three corrals, there was nothing else but open space for miles around. He had to be looking at his sister's home.

What would she think of him? What would he think of her? Ella had been the younger of the two siblings. Will tried to remember what she had looked like the day he left to go to war. He had been sixteen. Ella was only twelve back then. That would mean she be about twenty-six years old today. Fourteen years had been missed. Fourteen years to catch up on.

"You nervous?" Beth asked the question as she looked in Will's direction. He knew she was watching him observe the scene out in front.

"A little. Just thinking of the last time I saw Ella."

Will looked back at the shack in front of them. There was movement at the structure. A young man who looked to Will to be in his twenties came out of the door. Armed, he watched Will walk Powder in the direction of the house.

Will told Beth, "Stay here. I'm going to move forward a bit, but you be careful until we know where we stand."

By the manner of his stance, Will knew he was being assessed. Will stopped a good hundred feet short of the structure. He realized with his scarf pulled up and hat set low he might not look friendly, much the opposite. He figured it would be good to take this slow and easy.

Will pulled down his scarf and yelled out, "Name's Will Toal. Might Ella Toal live here?"

"Will!" A semi-scream came from inside the shack. The man at the door turned just in time to be shoved aside as a young lady in a full-length garment barreled through the door. He would have called the costume a dress. But it looked overly formal with its puffed sleeves above the elbow. She also wore a bonnet of matching fabric sitting atop thick, dark curls framing a round, full face. The dress and bonnet seemed out of place here in the middle of an open range. Will would have expected something a bit more functional. But despite the addition of years and several pounds, Will could see the likeness to the sister he had not seen in years.

"Will, is that you?"

"Ella?"

Will dismounted. He looked at the man cradling the rifle. While Ella moved toward Will and Powder, the man remained stoic and stationary. His expression did not extend any form of welcome. Much to the contrary. Will quickly decided to defer to the man before taking up with Ella. After all, he held the firearm.

"My wife and I decided to ride up and meet my sister. Mind if we tie up our horses over in the lean-to?"

No response. No change in the facial expression. No change in the position of the gun cradled in his arm.

Ella turned back to the man in the door. "Nate, this is my brother."

"You sure? He looks like another of Ferguson's cowhands."

Will waited. For a moment, no one spoke. Seeking to dispel any confusion, Will said, "I do have a ranch, and work cattle and horses down south in Jack's Valley. I do not work for Angus Ferguson. If I did, why would I bring my wife?"

Apparently still not convinced, Nate responded, "How do you know the man's first name?" He persisted in the small standoff.

Will tried to appear relaxed and decided to offer a more extensive explanation of his interplay with Ferguson. Maybe that would work to allay Nate's fears.

"There are not that many ranch owners here in northern Nevada. Most know of each other, or have heard descriptions of land and operations. I ran across Angus Ferguson last year during the draught. I have another spread up on the Truckee which butts up to Ferguson land. We had moved our stock north as the Carson River had dried up. Ferguson was not very welcoming. I wanted to try and talk to the people who controlled the dam of the Truckee at Tahoe to allow more water to flow down river for those who needed it for their stock. He wanted to blow up the dam at Tahoe City. He tried to do it, but he lost his only son in the process. I never saw eye-to-eye with Angus on the whole thing."

Will's effort seemed to work. Nate relaxed the gun, swinging it downward and moving back toward the door. "You were at the shootout with the railroad's men?"

"I was."

"We heard about that from other folks. We come just after it all happened, but people still talk about it."

Will looked away and then returned his gaze to Nate. "It was something that got out of hand unnecessarily. Could have been avoided."

"Sorry to be contrary. Been harassed and threatened by Ferguson's men. I gotta be real careful. Please, tie up your horses and come inside out of the wind."

With introductions now accepted, Ella then ran to Will and wrapped him in a tight hug. "Will, I only found out you were here in Nevada a short time ago. I never thought I'd see you again. I sent the letter and still did not know if it was really you."

Will smiled and pushed the front brim of his hat upward with his forefinger. "We have a lot of catching up to do."

"And who is this on the other horse? Did you say it was your wife? You are married?"

"Yes, this is Beth, my wife. She wanted to come. She wanted to meet you. Not often does a surprise happen like finding a sister you thought dead long ago."

Ella turned to Beth. "Come. Our place is very small, but you are most welcome."

Will gave Beth a smile, knowing she would understand that the facial expression confirmed Ella was his sister.

* * * * *

Inside the Crampion home, Will peeled off his jacket and hat, then lowered his scarf. He then helped Beth do the same. With the door closed, one could almost breathe air devoid of dust. But the winds blew through several cracks in the haphazard walls. The side boards should have been overlapped but they were not. It would have helped to keep the weather more on the outside. Uneven edges butted together left gaps through which wind and dust found its way.

Nate offered Will a seat. "Please, sit. Be interested to hear about the shootout at the dam." Nate leaned forward in Will's direction, a tangible sign he did want to hear about the confrontation.

Will chuckled as he sat down opposite Nate. He noticed Beth and Ella were now sitting on the sole bed and had already begun talking.

"Not much to tell. The railroad barons needed the dam and flow to float their logs down river to their sawmills. The logs became fuel for the locomotives to keep steam up. There were other folks who had ideas of taking Tahoe's water down to San Francisco. Made for a tense set of interests. Both sides hired guns. It all got set off by a man crazed with the thought of protecting Tahoe and the forests around the lake. But he was the one who started the shooting."

"We heard several died."

Will nodded. "Yep. Several did. Shooting started, and apparently, Angus sent his son into the fray with a lighted stick of dynamite. One of the parties, no one really knows who, shot the son who fell and was killed for sure in the resulting explosion. Angus and his men then charged one of the camps and wiped everyone out."

"Ferguson have any other children?"

"No, that was his only son. While I don't claim to know the man, I've heard Angus has become morose. Might understand, but the whole dynamite thing was his own idea. He might take it worse because of that. When something bad like that happens, people often try to find someone else to blame. But here, the blame falls to Angus himself. Might be hard to live with that on one's mind."

Nate sat back in his chair. "Thanks for telling me. But you are here to see Ella. I'm keepin' you two from talkin'."

Will watched as both Ella and Beth now joined the men at the table.

A childlike anticipation spread across Ella's face. Though he had thought about this conversation all along the ride north, he struggled to begin.

"I have so much to ask. How did you find out I was here in Nevada? When did you move West? How did you come? But most of all, tell me about Ma and Pa. What happened? The hands told me you were dead."

Ella held up both hands and laughed. "Hold on, I can't answer ten questions all at once. By the way, I have just as many for you."

Will felt a relief at getting beyond the start. "Okay, you go first. Tell me what happened at the farm and your trip west. Then, I'll tell you my story."

Ella took a deep breath. "We knew the Yanks were gettin' near. The main body of the army was to the north, and we were hopin' they'd miss us. But some of the neighbors had told us about raids not far away. They'd ride in with fifty or so soldiers and take everything they wanted. If you resisted, they shot you. Those that didn't get shot watched as the Yanks burned their farms as they left. Everyone was scared. Ma sent me to Aunt Leona and Uncle Desmond's farm to the south. You remember, they had a farm down in Valdosta, Georgia, near Florida."

Will tried to remember. "That's right, their farm was down almost on the Gulf Coast, wasn't it?"

"Right. Pa said he'd never leave our farm. He'd fight if they came and tried to take what little we had left. I sent one or two letters while I was at Aunt Leona's and got one or two from Ma. I was there almost six months. But the mail didn't run well back in those days. Then, I heard nothin'. For several months, no mail, no letters. It seemed like forever. Time dragged. We were all worried. Then, word came the war was over."

"That about fits with how long I was in Johnson's army. I fought for about six months before the war ended."

"Uncle Desmond was concerned for his older brother and said he'd go up to our farm. We all expected Ma and Pa to send for me. But Uncle Desmond didn't want me to go as it was crazy and dangerous to travel in those days. No one had anything. The roads were full of robbers and thieves. He wanted to find out if everyone was okay."

Will listened intently. He'd lived for fourteen years not knowing what really happened while he was away during the war. The hands who approached him when he returned obviously did not know the whole story. Ella could tell more about his family's history and family that had been taken from him.

"Uncle Desmond got back and told us the farm was burned, crops ruined. The farm hands had told him the soldiers killed both Ma and Pa. Most of the hands had left. There was no work. I stayed with Aunt Leona and Uncle Desmond until I was twenty. I met Nate at a church function. Churches had been burned. Houses had been burned. No one had any money. The church services were held outdoors. Nate and I would move slowly to the rear of those standing and slip out into the woods to sit and talk. He wanted to leave Georgia and come west. I'd told him to take me with him. We ran away about six years ago."

Will cast a stern look. "You married?" Almost instantly, he saw Beth shoot him a frown and the slightest of negative shakes of the head as if to tell him it was not a good question.

Ella's cheeks colored. It took her a moment to answer. "No. I haven't felt strange about that until now. Havin' my older brother ask is different. We love each other and do plan to get married. Just haven't done it yet."

"Ella." An exasperated exhale erupted from somewhere deep below. Will caught himself. He'd slipped into the older brother posture before he knew it happened. Beth must have been thinking the same thought as her expression had not changed. He decided to back off this line of questioning.

"I suppose I'm not the one to judge. Times have been more than strange since the war. Not many preachers way out here, either. When did you get to Nevada?"

"We worked our way up the Mississippi on jobs here and there to earn money for the train west. After several years of odd jobs, we had enough to buy our tickets. We picked up the train in Missouri and arrived in Reno about a year ago. Nate has always dreamed of ranching. We heard about the open range north of Reno and decided to come see. We liked the starkness of it all, the openness. Not many trees, though. We picked this spot as it has the only tree for miles. We tried to file a homestead claim, but the man in town keeps makin' excuses as to why the claim is not final."

"You got your own beef?"

Nate now interjected. "We bought thirty head of cross breeds. Branded them with the KC brand and turned them loose on the open range. I try to keep track of the new calves attached to heifers with my brand. Me and my two part-time hands try to collect and brand those little ones real quick. I watched as the big ranches started their roundup last spring and they took everything. I probably had ten head left after what they called their 'roundup'."

Will heard this and tried to hide a cringe. He had a bad feeling that what Nate would say next would not be good.

Nate continued. "I hadn't branded the new stock last year. So, this winter, I've been culling out new calves that seem to be attached to my heifers and brand them right away. At least I won't be losing my mavericks come this spring."

"How many head do you have now?"

"Between fifty and a hundred."

Will knew that ten head would not generate fifty offspring, no less a hundred. Nate had been taking random mavericks. But if he had truly come to the range with thirty head, then he would have had at least fifty by now. Maybe he was only recouping that to which he was entitled. But he was walking a fine line. If caught branding mavericks from other herds, the ranchers would consider him to be rustling. The young man seemed earnest. But he had a hard edge to him, too. Will was unsure what to make of what he'd just heard. Best keep his thoughts to himself.

Ella then said, "Tell me what happened to you."

Will gave her the long and detailed story of going home, finding the farm destroyed, coming West, working as a Texas Ranger and then on ranches in New Mexico. He described the trip west with Juan and Raul. He also told Ella about how he met Beth, their troubled beginning, but also how it had worked out so well in the end, and about the twins and Juliette.

"Sounds like you've done quite well."

Will now looked down at his boots and back up to Ella. It was time to tell his sister the whole truth.

"Ella, Pa kept money. Kept it buried near Grandpa's grave. I knew about it. When I came home and the folks told me the whole family had been killed, I waited until everyone had left and dug it up. That was the money I used to buy the ranch and seed stock. You're entitled to half of what I took."

Nate spoke up. "We don't need any charity. We intend to make it on our own."

Will gave Nate a stern look. "It's not charity. It's family money. Ella's entitled to her share. I'll arrange to have an account set up at a bank in Reno. I'll deposit a sum equal to half of what I got from the grave. It's only right."

Nate did not seem comfortable with the conversation. Ella looked back and forth between the men in the room. She came back to Will and reached out with both her hands to take his.

"Will, that is real nice. We could use the money. Maybe we could buy more stock and even a bull." She looked at Nate as she spoke. "We could keep the bull in a pen close by. Maybe build a barn."

"That's what the money did for me. Should do the same for you." Pleased to hear the hope in his sister's voice, Will was glad he'd brought up the family money. Dreams sometimes came true. Hard work helped, but hope fired the thought that those dreams could become reality.

Nate strode out the door. He didn't seem happy at all. Will looked as he left and then back to Ella.

Will could see Beth looked a bit anxious at Nate's exit. She turned to Ella. "He doesn't seem to like the offer."

Ella nodded. "Nate's independent. When we left Georgia, we agreed we would take nothing. We both wanted to leave the chaos and sadness all behind. We did well workin' at jobs. It was hard gettin' enough money for the train and our first stock, but we did it. He wants to make it all on his own. We've sold some beef and can make ends meet. But Ferguson is makin' things difficult."

"I can try to talk to Angus. He's a hard man. Built his own ranch from nothing. Now his son is gone. I am sure it's left a hole in his being. I know if I lost either Sean or Luke it would leave a hole in mine."

"Oh, Will, anything you can do would be wonderful. The last man who came out here was a Dale Paris. He said he knew you."

"Dale came here to the house?"

"Yes. Said he worked for Ferguson."

Will was puzzled. "That's strange. I do know Dale. He's a good man. I'll have to look him up. Don't think he'd be involved in harassing folks."

Will squeezed Ella's hands with a little extra feeling. "We've got to get started back home. I'll set up the account and come back to let you know how you can get money out of it. But you and Nate must come to our ranch. You have to meet the kids."

"I can't wait to come. Work is pretty constant here right now, but I'll try to get Nate to take a day off soon."

Will stood to leave. Beth walked up to his side. He saw that Nate was out in the corral saddling up a horse. He turned to Ella.

"Ella, Nate has to be real careful if he's taking unbranded mavericks early. If he takes any calves attached to heifers with other brands, he could be caught. Out here, they'll call that rustling. He could get hung."

Ella nodded. "Nate works hard. He only wants what's his. He's like you. Used a gun from the time he could walk. Says he's not scared of Ferguson. I do what I can to help. I've been doing some mending for local people. I learned to sew from Aunt Leona. It doesn't bring in much, though every little bit helps. But I worry, Will. I worry a lot."

Chapter Five

Spring 1878
Open Range District North of Reno, Nevada

A crisp early morning vista spread before six horsemen stopped atop the highest point on a string of low dirt mounds. Though the mound they had climbed was not tall, they were high enough to see for miles in all directions over the otherwise flat open range before them.

Tate Snyder lifted a leather gloved hand and rubbed his chin covered with a six-day stubble. A square jaw framed sun-wrinkled cheeks set below eyes that squinted into the rising sun. He had led his group here. It was a return trip. He hoped this raid would be as successful as the last.

Snyder and his gang had ridden over a good chunk of the unsettled West. He and his men had left their mark from Colorado to Johnson County, Wyoming. They had rustled cattle in Utah with its Hole in the Wall, and also in Nevada. But eastern Oregon was his home of choice. Open, dry, and untamed by any law, the east side of Oregon was the perfect place to raise and sell cattle taken from others. Settlers kept coming west over the Oregon trail, building multiple new towns all with the need for beef. They were novices in the ways of the West and never asked about his small herds with muted or burned brands. They needed beef. He could sell, and sell at high prices to food starved travelers.

The sides of their horses heaved, no doubt a result of carrying their masters up the hill. Of the six riders, some rested leaning back in their saddles; others moved forward, putting an elbow on top of the saddle horn. All but one wore a red sash around their waist. The last wore a red bandana around his head under a hat with the front brim upturned. The end of his red bandana hung the length of his back to the top of his gun belt.

The group faced south. To the west lay a fifteen-mile deposit of blue water left by the Truckee River known as Lake Pyramid. To the east was Winnemucca Lake, much smaller than its neighbor and so shallow it might go dry soon. Further west beyond Lake Pyramid was a valley bordered by the lofty Sierras. Low, purple clouds sagged in suspension like an artist's stroke across Pyramid taking on the hue of the mountains behind.

Morning broke calm.

"Where's the grass? This place looks like Utah—nothin' but desert." Brock Smythe scanned side-to-side, taking in the view before him.

Snyder grinned in repeated amazement at how it was always the youngest among them who spoke first. Barely twenty and unfiltered by the challenges of age, Smythe always seemed to be the first to speak, no matter the circumstance. The more aged of the group tolerated Smythe's neophyte approach to life, probably because he was good both with cows and with a gun.

"Cows don't need grass," said Snyder. "They can live on scrub. This here's a land of scrub."

"What do ya care what they eat? We're just here to take 'em." Clay Cooper had succinctly outlined their coming purpose. Cooper was the eldest of the gang. Snyder and Cooper had been riding together now for almost eight years. Slender and slow of movement, everything about Cooper was deliberate, reasoned. Snyder knew Cooper was the smartest of the lot, including himself. What Snyder liked was that most of Cooper's deliberations revolved around how to take cattle and not get caught.

Snyder agreed. "Clay's right. It don't matter what they eat, but the lack of trees and cover is a problem."

Cooper nodded in the direction of the near-dry bed of Lake Winnemucca. "We can collect the stock around that dry lake. These low hills will block any view from the east or west as we take the steers back north to Oregon. It might be a better hidin' place than the one we used last year. We were too exposed out there next to Pyramid."

After considering the suggestion, Snyder concluded, "That's what we'll hafta do. We can make three or four raids out into the herds but bring them back here to the lakebed. It's not protected like the space around Hole in the Wall, but it'll hafta do. We'll have to scout out a good spot to keep the stock, but we should start collecting cattle soon. I'd like to start tomorrow. Don't like being in one place too long."

Smythe rejoined the discussion. "Yeah, it was easy takin' cattle from those ranchers in Wyoming and using the canyons near Hole in the Wall as a place to keep them."

"Last year we got lucky here. Found enough stock quick and snuck out in the dark. We stayed out next to Pyramid until we collected enough head." Snyder looked back and forth from Pyramid to Winnemucca as if to assess the different locations for their purposes.

Snyder continued, "There are no forests to hide in like back home. But the country up the length of that dry lake is flat. We can make good time drivin' the stock north."

"The lakebed might be a better hidin' place, but what'll we do for water?" Again, it was Cooper asking the important questions.

Snyder gazed down the length of Lake Pyramid.

"Depending on where we take the stock, we follow the Truckee River up here to Pyramid and then cut off east to the dry lakebed. We can water them in both the river and in Pyramid until we get between the hills on either side of Winnemucca. Looks like there's a little water in the middle of that lake. It should keep them fine until we start to Oregon."

"I suppose it won't be long," said Cooper. "As you said, if we start soon, we'll need to keep them there only a day or two before we head north."

"I wasn't here last year; how many head do you think we can get?" asked Smythe.

Snyder answered the newcomer. "Last year we took about three hundred head. It didn't take long to round up that many. Speed is the key. We can't do any re-branding until we get to Oregon. Need to high tail it out of Nevada. Now with six of us, we should be able to handle up to four hundred head."

"I hear south of the town they use to call Lake Crossing and now call Reno, there is tall grass that grows all year. Those cattle might be better stock." The comment came again from Cooper. But it struck Snyder that Cooper was musing rather than making a strong suggestion.

"Too many people down to the south," Snyder responded. "Bringing stock up through Carson City and then Reno would have to happen under too many eyes. It's not open range down south. 'Member? We rode down there last year first and heard that all the ranches south of Carson City are on deeded property. This here's open range."

Cooper offered a simple nod. Not so much in agreement as just acknowledgement of a fact. "Suppose you're right. Ridin' in to deeded land would be a lot riskier. This here space is wide open, just like the name says."

"You see smoke over there?"

Jim Thurston pointed across Lake Pyramid to the south and west.

"I see it, you're right," said Snyder. "Looks like three cowhands doing some branding. That can't be men from a big outfit. They don't start their roundup until later in the spring."

Cooper grinned. "They must be doin' what we want to be doin'. They're just getting the brands on right away. They've gotta be takin' mavericks."

"Probably not bein' particular about the brands on the mother's next to 'em either." This came nonchalantly from Russell "Russ" Ball. He'd been watching the activity below, looking in the same direction as Thurston.

"If they're maverickin', they'd better be careful. Any hands from the big ranches will consider that rustling," observed Johnny Fenton, the last of the group.

Cooper then smiled. "You're right Johnny. But we should talk to those boys. Maybe we could work with them. If they refuse, we could let them know it might not be good for their health if someone told the ranchers what they're doin' out there. It's a stretch, but they might consider workin' with us if the threat is made clear enough."

Snyder felt a grin spreading across his own face. "Clay, I like the way you think. We could use the extra hands. Rounding up stock would go quicker. We could split the head we collect. Might not be a bad idea at that."

Snyder took time to consider his next move. As any leader of men, whether nefarious or otherwise, decisions and planning were the keys to holding that position. Snyder considered his personnel; which men fit which job.

"Jim, you and Russ head down to the dry lakebed area and scout for a place to hide the stock. Brock, you and Johnny ride out and take a look around. See if you can find where the cattle naturally collect. Think about the numbers. We don't want to take too many. Not lookin' to make it obvious we've been here. Also, think about routes to get them to the dry lakebed. Clay, let's you and I ride down there and have a talk with those boys. We all meet here at this spot before dark. We start rounding up cattle tomorrow."

Chapter Six

Spring 1878
Toal Ranch—Jack's Valley, Nevada

"The boys are finally asleep. Juliette always goes down to bed earlier than the boys, but we both know she'll be up before the crack of dawn."

Will looked up from his porch rocker and watched Beth exit the main door to the house and drop onto the small bench to his left. The simple piece of furniture looked out of place, but it had rested in the same spot since Will built the house. He sensed Beth was tired. Such was life on the ranch.

Soft light strained its way through the open doorway from the fireplace inside. It was not a strong beam. While it tried to carve its way into the shroud of night, the feeble beams lacked the power to extend more than a few feet beyond the door before darkness took over. The rest of the world was black.

After taking a moment to catch her breath, Beth looked at Will. "So, we talked on the ride home from meeting your sister, but you said you needed time to think about what we saw. I haven't pushed to talk about the trip. Lately, you seem a little distant since we returned."

Will took some time to answer. He knew Beth had not pressed him to relay the results of what she knew was a significant event in his life. His sister was not dead. And she was now only fifty miles away from Toal Ranch. That she had not pushed for him to talk about it he considered a measure of how close they were as man and wife. She probably could tell he was troubled about his visit. He had struggled with his feelings about what he had seen on the entire ride home. Beth could see it, sense it. Will stopped pushing the rocker and turned to face her.

"Honey, I would describe the meeting as strange. Ella is the same, as if nothing has changed. Oh, she's older and she's a lot heavier than when I last saw her. But she's the same as I remember her. She is a bubble of energy and dreams. It was if we had never been separated. Problem is, she's attached to that man Nate Crampion…living unmarried. As you saw, he was not very welcoming at all. Stood at the door with rifle at the ready claiming I looked like another of the ranchers' hands. Nate almost didn't let us come in. You heard when he said he's been harassed by men from Angus Ferguson's ranch."

"Angus Ferguson," said Beth. "From what Nate and Ella said, it sounds like Angus hasn't changed since he rode to the Truckee River Dam last spring and tried to blow it up."

"Yep, and it didn't help that he lost his only son in the explosion."

"Why do you think he's harassing your sister?"

"Because I think Nate is rustling mavericks off the open range. I think that's what Nate is really doing, based on our conversation there at the table."

"Oh, that's not good. I got the sense Ella was uneasy. When she told me they weren't married over on the bedside, I thought that was the reason. Maybe her real fear is what Nate is doing."

"Could be." Will sat back and began to rock again.

Beth did not respond. Will sensed she was waiting for him to further explain his concerns. He took some time before he continued.

"Angus was short tempered before the events at the dam. Now that he's lost his son, I would guess he's damaged in a way. Sittin' all alone day after day his loss might begin to eat at him. If he thinks someone is stealin' his cattle…well, that hair-trigger temper could easily lead to someone getting hung."

Beth looked out beyond the compound and then came back to Will. "Well, if Nate is stealing his cattle, Angus would be within his rights to take action would he not?"

"Maybe. Crampion says Ferguson's men took some of his unbranded mavericks in the general round up last spring. From the number of cattle he started with, and what he has now, I think the man was trying to tell me he's just getting his stock back and collecting what he should have. But if he takes a maverick attached to a Ferguson branded heifer and gets caught, there could be serious Western justice dispensed on the spot."

The two were quiet for a moment as the significance of the situation sunk in.

Will broke the silence. "It was great seeing Ella. I couldn't wait to hear how she came to be so near."

Beth leaned forward, "It was an amazing story."

"The story *was* amazing. It makes sense that she was not at the farm when Ma and Pa were killed. My mother was worried about the oncoming Union Army and I can see Ma would have sent her further south in Georgia to our Aunt Leona's farm. Leona's farm would be away from Sherman's path as it is down near Florida. Ella also made a point to say most of the regular hands had left our farm before the army attacked. Pa sent them away. I can see Pa doing that, too. It also makes sense, if you know my Uncle Desmond, that he would ride up to see what was going on when they didn't hear from my parents.

"Please take this in the right way." Beth shifted on the bench. Will could tell the next comment was going to be sensitive. "Do you think Ella's story is true? Could it be something entirely created to explain her departure from Georgia?"

Will shrugged. "I think the story is real. It could have been something they either heard from others or just made up, but I don't think so."

"Strange how she got to Nevada…" Beth let the comment hover between them. She obviously wanted to probe Will's assessment further.

"From how she relayed it, I do believe she met Nate Crampion at a church function in Georgia. They obviously have feelings for each other, anyone can see that. The South was a mess after the war. They both wanted to leave. So did I. One day they set plans and just left together. I can see that."

"But never got married?"

Will shook his head. "Nope.

Beth added, "While we were on the bed before we reached the table, Ella said they always planned to get married. But with all the jobs and work there was just no time to get hitched."

Will had no response. Beth cracked a small smile and continued.

"Maybe it's just a hereditary Toal problem. You didn't exactly rush to the altar." A merry, shrewd grin spread across Beth's face.

"But, with you and me, there were circumstances."

Beth could not resist another playful jab. "Ah, what circumstances? One little tap on the head and it sent you into a spin that prevented you from bending your knee for four years."

"That *tap*, as you call it, knocked me out for three days. They didn't know if I would ever wake up."

Will could now smile and jest about an unsettled time between him and Beth. She had smacked him on the back of his head with her handgun after a shootout with a man who wanted money from Beth. At the time, Beth had thought it was the only way she could draw the outlaw away from Will. He had doubted her motives in ever lessening degrees for four years. It took an attempted kidnapping of Beth to finally solidify his love for this remarkable woman. But she was right, it took him four years to finally ask her to marry him.

"In the end, it was great to see Ella; to know I have relatives who are alive. But I'm worried about her."

"I can tell by the way you've been walking around here at the ranch since we returned."

Will sighed. "I asked Nate about his stock. You heard. He tried to lay out the numbers. Claimed he bought thirty head, branded them, and turned them loose on the open range. But after losing some to Ferguson in the spring roundup, he's now collecting what he claims are his mavericks and branding them throughout the year. That way, he doesn't have to work to protect them from being included in the big ranch roundup."

Beth spread her arms. "Even if he had the best breeding winter in history, there is no way his thirty head could grow to one hundred."

Again, impressed with Beth's acuity, Will just nodded. "Yep. If you know ranching, those numbers don't make sense, do they?"

"So, that's why you think Nate is rustling?"

"I think it's a good possibility. And if he is, then Ella could be in danger."

Beth sat back on the bench pressing her spine to the front wall of the house. "Now I understand why you were so pensive lately."

"That's not all. Remember, Ella said Dale Paris was working for Ferguson. He'd stopped by their ranch to warn Nate."

"I heard that. But Dale is an investigator. Maybe Ferguson is being reasonable as he tries to verify any taking of his property."

"I just thought it is strange that Dale would be working for someone like Angus."

"Will, even Dale Paris needs work."

"I know, it all just struck me as strange. You saw what happened when I told Ella about the money and offered to pay her an amount equal to half of what Pa had left. Nate wanted no part of it. But Ella said it would be 'well used'."

Beth tried to be positive. "Maybe this Nate Crampion will eventually use it to *buy* stock rather than collect mavericks."

"Maybe, but he's dealing with a lot of big ranchers, all who turn their herds loose in the open. Those men don't want small-time operations to run cattle on their range."

"I never really understood the whole open range concept. I am so glad you bought your land, and we don't have to deal with other owners splitting up cattle in a roundup. I'm not sure you would ever be able to tell what stock belongs to what ranch."

"It takes a lot of cooperation. The big ranchers all have similar interests. And it's a system they're used to."

Beth looked up at Will. "But will they ever come to accept a small rancher like Crampion?"

Will paused, and then answered, "Doubt it. As I understand it, there are many new homesteaders out on that range. The large ranchers want them all gone."

"They wouldn't resort to violence, would they?"

Will shrugged. "They might. Now you know why I'm worried."

Chapter Seven

Spring 1878
Open Range—North of Reno, Nevada

The stench of sweat lifted from Dale Paris's horse, and probably himself, too. He wore an ankle-length duster buttoned up against the early chill. He had camped out in the open for three nights straight. Not only his horse was beginning to smell ripe.

Intended to keep one dry in rain, his duster spread like a tent from the fastened collar down around Paris and his horse. He had been riding for two hours already today. Heat and aroma from his horse rose under the duster to his collar. It collected right under his nose as if smoke rising out of a chimney. Riding by day over stretches of ground broken only by low lying hills and sleeping on his horse blanket at night left both him and his mount with the same scent. A bath for him and curry comb for his horse would do both good.

As the vision of bed and bath at home continued to invade his thoughts, Paris unbuttoned his duster. It was already warming. A soft morning breeze lifted the now-freed portals of the long coat and naturally pulled them back on his sides. The infusion of fresh air smelled clean. He had to admit he'd become accustomed to his familiar bed and daily bath. Maybe he was getting soft. Maybe it was age. But he had stayed out under the stars out of frustration. He had not seen anyone taking cattle. He felt a duty to his employer. So, he had stayed out here in the solitary spaces.

Paris had made a large loop on the open range. He began his trip stopping by the remote corrals of Nate Crampion. Traveling west toward the Sierras, he had traversed the open range further to the north, and as of yesterday, turned south on his return. Stopping to catch their collective breath, both he and his horse were atop a small hill where he could see the Crampion home. He estimated he'd ridden over sixty miles yet had seen no rustling.

In the distance, dust elevated from a little used two-track road. A pair of wagons looked to be headed to the Crampion home. The motion of the dust caught his eye. There was a distance between the two rigs. They did not appear to be together.

Paris watched as the first wagon pulled up to the house. Ella Crampion came out of the front door and two men grabbed something out of the back of the wagon and followed her back in. They were inside maybe ten minutes and then came back out. The men climbed back on to their wagon rig, wheeled it around and headed off. The first wagon passed the second as it, too, neared the home. The drivers of both rigs waved with a casual raise of the hand.

Ella came out and greeted the second wagon just as she had the first. Again, the driver swung down and grabbed something out of the back. Paris strained to see what items had been collected, but the distance was too far. He had a field glass, but it was back in his saddlebag. Again, both entered the house. This time, the driver did not return for at least fifteen minutes. Upon exiting, he turned his rig around and headed back out on the two-track.

Paris wondered what was taking place. He could not see Crampion's horse tied to the lean-to. While there were a few head of cattle in one of the corrals, there were only one or two horses in the other. Not like the four or five that had been there when Paris visited days ago. He watched. There was no sign of Nate. Paris considered riding down to see if he could find out what had taken place, but decided against it. If Crampion was not home, he was out on the range. Paris decided to ride out to

Crampion's corrals. But the meeting of Ella and the two wagons intrigued him.

* * * * *

The calf squealed as the hot iron hit his left hip. Smoke and an acrid smell of burning hide punched his nostrils. Nate Crampion loved everything about ranching. Everything but the smell of a branding iron scorching the side of a steer.

"Hold him steady, now." Crampion spoke to his two part-time hands, each mounted on a horse with a rope attached to the steer. Nick Ray had done the heading. His horse pulled from that end. Reese Kindell had both feet looped and pulled opposite. The young calf lay stretched in between.

"I'll do the honors, and this young'un will no longer be on his way to becoming a bull."

Crampion then pulled his knife, swiftly cut a small section at the bottom of the scrotal sac, and pulled out the animal's testicles.

Without looking up from his efforts, Nate said, "It always surprises me how little blood flows when we do this. I have always imagined the exact opposite would happen."

Nick answered, "I'm just glad it's that steer that gets it and not me."

Reese went one step further. "What puzzles me is that they don't scream, don't even flinch for the most part. I can't imagine how that would feel if it were me." Kindell who had the rope connected to the heels almost squirmed in his saddle at the thought.

Nate smiled. "It is strange. But we'll watch them here in the corral for about four hours and you'll see, they do amazingly well. By tomorrow, they're actin' like nothin' happened."

Nick looked up. "Someone's comin'. Looks like two riders, cowhands."

Nate turned in the direction of Ray's gaze. He sheathed his knife and reached for his rifle. "Turn this one loose and get ready. Don't know what we'll be facin'."

Reese watched as he snapped his lariat loose from the calf. Nate and Ray both were now watching the oncoming riders. As he wound up his lariat, Reese said, "Those red sashes around their waists?"

"Could be," said Crampion. "If they *are* red sashes, it's not good."

* * * * *

Clay Cooper raised his hand and pulled up on his reins. "Hold on, Tate. Looks like they're reachin' for weapons."

"You're right. They've stopped with the brandin' and look like they're ready for a fight."

Cooper held his horse at a complete stop. Snyder did the same. Both gave the situation some thought.

"It's only the two of us," said Clay. "Maybe we walk real slow and keep our hands clear of the guns to show we mean no harm—at least, yet."

"Seein' as there are three men up ahead with both rifles and six shooters, I'd agree. Any reach for ours could lead to bullets flyin' and they got more shooters."

Clay gently touched the sides of his horse and started a slow walk toward the corral. He tipped the front bill of his hat and did his best to sound welcoming. "Mornin', thought we'd stop by and have a chat."

"Funny place to want to chat."

Cooper assessed the man who had answered. He looked no more than mid-twenties, maybe. His build was solid, and he also stood tall. The top of his head carried a tan-colored hat with front bill raised. The face looking at him was calm, but it had a firm tightness of resolve to it.

He seemed older than he looked. The young man held a medium-length rifle across his chest with the barrel cradled in his left elbow. His right hand covered the trigger and lever action. One quick motion, and the rifle could be whipped forward. If the trigger was pulled, he'd be ready to jack another round into the magazine of the repeater. The posture gave Cooper the impression that the man, albeit young, knew how to handle the rifle and possessed the mien to use it, if necessary.

Tate Snyder tried to fill the silence. "Funny time to be out brandin' cattle. Isn't that something all the ranches do late in the spring?"

Without changing his unmistakable suspicious expression, the young man in the upturned hat said, "What business is it of yours?"

Cooper could tell this was not going to be a congenial conversation. Best move to the real reason they were here. "Might be a problem for you if we were to tell some ranch owner you're out here brandin' his cattle."

The man in the upturned hat turned to face Cooper. "First, these are my cattle. No iron marks any maverick that is not attached to a heifer with my brand. Second, if someone were to say different to any rancher hereabouts, it might be detrimental to that person's health. And, if that person making the false claims wore a red sash, he might just find a rope around his own neck."

Realizing a bluff had been thoroughly called, but not one to back down early himself, Cooper took the challenge.

"We came into these parts looking to see if folks might want to work with us. But I'm not gettin' the feelin' you're the type to join up. Maybe that means we end up on opposite sides."

"Join up with who? What outfit do you work for?"

Snyder replied, "We have our own outfit."

"Yeah, where?"

"Up north."

Upturned Brim looked down, then returned his gaze to Snyder. "The name's Nate Crampion. I work nothing but my own stock. I'm small and don't want the big boys to take my mavericks like they did last year in their big spring roundup. But I work alone and intend to keep it that way. And I especially would avoid working with anyone wearing a red sash."

Cooper moved his right hand closer to his six-gun.

Crampion braced his feet as if anticipating a need to shoot. "I wouldn't do that. I think right now, you should keep your hands nice and quiet. It would be a bad fall from top of your horse after a .44 magnum from my Henry hit you in the chest."

Crampion had not moved his barrel from his elbow. But confidence oozed from his stance and demeanor. Cooper decided not to test it. Might be best to resolve this another day when the odds and circumstances were more favorable.

"As the man said, we had hoped we might find someone here local to work with. Seems it's not going to be you."

Crampion now let a wry grin spread across his face. "You got that figured correctly. And I keep close track of my stock. Should any go missing, I'll come looking for you."

Cooper could not resist. "Best you keep a constant watch on your stock. Never know where they might stray."

Snyder turned to Cooper. "Let's go, Clay. Nothin' more to discuss here."

Cooper nodded and pulled his reins to the left. His horse sidestepped around, and he and Snyder began riding away at a slow trot.

As they cleared what Cooper estimated might be the range of a Henry rifle, he spoke out of the side of his mouth to Snyder.

"I'm going to make it a point to grab some of that man's stock. Did you see the brand? It was a KC. I'll be lookin' for some with that mark.

He spoke as if he was educated a mite, but he isn't smart enough not to get some cattle stolen. No one is."

Back in the corral, Nick Ray asked Nate, "Who are they?"

Nate set the stock of his Henry rifle down against a near fence post in the corral. "Those are members of the Red Sash Gang. They are known rustlers from here to Wyoming. If they've a mind to, they will try to take every one of our steers."

Kindell chuckled. "Seein' as how neighborly you were, I would suspect they might just make it a point to take all of our stock they can get their hands on."

Nate watched as the two riders headed off.

"That's why we are going to stay out here in the line shack all night again tonight. We'll be ridin' circuit around the area watching out for their return."

* * * * *

Dale Paris had seen the entire exchange. He slapped the eyepiece of his small field glass, collapsing the multiple sliding parts into its smallest size. He then reached back to put it into his saddlebag. The riders who had approached Crampion's corral wore red sashes. Angus Ferguson had mentioned them. Ranch owners all across the mid-western plains knew of that gang. Butch Cassidy, Bill Booth, Tom Waggoner, and the Red Sash Gang were all known rustlers.

"If Nate Crampion is working with the Red Sash Gang," Paris muttered, "I'd better tell Will Toal to look out for his sister."

Chapter Eight

Spring 1878
Along Truckee River, Open Range

Daylight lasted longer here toward the end of spring. Paris had hung close to the Truckee River headed south and back to the Ferguson Ranch. He planned to stop briefly at the ranch and report to old man Ferguson, after which he would continue to Reno. Thoughts of his bed and a bath got stronger after he committed to end this tour of the range. But he also knew there was someone else in town he had to talk to. That someone needed to know what was happening out here on the range.

Cottonwoods and the shorter horse chestnut trees clung to the constantly moist soil adjacent to the riverbed. Both were gaining their leaves back after shedding them for the winter. The cottonwoods reached over a hundred feet tall and spread out covering almost as much ground below. Their triangle tooth-edged leaves fluttered in the usual breeze creating a soft sound and giving motion to the invisible gusts. The horse chestnuts were much different. Gnarled strands banded together to form the stout trunks. Those trunks looked like a woven leather lariat in wood. Back home his family had chestnut trees too, but they called them buckeyes. Yet, here in the West, folks called them horse chestnuts. Everything here in the West centered around the horse, even the trees.

Paris saw three riders coming north. He recognized both riders and horses. They all worked for Angus Ferguson. Bo Richards rode a distinctive paint horse. Levi Wallace and Roy "RR" Reddiker both rode bays out of the ranch's string. All three had bedrolls tied to the back of their saddles. They were obviously headed out for more than just a day ride. The group pulled up before Paris.

Usually, Bo spoke for this group. Holding to form, Richards did not take long to inquire.

"Seen any rustlers? Mr. Ferguson sent us out to check the range for a few days."

Paris shook his head in the negative. "Didn't see any rustling but might have seen some rustlers."

Reddiker perked up. "Do tell."

Paris leaned forward on his saddle horn. He told the group of seeing the Red Sash riders talking to Nate Crampion.

"That Crampion is taking steers. We all know it."

Paris shrugged his shoulders in a physical display of uncertainty. "Maybe, maybe not. I did not see him take any steers. He was branding in that remote corral of his next to his line shack, but all the heifers showed a KC brand."

Levi raised his finger and pointed at Paris, remarking, "But he could've taken mavericks and already branded them."

"True," said Paris. "But he's not rustlin' by taking mavericks. Mavericks on the open range are open to anyone who can take them. That's the law."

"Yeah, but not mavericks that are attached to their mommas. If he claims all his heifers are havin' twins, you and I both know that don't happen in open ground. Almost all cows have only one calf."

Paris did not want to argue. The bias on the part of these hands was clear and reflected the push of their boss, Angus Ferguson. Paris offered one last comment.

"Can't do much about it unless we see them actually take a branded steer, or a maverick and a branded one together. Until then, we have to watch and wait."

"Mr. Ferguson ain't gonna wait too much longer. He's ready to move these nesters off the range right now."

Paris tried to change the topic.

"Better at the moment to watch out for those riders wearing a red sash. From what we're told, they could be the outright thieves. Catch them in the act and things are simple."

The more mature Bo Richards continued with Paris's thought.

"It's gettin' dry quick. Most of the stock will be collecting near the Truckee. Maybe we will keep ridin' along the river and keep a lookout for anyone with a red sash."

"Good luck," said Paris. He tipped his hat and pulled around the group and continued south. As he passed, Levi chuckled, saying, "Hey, Paris, when are you gonna get a decent hat? That bowler looks like it belongs in a railway station." All three hands laughed.

Paris just smiled and rode on.

* * * * *

Evening was setting in. The sun had slipped behind the Sierras to the west. The only light left was a muted purple. Dark crests silhouetted high on the horizon.

It had been three hours since they had talked to Dale Paris. The ride had not been rushed. The three Ferguson cowhands were simply out scanning.

"There, see those two hands driving about thirty head?" Bo Richards pointed as he spoke.

Levi Wallace pulled up and squinted against the shadows. "I see them. Ain't that the yearling with the white hind leg in that group of steers?"

Roy Reddiker stood up in his stirrups. "I think it is. We've never seen a steer with a white leg anywhere else on the range. He was hanging close to one of our branded heifers when we saw him a week ago.

Must be the same animal. That heifer is ours. The whole group has to be ours."

Richards reached down and unhooked the leather safety strap on his handgun. "Get ready, boys. If I'm not mistaken, those two out there are wearin' a red sash. Paris told us to keep a lookout for them."

Wallace now looked at Richards. "What ya plannin'?"

Richards responded without turning to Wallace. "Get your guns ready. We're gonna charge them. Shoot at 'em if you can, but only take good shots. The gunshots will spook the stock and they'll start to run. So much the better. We can always round them up later. But they'll be out of control for those two."

Wallace kept looking at Richards. "Then what?"

Richards now turned to Levi. "We keep after those two until we catch 'em. If we do, we string 'em up. Mr. Ferguson said we was to stop any rustlin' we see and deal out justice as needed. This here looks like rustlin' to me."

Both men on either side of Richards pulled their handguns out. Richards had already pulled his.

"Ready?" Richards looked back and forth to each of the men on either side of him.

"Let's go," said Reddiker.

Spurs raked across the flanks of three horses simultaneously. All three mounts jumped forward. The trio spread out some as the horses gathered speed.

Richards was the first to shoot. He simply raised his gun high above his head and shot a round into the sky. The combination of the riders fast approaching, and the report of the gunfire had the effect he intended. The cattle immediately panicked and started to run, scattering as predicted. The small herd dispersed almost as soon as they started running. *So much the better,* thought Richards. The quicker the cattle scattered, the quicker the Sash riders would give up any hope of keeping the herd together. Then, it would be a simple matter of running down the rustlers.

Richards then yelled out to Reddiker and Wallace, "Let the cattle go. Head after the hands."

* * * * *

Both men wearing their red sash quickly pushed their horses to a gallop heading north. Johnny Fenton leaned forward urging his horse to full speed flipping his quirt from side to side of the animals' shoulders to enhance the urgency. After three slaps of the quirt, he looked to his right at Brock Smythe. With his head almost sideways to the ground, he yelled, "We got a good start. They're not in range. Just ride hard until we can get to some cover and then we can start shooting back."

Smythe was leaning forward almost to the same degree as Fenton.

"Maybe we should let them have a few even as we ride."

"Too hard to hit 'em. Save the rounds for when we stop. We'll need to make the shots count."

Fenton watched as Smythe reached back to pull his gun anyway. Just as he cleared leather, Smythe was gone. Fenton heard the sickening sound of a bone snapping. Dust flew up around Smythe and his horse as the animal rolled forward in a complete flip, after which, both skidded to a stop. Fenton could only guess what caused the horse to tumble. Might be a prairie dog hole, a rock causing the hock to twist on its downward thrust, or the cannon bone of the horse just broke.

Fenton pulled his reins with such force it must have caused the plate of his own mount's bit to slam into the roof of the animal's mouth. The horse sank down on its hind quarters skidding to a halt. Fenton spun the horse around and headed back to where Smythe was sprawled out in dust. His body was completely still. He lay in a contorted position

Fenton could tell was not natural by any estimation. He looked at the horse. The front left leg was broken in two. The animal was trying to get up but could only plant one of its front feet to lift its body. It was not having any success. Fenton looked at the oncoming riders. They would be in range shortly. And now, he was even more outgunned. Should he check on Smythe? In the flash of a moment, Fenton decided: he spun his horse and took off heading back north.

* * * * *

Wallace yelled, "One's down!"

Richards leveled his pistol at the rider now headed away and pulled off another round. He missed. He squeezed the trigger again. The rider ahead kept moving without any evidence of being hit.

The Ferguson men reached the downed rider. The horse was still struggling to rise.

"Horse is done for," said Reddiker.

"That's for sure, and the rider don't look much better," answered Wallace.

Richards took in the scene. Not wanting to waste any more time, he issued orders.

"Levi, tie up the man's hands. Be careful. He may not be dead. Stay here and keep an eye on him. Reddiker, you're with me. Let's see if we can catch up to the other one."

Richards and Roy Reddiker then spurred ahead after the now lone rider.

Wallace stepped off his horse and pulled his lariat with him. He kept his gun in his right hand pointed at the inert body in the dirt. The man was lying mostly on his left side and facing away from Levi. He saw that the man's holster at his raised right hip was empty. It was a fancy holster. Had to be a fancy gun to match it somewhere. He carefully approached. The man did not move. Wallace could not see both hands, and worried the man was playing possum. He might flip over and take a shot. He waited. Still, no movement. Wallace reached out with his boot and shoved the man to the rear of his shoulder immediately jumping back and aiming his gun at his head. Nothing.

Wallace walked around to the other side of the man. His horse kept trying to lift itself, now issuing guttural grunts of pain with the effort all to no avail. Wallace kept his eye trained on the man lying on the ground. Still no movement. Now on the other side, he again used his boot to shove the body. No reaction.

Wallace could now see the man's six gun loose and down near his knee. There had been no movement to grab the weapon. There had been no movement at all. Wallace holstered his own gun. He stooped down and picked up the lifeless man's weapon, flipped out the cylinder and emptied the cartridges into his hand. He pocketed the cartridges and jammed the weapon into his belt. It was, indeed, a new-looking Colt .44 magnum single action revolver. Levi had heard Colt had only started making these five to six years ago. Definitely a nice gun to fit into the man's fancy holster.

Wallace then turned and moved to the side of the injured horse. He approached the animal's head, pulled his gun, and shot it, putting it out of its misery.

Levi knelt and pulled the man's hands away from his body. He then noticed that the man was still breathing. He tied both together and knotted them tightly. As he cinched the knot with a jerk, the man's eyes opened wide, wider than Wallace imagined any eyes could open. The body that had been lying in a contorted position did not move, but the man's head lifted off the ground. Startled, Wallace jumped back two steps keeping the rope taut in his left hand. With his right, he reached for his now holstered gun.

Wallace's tension on the rope pulled the rustler's hands and arms away from his body. Other than the lifting of the man's arms and the head rising, nothing else moved. Wallace now stood leaning away from the prone man, steadying himself with his hold of the rope. The rustler's eyes did not track in Wallace's direction. They looked upward. The man's eyes remained open only for a moment, then closed as if he was hit with a jolt of pain, or maybe remorse. Wallace couldn't tell. The body then went limp again. Levi could see he was no longer breathing.

Wallace waited, watching for another change. But nothing. His own heartbeat raced, not knowing what to anticipate. Still, nothing. He put down the rope and leaned over to feel the prone man's neck. No pulse.

Levi stood and walked back to his horse doling out loops of his lariat as he moved away from the man. Not knowing what else to do, he mounted his horse and dallied his lariat around his saddle horn. He backed up his horse until the lariat strung taut and waited.

* * * * *

Wallace had not waited long, maybe a quarter-of-an-hour, when he saw Richards and Reddiker riding back. Both of their horses were lathered with white foam running down the underside of their necks and covering their chests. He watched them approach at a collected trot.

Richards pulled up and looked at the man lying fixed in the same position he'd last seen him.

"He hasn't moved?"

Levi shook his head. "Nope, hasn't moved a muscle. He's dead."

"How do you know that?" asked Richards.

Wallace continued to just stare at the man on the ground. "After I tied his hands, his body didn't move, but his head lifted sudden-like. Don't mind tellin' you it caused me quite a start. With his body just layin' there limp, his head lifted up and his eyes opened up so wide I thought they'd pop out of their sockets."

Richards gave Levi an inquisitive look. "Did you shoot him when he did that?"

"Nope. Those eyes flashed open starin' at the sky and then he winced and flopped back down. He ain't taken a breath since."

"Hope he had those eyes opened long enough to make his peace," said Richards.

"Maybe he damaged his head in the fall. Maybe broke his neck." The observation came from Reddiker this time.

Richards pulled his hat off and wiped his brow with the back of his forearm. "We lost the other one. That man's riding a real good horse. Ran away from ours in about three miles or so. Lost him in some rocks. Didn't want to push it and get one of us killed. He could have jumped off his horse and pulled a rifle just waiting until we got close."

"What are we gonna do with this one?" asked Levi.

Richards sighed, and, while still looking down at the prone cowboy, said, "We're gonna hang him."

"Hang him?" asked Wallace. "He's already dead. Not only that, he looks young, just past being a boy."

"He was old enough to know better than rustle cattle," came Richards's reply. There was a stern resolution in his voice when he said it. "We're gonna string him up so's those ridin' with him will see we mean business. They won't know he was dead before we strung him up. Maybe after the sight they'll take off and move to some other open range."

Range War

Levi then asked, "How we gonna move him? His horse is dead. I had to shoot him."

Richards looked at the now deceased horse. "Only thing you could've done. Can't let the animal suffer."

"Want us to lift him up on one of our horses?" Richards looked at Reddiker to answer his question.

"No, Levi, just drag him over to that cottonwood there by the river. There's a horse chestnut tree next to it, and we could use that, too. But the cottonwood is taller. If we string him up there, he'll be seen at a distance. Might strike his partners hard if they see him hung up high. We'll use the cottonwood."

Ferguson's men then moved toward the river. Levi and his horse dragged the still motionless man through dirt and low scrub. The body simply flopped back and forth without any control or resistance. The group came up to the designated cottonwood.

Richards had taken the dead man's own lariat from his saddle. He tossed the dally stub of the rope over a branch and pulled it through the honda loop with a racer at the other end of his lariat.

Watching, Levi asked, "Do you think the racer will give way if you string someone up?"

Richards stood up, looked at his questioner and scoffed. "Levi, you know that little piece of rawhide at the top of the honda loop we call a racer is there to make the tightening of a loop thrown over the head of a steer close quick. It also keeps the rest of the lariat from burning over time with continued roping. You rope steers and drag them. Any steer is going to outweigh this boy here. Racers hold fast when you rope a steer. The racer will be fine."

Richards then returned to the action at hand.

"Roy, put the loop around the man's neck. Take Levi's rope off his hands. I'll dally up, and when you're ready, I'll get my horse to back and pull him up. When he's high enough, we'll all have to take a hold and pull the rope over to the tree and tie it off around the trunk."

Reddiker did as commanded. The noose was looped around the kid's neck.

Richards then mounted.

Reddiker then nodded to Richards all was ready. All three watched the young cattle thief begin to rise as Richards spurred his horse in the effort to lift him off the ground. After the rope was tied off, Levi stood next to the other two with a discomforted look. He did not want to appear hesitant. But he did not feel good about what they'd done. With a look to his right and left he could tell neither Richards or Reddiker felt any remorse. Their faces showed nothing but satisfaction. Levi decided not to say anything.

As the three men rode away from the now suspended body of Bryce Smythe, Richards looked back and said, "Hope the rest of his gang takes note. Same will happen to all of them if they stay around here. Best they leave—and soon."

Reddiker then added, "Let's camp near. Getting dark, anyway. Maybe some others wearin' the red sash will come lookin' for their friend. We might get some more."

Richards smiled. "Roy, that's one of the best ideas you've had in quite a while. Let's ride to the other side of that rise over there and set camp. We can keep out of sight but watch for any of his partners. If they don't come back before morning, we'll move on. Mr. Ferguson should be happy. At least we got one."

Chapter Nine

Spring 1878
Toal Ranch, Jack's Valley, Nevada

Strands of deep emerald grass abounded like dry waves in the wind. A gust would cause the knee-high blades to lean sideways as if a hand were somehow passed through a section of the pasture. Then they would relax and rise to full height waiting for the next breeze to push them down again. How different was this stretch of land from the open range north of Reno? Spring had amply supported the growth of grass all over this part of the southern Carson Valley. Paris knew the locals called it Jack's Valley. He did not know why. Bordered by fast rising Sierras to the west and stretching across miles to the east, the valley was scattered with cattle strewn across massive fenced in pastures. The landscape before him teemed with a kind of peace. He could almost feel the difference. There was a tension on the land up north. Not here. The unknown and struggle to survive permeated the north. Not here. The entire scene spoke of contentment and order. Some had called this area an Eden. They could be right.

Some time ago, Paris had ridden down this same road into the central compound of the Toal Ranch to deliver foreclosure papers on Will Toal. It had not been a pleasant day. At the time, Paris thought he was doing the right thing. He represented the railroads on that day. But it had led to a confrontation, particularly with Will Toal. Animosity resulted. Years went by before that animosity abated. It took an event where Paris had appeared in the nick of time and saved Will's life to fully end the tension between the two. They had worked together since. Paris hoped he had generated enough respect over those subsequent efforts to carry him through the meeting he was headed to today.

On that earlier ride years ago, Paris had admired the trees throughout Jack's Valley. They reminded him of home back in Indiana where he grew up. The same held true today. Water from the close Sierras coupled with regular seed carrying winds resulted in multiple stands of trees. The pastures cradled all kinds, large and small. Some stood alone while some sheltered homes. Everything was green here. The trees rose in healthy strength. Everything looked alive. He should have bought land here when he had the chance.

Paris walked his horse into the compound. While he was sure he'd been seen long before he arrived, he thought it best to call out a welcome.

"Hello! Is Will Toal in?"

A tall, long-legged blonde breezed through the doorway of the main house.

"Dale Paris. Get off your horse and rest yourself."

Paris immediately knew this fine lady as Will Toal's wife.

"Mrs. Toal, I would love to do just that."

"You call me Mrs. Toal once more and you can stay on your horse and head right back where you came from. Dale, you know better than that. I'm Beth."

"And Beth it shall be. Let me tie my horse up. Can I use the water trough over by the barn?"

"Absolutely. Go water your animal, loosen his cinch and then come into the house. I'll have a lemonade ready for you by then. We planted a lemon tree a couple of years ago and now twice a year we get more lemons than we can use. The branches on the little tree are not strong enough to hold up all the fruit. People questioned whether it would grow here, but it did well even with the drought last year. It's a hardy little thing but we have to use the lemons, or they just fall off and rot."

"You have no idea how appealing that sounds. I'll be right there. Is Will around?"

Beth rubbed her hands on her apron. "No, but I'll send one of the boys to get him. He's not far."

"That would be perfect. I do need to talk to him."

"Tend to your horse and I'll have the boys fetch Will."

Paris led his horse across the compound and let him take a quick drink. Looking around, he noticed there was a new coat of paint on the barn opposite the main house. The other two buildings to his left and right also looked freshly painted. He seemed to recall the building on one side was for Will's ramrod, and opposite that was the bunkhouse. The four buildings were all set in a square to form the borders of the compound. He walked back to the main house. He stopped at the entrance and rapped his knuckles on the door frame.

"Okay for me to come in?"

Beth came through a door across the room. Pointing to a low table with a couch and two chairs near the chimney she said, "Please, have a seat."

Paris looked around the room. "I was only here once before. Wasn't this the kitchen of the house when it was originally built?"

Beth laughed. "It was the kitchen, main room, and dining room all in one. The only other room then was Will's tiny bedroom which we converted to the kitchen, the room I just came from. We've expanded a bit as the family grew in numbers. Besides converting the kitchen, we have added three bedrooms to the rear. The boys are in one, Juliette in another, and Will and I are in the largest of the three."

"And with a fine settee here before the chimney. My, you've brought some culture to home and hearth, despite your rough-hewn husband."

Her smile became even wider. "Dale, thank you. I am glad someone here out on the wide-open spaces recognizes these are improvements. My dear husband, I am sure, would still be happy to be camping in the grass. He thinks a stall in the barn is a fine hotel."

"How is the ranch owner doing? It's been over nine months since the gunfight at the dam."

Beth placed two glasses on the table then sat opposite Paris. She paused before answering. Paris could not help but notice.

"The ranch is doing fine. The beef stock is building back up after the last couple of drought years. Will says this year's new horses will be the best we've ever put up for sale." She again hesitated. "But Will found out the sister he'd thought long dead is alive and lives nearby. He went to see her. What should have been—what I'd hoped to be—a happy event has left him troubled."

"Interesting. I came to talk to him about his sister, too. I think there's good reason to worry."

A voice, low and stern, came from the open door. "And why would you be worried about my sister?"

Paris immediately stood. Something was wrong. By posture and tone, he heard a healthy dose of suspicion in Will's voice. Will Toal was a just and straight man. Paris could tell right away that, for some reason, he was being judged through Will's prism of right and wrong. Toal must have heard he was working for Ferguson. Paris had cultivated their relationship with great care. He knew in an instant the next moments might lead to irreparable damage to that bond. His first words would be crucial.

"Will, I've come to tell you I think she's in trouble. I'd like to figure a way we both can work together and help her out."

Paris watched as Will's head tilted slightly upward and to the side.

"Ella told me you were working with Ferguson, and that Ferguson was harassing her and Nate to move out."

Paris had guessed right. Will had heard he was working with Ferguson. Knowing the source of the problem made reaching the solution easier. Paris moved across the room toward his host.

"Will, I'm being paid by Ferguson to find rustlers, not to harass them or dispense justice. But I'm also reporting to Leif Svensson, Sheriff of Reno, on the activity of Ferguson and the Nevada Stock Grower's Association."

Still sounding yet to be convinced, Will asked, "Why Svensson?"

Paris continued to move toward Will. He now stood arm's length away, man to man. "Because Ferguson is out of control, and along with the Nevada Stock Growers Association, aims to rid the range of homesteaders—whether it's legal or not. Your sister sits right in the middle of his crosshairs. What makes it worse, the man she's living with is acting strange. He could be just protecting what's his, or he could be taking cattle belonging to the big ranches. Right now, I can't tell which of the two paths he's following. In the end, it doesn't matter which of those is right, he's putting your sister in harm's way. I came to tell you and try to fix it."

Paris held out his hand.

"You're not pushin' Ferguson's agenda?"

"Nope."

"Didn't think you would be. Glad to hear it from the horse's mouth." Will grabbed his hand. "Nice to see you again."

Will turned to Beth, "Any more lemonade?"

"Depends."

"Depends on what?"

"Depends on how I'm greeted and how I'm asked."

Paris smiled. He'd seen Will Toal face fast gunmen, stare into the barrels of rifles pointed at him. But he'd never seen him as uncomfortable as he was right now.

"So, if I were to try and show my friend, here, that I am the man of the house and demand a glass of lemonade, I'd go thirsty?"

Beth leveled her most austere gaze. "You would."

A knowing grin cracked at either edge of Will's mouth. Though he responded to his wife, he looked at Paris.

"You would go out of your way to embarrass your husband in that manner?"

Gaze undeterred, but with an equally slight grin of her own, Beth replied, "I would."

Will used his index finger to push up the front brim of his hat.

"Then I suppose I should humbly ask my lovely bride for a glass of lemonade."

"Properly done. And yes, you may." With that, Beth returned to the kitchen.

Having watched the little scene, Paris grinned himself. "Always this way?"

Will answered as he moved to take a seat. "Nah, she only does it to show off for company. I let her get away with it, part of the performance."

"I heard that!" came her retort from deep in the kitchen.

Both men now openly smiled.

"Can you stay?"

Paris shook his head. "I can't. I must get back to the range. But I had to see you about Ella."

"I appreciate you coming. You probably know more about what her Nate Crampion is up to. I have to confess, he told me what he does…and I'm a little skeptical myself."

"You should be. I've seen him out on the range collecting and branding mavericks. I have yet to see him take a maverick attached to another brand, but that's hard to tell sometimes."

Will agreed. "I know, brands can be changed."

Paris opened his hands, palms up. "But I've not seen him changing any brands, only putting his KC on new mavericks."

Will then asked, "Aren't mavericks open game for anyone who takes them?"

Paris sat back. "That's the law in Texas. But in Wyoming, all unbranded calves attached to mothers, what we call mavericks, are deemed the property of the Wyoming Stock Growers Association. The Nevada group here feels the same should apply to them."

Will looked puzzled. "What's the law here in Nevada?"

Paris lifted his hands into the air. "Anybody's guess."

Beth walked back into the room with a fresh round of filled glasses. "That sounds like a legal quagmire. Maybe you should talk to Sam Grande, Will."

Will nodded. "Probably a good idea."

Paris then added, "Svensson is not even sure what is legal and what is not out there. He knows you can't rustle cattle. But he and many define that as someone stealing a branded animal belonging to another. As for mavericks, he's uncertain too. To make matters more difficult, that open range is federal land. Svensson questions whether he has any jurisdiction when it comes to dealing with homestead claims versus grazing permits. Svensson believes that falls within the jurisdiction of a U.S. marshal because those are federal laws applicable to federal land. He doesn't want to get involved unless the Stockman's Association starts hurting people."

Paris watched as Will displayed open disbelief. "They wouldn't do that, would they? Ferguson wouldn't do that. Right?"

Paris looked down and back at Will with sorrow in his eyes.

"Angus is broken, lost. With his son Dirk gone, he's become a bitter, angry man. And he is pushing the Stock Growers down the same road."

Will pursued. "But intentionally out to injure and harm people?"

"As best as I can tell," Paris began, "Angus truly believes that these homesteaders are breaking the law. Not only squatting on lands licensed for grazing, but taking his mavericks, which, he believes, belong outright to the ranch owners. He thinks they should be run out. If not run out, burned out. If not burned out, simply hung."

Will was silent. Paris could see he was stunned by the stark assessment.

Dale continued. "But that's where Svensson draws the line. He feels issues with cattle on government land is the government's problem. People injuring others without justification makes him ready to act."

"Ready to do what?" asked Will.

"Get a posse together and arrest anyone responsible, even if it is one or more of the powerful ranchers. He doesn't like Ferguson. I suppose that goes both ways. Svensson thinks the man is obsessed. The two men don't see eye-to-eye on much of anything."

Will sipped his lemonade. He then extended his glass out in front of him as if it held the answers to life, and not just a liquid to quench thirst.

"Can you count on Svensson to stand up to Ferguson?"

Paris nodded. "I'm sure of it."

Will continued to twirl his glass. Paris could see it was a simple act to suspend the conversation long enough to collect his thoughts. "Then, let's do this. I'll go talk to Sam Grande tomorrow. You tell Svensson that I'm going to try and convince my sister to come stay here on the ranch. I'll try to get Nate to bring his stock here, too. But I've already suggested that once and he refused. Kind of stubborn. I'm not sure I'll have any success. Lastly, hope you will let me know if you hear Ferguson is going to take more drastic steps?"

Paris stood. "Agreed. I've got to get back. I'll spend the next couple of days in Reno. There's a meeting of the Stock Growers Association and I'll try to be there just to see what they're up to. Then I'll head back out on the range to keep a lookout. But if any of Ferguson's hands think Crampion is rebranding or taking their stock, they're liable to try and hang him on the spot."

"I know," said Will. "I'll have to be more convincing when I see them the next time. Problem is I might not be able to head back north for a week or so. I have buyers coming to bid on our new horses."

Paris nodded. "If I hear anything, I'll send a wire message."

Paris shook Will's hand and walked out the door. Will stood in the doorway and watched him go. Beth came up behind Will and wrapped her arms around his waist while she looked over one shoulder.

"Nice of him to come."

"It was."

Beth squeezed a bit harder. "You have to convince your sister to come here to the ranch. This sounds more and more dangerous."

"Plannin' on it."

Chapter Ten

Spring 1878
Reno, Nevada

Smoke, sweat, and emotion filled the confinement of the room. Teeth clenched on every manner of smokable device from cigars to S-curved dropped down pipes. A white mist of exhaled tobacco floated in the rafters looking for an escape. As with the issue at hand, there was none.

The discussion had lasted almost an hour. Angus Ferguson and Carter McKinnon had called this meeting of the Nevada Stock Growers Association. Originally pleased with the way the meeting had started, Angus now felt his stomach tighten at the possibility the group would be swayed away by those who object to his suggested solution. As he saw it, they were the ones with little resolve. While everyone could agree rustling was a problem, there were many who disagreed as to what to do about it.

Angus Ferguson could not contain his frustration. Seated next to Carter McKinnon, he touched his neighbor's upper leg. McKinnon wore a suit of fine woolen material. The fabric had been imported from England. But Ferguson did not notice. Angus used his index finger to poke again at McKinnon as if to emphasize the importance of the moment. He leaned in close to Carter.

"This has to end." With Ferguson's Scottish brogue the word *to* came out sounding as if spelled *tew*. "About half of the group sees things our way, the other half are doing their best to kill the idea."

McKinnon gazed around the room before he answered Angus.

"You can see the strain on the faces of those undecided. They puff on their smoke of choice, but they draw quicker despite trying to look relaxed. You can tell by the way they smoke who agrees, who is against, and who is undecided."

"Funny, the things you see, Carter."

"Am I wrong?"

"As I look at those doing the smoking, you might just be right."

McKinnon then nodded to a far corner of the room. "Who invited Sheriff Svensson to this?"

Angus followed his gaze.

"I dinna know. It certainly wasn't you or me. Someone else must have thought he could be convinced to help matters."

McKinnon tucked his chin toward his chest in a physical act of mild disagreement.

"Or they brought him because they were worried about what the Stock Growers might do."

Ferguson considered how he should approach his next move. He'd told the collected group about his idea to hire Frank Canton and designate him as a Range Detective. Wyoming ranch owners had recommended Canton to Angus as a man who could clear Nevada's range of rustlers. He'd done the same in Wyoming. Canton would also be allowed to hire several men from Texas to ride the range in search of rustlers. He had used the term "patrol". But then someone asked what they should do about the homesteaders who did not have a proper finalized title to their claim. In a quick answer, without giving the question much thought, Ferguson had said they should be driven out. The meeting became chaotic after that.

Men were now talking over each other. The accumulated combination of comments, shouts, accusations, and retorts produced the current din of incomprehensible miscommunication. The meeting was devolving. Some agreed with Angus. Others felt the homesteaders had a legal right to be out on the land, and any attempt to physically remove them might be found criminal. Ferguson stood.

"Enough!"

Silence followed. The chairs in the room had been arranged in a large series of quadrangles. An open space sat at the center of the arrangement. Angus moved to the center, spun around looking at the entire collection of ranch owners, politicians, and investors, all of whom made up the membership of the Nevada Stock Grower's Association. He was the center of attention.

"I have no problem with the Homestead Act. But no one should be allowed to flop themselves out in the middle of an open range and claim land that has already been designated under a grazing permit. There is only one reason anyone might want to do that: to steal cattle."

A stir arose, but Ferguson held up his hand to quell any start of discussion. He intended to drive home his point before anyone could object.

"We all have lost stock. Some more than others. And it comes on the heels of two winters with little rain where hundreds, if not thousands, of our cattle died in the drought. These nesters come with no stock of their own. Then, like magic, they have a hundred head under brand. How did that happen?"

Angus stopped his constant twirl. He stretched open the front of his coat and pulled it wide as he slid his hands down the length of the lapels. As his hands descended along the fabric, while still spreading the jacket, he tucked his thumbs into the pockets of his vest. No one had taken up his challenge. He knew he was pushing the argument in the direction he wanted.

"I'll tell you why. These nesters don't bring cattle with them. They had no starter herds. Any stock they have now came from us." Angus's voice now raised. "They've taken our beef! *Our beef*! These nesters are nothing but grease spots blotting our range. There are some here who worry it might be criminal to drive them off. What about the criminal act of rustling? They take our mavericks and call them their own. That is theft! *They* are the criminals. And our own sheriff stands by because he says he can do nothing."

Ferguson, pleased with himself and his manipulation of Sheriff Svensson's presence, now thrust his point home lifting his hand in the direction of Svensson. "Sheriff, did you not say there was nothing you could do about those taking our mavericks?" Ferguson shot the sheriff a feral stare, daring him to contradict what he'd told Angus earlier.

Several sets of eyes turned to Svensson. Trapped by the challenge, as he knew others had heard his answer to this same question weeks earlier, he did not respond.

Angus waited for the sheriff to say something. Grinning at his minor verbal victory, he now spun again. "There. *There* is your answer. The law will do nothing. It is left to us. If we do nothing, we will all be broke. If we do not stop the flow of our cattle out to illegal brands, then it will continue. If no one moves to stop them, the grangers will only take more and more. I did not work my land and build my herd to see it taken by usurpers, these sheepherders, and nesters. They are the criminals."

Doing his best to be supportive, McKinnon floated a question, the answer to which he already knew. "How long to get Frank Canton here to Reno?"

Ferguson turned to face McKinnon. "Carter, as ye know, Frank Canton is already here. He stands in another room in this very building."

A minor uproar followed. Ian McBride stood and pointed a finger at Ferguson. "You had no right to hire this man on behalf of the Growers Association without our approval."

Angus did not miss a beat. He turned immediately, confronting his adversary. "Ian, I have hired Mr. Canton myself. I have made a recommendation to this group that we should all agree to hire this man. But if there is no such agreement, I fully intend to hire him myself. If I do that, he will protect only my herd. If the group agrees to hire him, he will protect everyone's."

"You've no right, Angus." Again, it was McBride.

"Ian, if you and your European investors do not like the idea, then you go back to your home and sit yourself down and watch. The rest of us will stop the losses."

This time, there was a more positive stir in the room. Angus could feel momentum building to go along with his plan. Sensing it was time to bring matters to a head, Angus took one more spin on his heel.

"It is time, gentlemen. Those who want to help and be part of the solution, stay and meet Mr. Canton. Those who do not, it is time for you to leave."

Ian McBride, Sheriff Svensson and three other ranchers stood and moved to walk out of the room. As he walked by Ferguson, McBride leaned close and said, "Angus, you make a grave mistake here. Those people have a right to homestead government land. You have no right to take it from them."

Ferguson just glared at McBride. He knew there was nothing more to be said. After the objectors left the room, Angus turned back to McKinnon and asked, "Carter, I think it is now a good time for the group to meet Mr. Canton. Would you please go fetch him for us all?"

"My pleasure."

McKinnon left and returned shortly with a man wearing a long black duster. The outer boot-length jacket covered a dark suit below. A white shirt collar collected underneath a black string tie. Well-trimmed strips of graying hair could be seen just below the edges of a dark woolen cap. The cap had a flat leather top and bill, but the sides looked as if it had been sheared from a black sheep. He was about forty years old, skin wrinkled and darkened by the sun, standing almost six feet tall. Broad in the shoulder, from which his duster draped and flowed to his rear as he moved, Canton cast an imposing figure.

The invited guest entered the room and moved close to Ferguson.

"Mr. Canton, welcome to the Nevada Stock Grower's Association. I have suggested to our group that they consider hiring you to protect our range. Please tell them how you would do that."

Though Ferguson had told him he would ask this exact question, Canton paused, looked around the room and took off his cap and duster. He laid them down on an empty chair. All present waited expectantly for the man's response.

Returning to the center of the room, Canton stood opposite Ferguson and answered. "I would hire deputies and along with them ride your range watching for people taking mavericks. If they have taken an unbranded maverick, I'll treat them like the rustler they are. Branding takes place once a year in late spring. All the stock is collected and separated by the brands of the heifers. The mavericks who follow those heifers are the property of the owner holding the brand. That's how things have been done for a decade in Texas, Nebraska, and Wyoming."

"What about homesteaders?" The question came from one of the ranchers sitting in a ring of seats furthest away from the center.

"I'd watch their property carefully. If I see any branding going on outside of the spring roundup or any unbranded mavericks collected in corrals, then I'd treat them as rustlers, too."

Ferguson then asked, "How many men will you need to hire?"

Canton answered with a casual confidence. "About ten should do."

"And where would you get these men?"

"Texas. I've contacted five good men who are already on their way here. They will arrive on tomorrow's early train. I could have up to twenty come soon, if needed."

"Are these men familiar with the job at hand?"

"Each one has ridden with me on range duty in either Texas or Wyoming."

Ferguson stretched the introduction in an effort to convince any lingering doubters. "And did your efforts work in Texas and Wyoming."

"You can talk to the cattlemen's groups in both states where I have been hired. Rustling was reduced by more than half. In Wyoming, it was reduced almost to nothing."

Ferguson smiled. "I have talked to the Wyoming Stock Growers Association. You come highly recommended. That's why I hired you, and why I recommend our group here in Nevada do the same."

Canton did not respond.

Angus then looked at the collected ranchers.

"Two days ago, several of our ranch hands came upon a pair of riders wearing a red sash. These riders were herding mavericks and stock bearing my brand headed north. My men pursued the thieves. They captured one of the riders and hung him. The point here, gentlemen, is that organized bands of rustlers are working our range. We need to stop them now. The homesteaders claim herds that are growing. Ours are diminishing. We need to hire this man, and do it now. Anyone disagree?"

No one did. To the contrary, many of those in the room nodded their heads in agreement.

"Then, it's done. Mr. Canton, hire your ten men and get to work. We will have badges made. You and your men will be Range Detectives in the employ of the Nevada Stock Grower's Association. Your charge is to end cattle rustling on Nevada's open range."

Canton nodded, but then lifted both arms along with posing a question of his own. "And what are you men prepared to do?"

The comment took some aback. Taking in the silence, Canton continued.

"In order to make it plain and clear to everyone, I've found it best that the ranch owners and their hands join in specific efforts to pursue those found to be stealing."

"I'd be willing to ride with you and could provide several of my hands to join us, too," said Ferguson.

Others, the most enthusiastic of the group, raised their voices. Carter McKinnon, along with Senator Ronald Tisdale, and Attorney General Gentry MacDonald, all offered to ride with the group and bring additional men if needed.

Ferguson looked at Canton.

"From the sound of those answering, I think you can count on over forty men all total." Ferguson thought he could see a sign of approval on Canton's face.

Canton swung back to face the rest of the group. "That should do. With those additional men, we should be able to deal with anything we meet out on the range."

"When can you start?" Ferguson wanted the group to have a good idea as to when the plan would take effect.

Canton looked directly at Angus to answer his question. "The first of my men will arrive tomorrow. Give me a day after that to arrange for horses and equipment. Two days from now we should be out on the range."

"The sooner the better," responded Angus. "Gentlemen let's move to the bar. For the first time in years, I feel like this group is going to do something of value, value to us all. After the last couple of years, our bank accounts can use it."

* * * * *

Dale Paris was about to step into Sheriff Leif Svensson's office. As he stood poised in front of the door, several men approached. Each was dressed in a manner making it known immediately that they were men of wealth. Paris thought he recognized one or two as wealthy landowners. They were led by a small man wearing a dark, expensive woolen coat reaching almost to the man's knees. The lapels were of black silk. His boots were highly polished and clean. Here in the middle of Reno, that alone was remarkable.

"Do you work for the sheriff?" The small man was abrupt, almost commanding with the question.

Paris did not want to reveal the double-sided nature of his efforts both for Angus Ferguson and the sheriff. "I am a private investigator. I have many cases I work simultaneously. I try to keep the sheriff apprised of my efforts."

"Is the sheriff present?"

Paris looked through the door into the office. The sheriff's desk was empty. The only person inside was a deputy. "Apparently not," he answered.

"Then I would ask you to relay to our good sheriff that he better keep a close watch on the Stockgrowers Association."

Intrigued, Paris asked, "Why?"

"Because they are about to take the law into their own hands."

Paris did not have time to reply. The man and his entourage walked by without saying another word.

Chapter Eleven

Spring 1878
Carson City, Nevada

It was a small bell, a small sound. A soft rattle vibrated from the inside of the door to which it was attached. He wondered. A signal? An announcement? A warning? Will Toal chuckled at the fact that no matter where his friend attorney Samuel S. Grande moved his office, this little bell went with him.

Will shook the door a little extra to extend the muted message. He always did. For Will, there was something strange, almost ostentatious about the little bell. Yet, while he would never have attached one to any office he might have, he thought it fit Sam's personality. It made him smile every time he entered Sam's office. Maybe that was the point.

"Toal, is that you?"

Sam knew the routine.

Will knew the proprietor of this office well. Grande had helped him homestead his ranch when no one else would lend any assistance to someone from the south. He then created the legal solution to save not only Will's ranch but the other ranchers in the Carson Valley when the railroad was trying to foreclose on them all. And he'd recently won a major battle for the Nevada folks in a legal fight with Californians over the rights to water from Lake Tahoe during one of the worst droughts in recent memory.

"Yep, it's me. You coming out here, or do I have to hunt you through this massive new office with all its rooms?"

Will stood for a moment just inside the door. He had been here only once since Sam had changed offices. As no one moved or spoke, Will decided to further explore. He moved toward one of the three open doors out of which had come Grande's initial response.

"I kind of liked your old office. It had one room and I knew right away where you were and what your mood was. Knowing your mood is important. Changes quick. You still married?"

"What would you know about my moods? The only thing you can read are funny markings in the earth, which you call *signs*." Grande never lacked for the offense in any conversation. Will needed to keep the balance.

Grande came to the threshold of his office and the small lobby. The lawyer stood an impressive six-foot-five-inches tall, with a wide, barrel chest resting atop a frame that was solid all the way to the ground. Will found it hard to hide his amazement as to how much of the doorway Grande's physique took up. With the sunlight framing Grande from the rear, had he not been a good friend of the man, the vision, along with his tone of voice, could almost be intimidating. In the deepest, fullest baritone he could muster, Grande issued his response to Will's not-so-subtle challenge. "We've only been married six weeks."

Will smiled, thinking, *got him where I want him.*

"Long enough for her to know what she got in the bargain and decide to show you out."

Not to be dissuaded, Grande thrust with a jab of his own. "You should talk. Your wife is liable to take you for all you're worth any day now. The only thing holding her up is the fact there is nothing of value to take."

"Oh, I don't know. Three thousand acres, eight hundred head of cattle, and sixty horses of high quality ain't 'nothing'."

"Could be gone in the next storm. Or even more probably, gone with the next group of outlaws you irritate. As you never come to my office unless you are in some type of trouble, maybe you are here to discuss events which will finally lead to lovely Beth's widowhood. Maybe then she can get on with her life in peace."

"Naw, things are quiet."

"That's a relative term in your world."

Will sensed the verbal fencing was coming to an end.

"So, are you and Sandra coming out again for dinner this Sunday?"

"We are. Your wonderful wife has been most gracious to continue our weekly Sunday dinners after the wedding. Before that, it was if she took pity on me as a single man stuck in the confines of the city. The two ladies seem to get along quite nicely, and it is such a pleasure to get out of town. We should have you here to our house sometime, but Beth insists on our traveling out to the ranch. I have to say, Sandra and I do enjoy the ride out in the open."

"Sandra is great. Gotta admit, you're lucky man. Can't say as you deserve her, though."

"The same goes for you, my feckless client."

"Feckless? Where did you come up with that word?"

"Education."

Will shook his head. "Naw, probably something some other lawyer accused you of."

Grande let go of a hearty laugh. Will had rarely seen the attorney's face light up so completely.

"Actually, it was a term thrown at me by a judge in the heat of an argument I had with him. I didn't know what it meant until I came back to the office and looked it up. Oh, I knew it wasn't complimentary by the way he used the term. Up to that point, I always thought that judge was dumb as a post. I had to reassess after he used a term I didn't know."

"With your warm welcoming personality, I'm surprised someone hadn't called you that before." Will's grin spread even further, thinking he'd got him on the run.

This time, Grande had no immediate answer. Will noted a rare win in the pair's verbal battles. Grande silently motioned him to follow into his office. On their way, Will looked left to see an Asian male, short in stature sitting at a small desk in another office. Will stopped. He'd never seen anyone else in any of Grande's previous offices. Sam always worked alone. Will pointed to the occupied office.

"You hire a Chinaman?"

"I'm Japanese," came the loud retort. From the shrill tone of the law clerk's voice Will could tell he had hit a sore spot.

Embarrassed, Will contritely offered, "Sorry. Should have been introduced, but my lawyer here has poor manners."

Grande returned to the doorway pushing his large frame passed Will.

"His name is Warren Fujimoto. He is my new law clerk. He was born into a solid Japanese family, any member of which would take great offense to be called Chinese. The two cultures are not big fans of each other."

"I'm not sure where Japan is," said Will. "Rare to hear anything about it here in Nevada."

The clerk glared at Will. Grande stepped into the silence as something of a peacemaker. "Warren is quite brilliant, but no law school would admit someone of his background. So, I'm guiding him through the process of learning the law. It is called 'reading for the bar'."

Warren stood behind his desk. Will could not tell from the look on the young man's face if he was mad, upset, pleased, or relieved. His expression revealed no indication of the thoughts behind the mask. He wore a rumpled ill-fitting suit, but his tie was immaculately turned. Will had never worn such a tie, but he'd seen other wealthy men who had. The tie alone told Will this young man was trying to make something of himself, to fit in to this culture of a foreign land.

"What does 'reading for the bar' mean?" asked Will.

"He will work under me reading cases and laws, applying them in written documents or motions he'll write under my supervision. When I believe he is ready, he will be tested by our local judge for fitness to stand as a lawyer at the bar. As I still believe our local judge is no smarter than a weathered fence post despite his command of verbal insults, I believe Warren will have no problem passing. He'll be the first Japanese attorney in Nevada."

Will looked at Warren. "You American?"

Warren responded with a healthy dose of offense, "I was born in Hawaii, currently a territory of the United States. I'm an American."

Will laughed. "Good luck to you. Working for Sam Grande will be a test in itself."

Grande cut off the conversation. "Enough. Warren has work to do and so do I. What did you come here to waste my time for? I am sure it requires advice for which you have no intention to pay."

"Just another dinner next Sunday. Pay enough."

"Here, sit." Grande led the pair back into a separate room now functioning as his office.

"You are right, though. I do have a question to ask."

"Why am I not surprised?"

Will had a serious look on his face now.

"Has to do with the laws of the open range."

Grande's tenor changed. "You look concerned all of a sudden. Why are you worried about anything to do with open range? Your home sits on deeded acres. You have title to the ground you ranch."

"It's not about me, it's about my sister."

"Your sister? I thought you told me your entire family was killed during the war."

"I thought so, too. That's what our old field hands told me when I returned from the war. But I just got a letter from my sister Ella. She was staying with my aunt and uncle when my parents were killed by the Union soldiers. She's now living with a man named Crampion up north of Reno. They're trying to make a go of starting a small ranch out on the open range. I went up to see her last week. I'm worried about her situation and need to know what to tell her."

Grande pushed his chair back from his desk and crossed his legs. "Did they homestead the property?"

Will shrugged his shoulders. "They said they did, but the paperwork has been held up. They told me Angus Ferguson and his men are harassing them at every step. They've been told to leave, or things could get ugly."

"Isn't Angus Ferguson the man who lost his son in the battle for the Truckee Dam?"

Will nodded. "Yep, one and the same. Ella believes Ferguson or someone at his direction has held up completing their homestead application."

Grande looked around for a book, something he regularly did when advising a client. "As I've told you many times, you have to *read* the law if you want to know where you stand with your adversary." As usual, he placed great emphasis on the word *read*. Grande had given him the same instructive advice every time Will had asked for any legal opinion.

Will waved his hand around the room where stacks of thick books with ancient bindings rose from desktops, shelves and even the floor. "As always, you have the books. It's easier to just ask you, seein' as you've already read all these things."

Grande answered with a healthy dose of condescension. "That's why lawyers charge a fee. Most people must pay for that value delivered. You have a unique ability to circumvent the customary pay for service relationship."

Will smiled. "Don't go using them big words. They might cost me an extra steak next Sunday."

Grande exhaled in derision, "It should cost you a quarter of your herd."

"You're good, but you ain't that good," countered Will.

Grande was thumbing through the book now placed in his lap. He did not respond to Will's latest quip. The two friends could keep this up all day. Their regular Sunday dinners at Toal Ranch were a constant series of good-humored thrusts and parries. Both enjoyed the word play.

But Grande took his time before any further comments. Will waited. He knew Sam was one of the sharpest lawyers in Nevada. Not only was he quick to discern issues, but he was also even quicker in arriving at a suggested solution, often one no one else had thought of.

Grande eventually closed the book and looked at Will pensively.

"Normally, I find answers in the law. You have hit upon an issue which has no clear direction, either in statute or case law. I've been asked to represent other ranchers who have range rights, but my work for them has been with contracts for sale of beef and the like. However, while I was working for them, I tried to check on the status of their rights to the land they claim. Ownership rights on that land come into play with ownership rights to the beef out on the open range. I have to admit, it's a gray area of the law."

Perplexed, Will asked, "What do you mean, 'a gray area'?"

"In doing the work regarding contractual rights to the sale of beef, I had to confirm my client's ownership of the stock to be sold. He explained to me how they round up all the cattle during some Spring event. As I understand it, a group of ranchers essentially divvy up the herd among themselves. There is no prior paperwork to prove ownership, no bill of sale. Technical ownership was a little tricky to prove. Anyway, it got me looking into the whole open range thing."

Now even more confused, Will asked, "You mean the ownership to stock out on the range is not clear?"

Grande put the book he had been holding onto the top of his desk.

"The ranchers think it is. But from a strict legal stance, I would say it's not all that certain. For my part, it strikes me as a simple grab for as much as you can get. It's close to a free-for-all."

"What if someone like my sister homestead's property out on the range, can they take cattle just out there roaming about?"

"I found that Texas follows an informal semi-legal custom originating from its days following the Mexican Revolution. After Texas beat Santa Ana, lots of Mexican ranchers picked up their families and headed south, just leaving their herds run free. The Republic of Texas announced that any unbranded beef stock not attached to a branded mother were public property. Anyone could brand that individual animal and take possession. In Wyoming, on the other hand, the Cattlemen's Association pushed through legislation called the Maverick Act which says that all mavericks belong to the members of the Association."

"But that doesn't tell me who has the rights to stock on a homestead claim," said Will.

"No, it doesn't. The Homestead Act was passed by the Federal Government at the behest of Abe Lincoln in 1862. It gives the right to anyone who supports the Union to claim one hundred sixty acres. If they live on the land and improve it, they get title free and clear."

"What if that homestead is in the middle of an open space where some rancher has filed a grazing claim?"

Grande spread both his hands palms up. "Now you've hit the issue right between the eyes. There is no specific law here in Nevada. I just checked in that book in front of me. There are only sporadic cases with no definitive direction. So, you have cattle ranchers claiming quasi-property rights to graze cattle on land they really do not technically own.

At the same time, they are trying to protect stock they do own from being taken. This puts them in a situation essentially butting heads with local small landowners who want to interrupt the free use of range rights. Essentially, it's a free-for-all vulnerable to enforcement by vigilantism."

Will slumped. "The man Ella is living with appears to be taking mavericks and branding them before the rancher's regular spring roundup. He claims he tried to play the game by their rules last spring. He went to the roundup, but the big ranchers took almost all his mavericks. Sounds like they are acting as if the Wyoming rules apply."

Grande shook his head side to side. "If he's taking mavericks early, he risks the vigilante justice I spoke of."

"That's what I thought, too. Told him so. But Ella has asked me to help. What should I tell him?"

"Tell him to be real careful."

"I already have. But he seems hardheaded."

"Then, Will, stay out of it. I know you. When you get involved in something like this, bullets start flying."

"But, Sam, she's my sister."

Chapter Twelve

Spring 1878
Ferguson Ranch, Nevada

"Angus, good morning."

"Carter, welcome. Come on in."

Carter McKinnon stepped off his horse. One expensive leather boot touched the dirt and then the other. The collar of his outer coat had been pulled tight for the ride. He now loosened the front buttons. The coat extended only to his waist. Winter fabrics were thick. Whether wool or leather lined with sheepskin like McKinnon's, the purpose was to push out the biting cold. But here, spring kept things brisk only in the early mornings. The desert scrub of the open range warmed earlier than those ranchers nestled close to the base of the Sierras.

"It was quite cool this morning when I started out."

"I would have said it was cold, but then that might have been because I'm getting old, Carter. There is a fire inside. Let's go sit close and you can warm up a bit." Ferguson's cadence of speech never varied from his Scottish roots.

McKinnon watched to see if Ferguson's demeanor presented any cues as to how he might approach the day's coming events. But so far, McKinnon could discern nothing out of the norm. He had started out on the day's ride concerned. While committed to finding a solution to the loss of stock, he often found himself troubled over some of the steps Angus wanted to take. Angus had been a trusted friend for over a decade. Both men had carved out their veritable cattle kingdoms with their own two hands. Together, they had fought Indians, rustlers, droughts, market collapses, and now, nesters. But Angus had changed.

The loss of his son, Dirk, chiseled away a large part of Ferguson's life filter. He didn't seem to have the same care for the future. McKinnon worried that steps taken today would show a further erosion of concern for the time to come. Ferguson had become focused on the immediate. It might cloud his judgment. Carter often found himself wondering if his friend now made decisions based on evaluation and analysis as opposed to simple emotion.

"Angus, we are to meet with this Frank Canton and some of his men today, correct?"

"Canton, for certain; not sure if we are going to meet any of his men."

"And you wanted me here early so we can talk about this meeting before it takes place?"

Ferguson nodded, "Exactly. I think it would go much better with this man if the two of us join in making the suggestions for action."

"Angus, I am glad you decided to have me come. I am both interested and concerned as to how we move forward."

"We can talk. Did you eat? My cook has breakfast still on the stove."

"A little something would be good. Might help to warm me up starting from the inside out." McKinnon chuckled as he spoke.

The original Ferguson log cabin had been replaced with a two-story stone and wood structure. McKinnon thought it was large enough for two families. It had a kitchen, seven bedrooms, and a couple of rooms for staff in the main house. Attached was a separate long room to the rear which functioned as something of a mess hall for the hands and staff. With the barn and outlying houses for storage and dressing meat, the entire scope of the main ranch facility extended a sense of stability, of purpose. It fit its owner. But the best part of the house was the main downstairs fireplace. The massive open hearth was as tall as most men. Angus had to reach up to touch the mantel. Deep and wide, it could be stocked with enough wood that once lit, the logs would cast out waves of warmth. McKinnon walked straight to the mature blaze and extended his now bare hands to the expanding heat.

"Angus, who is this man Canton? What do you know about him? Can he be trusted?"

Ferguson sat in one of the two leather chairs facing the hearth.

"I'll tell you after he has left. Canton stayed here at the ranch last night. He is just finishing his breakfast. He'll be with us soon. Once he has started off on the day's duties, we can talk."

At that moment, Frank Canton walked into the room. "Am I interrupting?"

"Not a'tall," said Ferguson. "Come, join us. There is lots to discuss."

McKinnon turned in time to see the open welcome with interest. Ferguson had beckoned this man into the room as if he was another rancher, not the hired help. There was almost a deference in Angus's voice.

Dressed in the same clothes worn at the Stock Growers meeting, Canton again sported a fitted black coat covering a starched white shirt collected at the collar with a black string tie. He moved in a measured stride that seemed too short for his stature, as if he retained a portion of his energy from the movement. Canton advanced next to McKinnon and the fire. McKinnon felt a presence more than the man himself. Something he could not quite put his finger on. He retreated away, as if by instinct, to take the second chair next to Ferguson. It left Canton standing facing the two ranch owners.

A smirk grew across Canton's face. "Gentlemen, I understand you have a problem. Why don't you tell me exactly the nature and extent of that problem and what you would like me to do about it."

McKinnon heard little inflection in the man's voice. The effect was flat and modulated, almost serene. It resonated as a baritone invitation, a lure. With the combination of voice and sartorial covering, Canton could pass for a man of the cloth. However, both the attitude and the black-handled Colt holstered at his side brought a measure of insincerity to the man's manner of speech. It was if he did not really care if you saw through the false persona. He left it there in all its transparency as a dare to be challenged. *This was not a parson,* thought McKinnon. *The man was a predator.*

Ferguson replied to Canton's question. "For years, our range has been wide open. Ten years ago, there were probably only six to seven ranch owners who set stock free on the range. The Spring Roundup was a pleasant event. We met, set a date for collecting the stock, sent our hands out at the designated time and all of us worked ourselves to the bone separating and branding. At night, we would sleep on the ground around a fire and tell horrible stories, then laugh."

McKinnon cast a careful look at Canton trying to see how this information was being received.

Ferguson continued. "But then, about five years ago, homesteaders started arriving. The land to the south was deeded, taken. So, they moved to the north and started to file homestead claims on the same range where we had grazing rights. Most of these newcomers knew little about ranching or cattle and did not make it. But more came. Cattle got mixed up out in the open space. Now there are thirty to forty supposed ranchers at the roundup claiming stock. And somehow, in this new process, our herds do not grow—much the opposite. Where we used to see our herds increase over the winter, now we see them diminish."

"If your herds are becoming smaller, then someone is taking your stock. Am I correct?"

Again, it was Ferguson who responded. "Exactly!"

Canton pursued the thought. "Then, they are thieves."

Here was a simple assessment reduced to its fundamental core and devoid of any effort to overthink. McKinnon could not tell if the man was exceptionally astute and capable of distilling competing arguments into fundamental truths, or if he was a simpleton playing to his new benefactor's persuasions.

Not stopping for long, Canton continued. "And if they are caught in the act of stealing, then they deserve to be punished. The key are the mavericks. If found to be taking an unbranded calf attached and following a branded heifer, that is theft."

McKinnon could not argue. He felt the same way. But for some reason, he hesitated to agree.

Ferguson looked at McKinnon obviously sensing that hesitation. "Carter, do ye not agree?"

McKinnon paused but then responded. "I agree. But the key is that they are caught in the act."

Canton shifted to one leg crossing the other as his opposite elbow lifted to the top of the mantel and was now even with his jaw. "My men and I are quite experienced at gauging these kinds of activities. We've worked in Texas and in Wyoming. We know the signs. If a man is riding with a straight iron, there is no brand attached. That iron can be used for one purpose only: to alter an existing brand. To alter that brand and then take the maverick is nothing more than plain and simple theft. No other way to view it."

The statement was offered as incontrovertible fact. McKinnon marveled at the lack of emotion in the delivery. Canton knew his audience. He'd made this pitch before. But now he turned serious. The smirk disappeared.

"But you have not said what you are prepared to do about it."

As if transported across oceans, Angus Ferguson's Scottish brogue exploded. "I'll pay ye one hundred dollars for every rustler ye string up."

"Does that go for any of my men?"

"Aye, it does. It goes for any man under your command."

McKinnon watched as the smirk returned.

Angus again turned to his friend. While he gave every evidence he was about to ask a question, McKinnon could tell Angus had long since made up his own mind and was looking more for affirmation than analysis. "Carter, ye agree?"

McKinnon now knew why he had been requested to be present. He was not only here for support, but as a witness, for good or bad. His friendship was at stake. Yet, he also knew his business, his livelihood was at stake. He could not continue to lose stock as he had over the last few years. He waited and then answered. "I agree. If caught in the act, I agree."

Canton now shifted his stance from right foot to left leaving his elbow still on the mantel. "And what about the nesters? How am I to deal with them?"

As opposed to questions regarding the taking of stock, Ferguson did not respond quickly to this question. "What do you propose?"

In the same matter-of-fact, even-toned voice, devoid of emotion, Canton responded. "If someone is on property subject to grazing rights without full homestead title, then they are trespassers. I assume that you are within your rights to deal with a trespasser here in Nevada just the same as in Texas or Wyoming."

Carter here stepped in. "And how is that?"

Through the ever-present smirk, Canton answered. "You ask them to leave. If they don't, you shoot them."

Ferguson displayed a smile of his own. "I'll pay ye one hundred dollars for every illegal nester killed who refuses to leave. And you can start with that usurper, Crampion."

Canton did not respond. He waited.

McKinnon watched to see if the face would give any evidence of a victory, to gloat. But Canton's face disgorged no indication of what was going on behind the mask. Canton looked back and forth between the two men. Hearing no objection, no retreat from the orders just given, he obviously took the silence as affirmation of the job description now outlined.

"Gentlemen, then I will get to work."

With that, Canton strode out of the room in the same measured gait he used to enter. He never turned or looked back.

McKinnon waited until he heard the front door close. "Angus, can we trust this man? What do we know about him?"

Ferguson sighed. "Ah, I know but a little. I am told Canton did some mavericking himself in Texas as a young man. But he became attached to a lawman who turned him around. He's worked for either the law or stock associations ever since."

"What does the word *work* mean here?" McKinnon asked.

"He'll do what we ask. He's rid Wyoming of rustlers and nesters. He can do the same here."

"But how many will he kill, Angus? How many will he kill?"

"What is needed, Carter. Anything that is needed."

Chapter Thirteen

Spring 1878
Ferguson Ranch, Nevada

The sun was about to slip below the mountain-crested horizon to the west. In another hour, the sky would transform from a translucent warm yellow to a dark horizon broken by purple summits. An orange-haloed sunset would succumb to indigo blue, followed by darkness. Each day lived and died the same way here on the range bordering the desert. Rarely would there be an interruption to this evening ritual.

Paris looked up at the spectacle of the day's end as it descended behind the Sierras. He had ridden more miles than he dared count over the last several days. Tired, he had just arrived at the main house of the Ferguson spread. He had left Toal Ranch yesterday, riding to Reno. Sheriff Svenson had told him about the meeting of the Stockman's Association the day before. Svensson had described the tension in the room when Angus Ferguson had made his arguments for the hiring of a man named Frank Canton. Some had disagreed with the proposed approach. Those who opposed the suggested plan ultimately departed. Svensson left with them. He felt relieved to be out of the room until he passed what he was later told would be the man Ferguson wanted to hire. According to Svensson, the man dressed to intimidate. Attired almost completely in black, his sidearm was prominently displayed with its gunslinger tie down. From his outfit alone, Svensson could tell this man would be trouble. The sheriff did not shy from relating to Paris his firm belief that the entire situation would soon escalate. He feared people were going to get hurt.

Paris had agreed to notify Svensson as soon as he knew for sure that Ferguson or this new hired gun had taken any overt steps to displace or injure anyone. Both had agreed to stay in close contact. Svensson would alert those townsfolk willing to consider joining a posse and tell them to be ready for a call to ride. That was the best they could do, at the moment.

Pulling up his horse in front of the main house, Paris saw that Angus Ferguson stood in the doorway. "Mr. Ferguson, I just saw a rider leaving. Was that Mr. McKinnon?"

"It was."

Paris took a stab at gathering information in his role as someone serving two masters. "Did McKinnon just stop by for a visit?"

"Nae, he came to speak with the man we hired to remove the rustlers."

"I had heard you have hired someone to patrol the range."

"Aye, Frank Canton. Carter and I both talked to him earlier today. Canton started out late morning with the first few men he has hired. There should be ten more men coming soon from Texas. Shortly, there will be a proper force to deal with these thieves and nesters."

"Texas?" Paris did little to disguise that he was perplexed.

"Aye, men from Texas who know how to handle a gun and have patrolled ranges in their home state, as well as Wyoming. These men are experienced with those who think they can elude the law."

Paris thought to ask for clarification as to what exact law was being eluded, but then thought better of asking. "Are these detectives going to have the power to arrest thieves and take them in for trial?"

Ferguson scoffed. "Nae, they'll dispense justice on the spot."

Paris now had no doubt what that meant. The mandate to rid the range of any small landowner had been set. From what Ferguson now

Range War

relayed, a collection of men would soon be on hand to pursue the orders; by force, if needed.

Ferguson had been watching the departing McKinnon as if lost in some thought or concern, but now turned to Paris. "I did not see you at the meeting of the Stockman's Association yesterday."

Paris answered warily. "I went to Carson City to pursue an inquiry with their sheriff. I had watched some men wearing a red sash out on the open range and wanted to find out if he had any wanted notices on the men I'd seen."

Paris knew Ferguson would have little or no contact with the pleasant if highly ineffectual Sheriff Zack Thompson in Carson City to check on Paris's story.

"You probably should have checked with our own Reno Sheriff, the slacker Svensson."

Ignoring the slight, Paris responded, "I did stop by and ask my questions of Sheriff Svensson, too. Seems neither has any direct knowledge of any Red Sash group. Both had heard of a gang allegedly rustling cattle in Utah and Wyoming, but there is little information or detail."

"Come in and tell me more about what you saw. Do you know that Bo Richards and Reddiker came across men wearing a red sash, too?"

"No. I met up with Bo, Reddiker, and Levi Wallace as they were riding out to survey the herds. Told them about the men with the sash I'd seen."

"Well, they caught two of them outright taking cattle with my brand."

Paris stopped at the threshold upon hearing of the contact. "What did Richards do?"

Ferguson turned and with relish answered. "They chased them off. One got away, but they caught the other. His horse apparently stepped into a hole and collapsed on the run. The man was killed in the fall. But

Bo strung him up even though he was dead. Fitting end for a thief. I told Bo he'd done the right thing. The rest of this gang should know right off how we intend to deal with them."

Paris had yet to move. He straddled the independence of the outdoors with the building risk of entering Ferguson's home, as if entry would be tantamount to inclusion into the activities of the house's master. Movement forward would have to be with caution.

"The boys told me they had met you. They also said you planned on heading on over to the Crampion shack to watch the goings on. Did you see anything of interest there?"

Paris entered the room as if on full alert. He knew he had a job to do for Ferguson. But he hesitated on saying anything that might be misconstrued by his employer. He did not want to say anything that increased Ferguson's already known hatred for Crampion, but he needed to provide a report. Crampion's posture in the building adversarial range dynamic had become much more complicated with the knowledge that Ella Toal lived with him.

"I did not see Crampion at or near his house. I watched for a good period, and I did not see him with any stock, either coming or going."

"What about his woman?"

"I didn't see her working with any stock, either. She had two visitors, two separate sets of wagons."

"Visitors? What type?"

Oh, no. I should have been more careful. Trying to cover his tracks, Paris quickly attempted to divert what he knew would be an over reactive interest on Ferguson's part.

"Two sets of men who looked to be both delivering and picking something up. It all looked pretty harmless."

"You said Crampion was not there. What could she be doing other than entertaining men? She's probably a prostitute looking to bring in more money."

"I didn't get that impression when I met her, Mr. Ferguson."

"But didn't you tell me she wears an inappropriately formal blue dress with head covering for living out on the prairie?"

Paris tried to think of some way to divert this conversation into any other topic. This was Will's sister. "I did, but I just think she was unprepared for life out in the open and didn't have the appropriate clothes. Did Richards and Reddiker get any names from the men with the sash?"

Undeterred from his prior focus, Ferguson continued pursuit of his inquiry regarding the woman at the Crampion ranch. "But wearing a full-length formal dress? There could be only one purpose. The only trade she is dealing in is herself. The woman must be a prostitute."

Dismayed, Paris could think of no answer.

Ferguson stood in front of his hearth. He did not move. Paris watched as the man investigated the pile of cooled ash as if some judgment phoenix would arise. Standing with crossed arms, he focused downward covering an extended silence.

Paris waited. Unsure of the direction the conversation going forward, he remained quiet until he could get a better read.

Finally, Angus turned to face Paris. His face looked troubled. Not angry, not heated. But troubled as if something was personally amiss. "Crampion and his woman must go."

Ferguson uttered the simple statement, but he lacked any emotion with its delivery. Paris had expected an outburst. But this was nothing of the sort. It was if the man was about to cry. Paris was completely confused.

As if Ferguson could read Paris's bewildered expression, he offered what he must have thought was an explanation. "My wife would have been utterly disgusted if any such activity were taking place on our range. Crampion and his woman must go. I owe it to my departed wife's memory to rid the range of this abomination. I'll tell Frank Canton to see to it."

In his effort to avoid saying anything derogatory about Nate Crampion's actions, Paris had inadvertently done something much worse. In an offhanded comment intended to divert Ferguson's focus, Paris had not only failed but lifted Ella Toal to a new height of notoriety in his boss's mind. Though based on speculation alone, she now bore a stain. Paris knew he had to get word to Will. Hopefully, he could get to his sister soon and convince her to move to Jack's Valley.

Chapter Fourteen

Spring 1878
Open Range north of Reno, Nevada

Frank Canton pulled the collar of his black duster tighter. A white scarf filled the openings between his neck and the duster doing its best to block out the intrusion of the pre-dawn chill. The prairie air had a bite to it this early. The moon looked close enough to touch as it disappeared behind the mountain crests of the Sierras to the west. The white orb seemed outsized, too large. Out on the flat plains of Texas he'd seen the same thing. From his vantage, the lunar arc looked as if it would crash into the mountains.

He kicked the burned-out remnants of the night's fire. Standing above the now cold embers, he grinned at the thought that these ashes looked remarkably like the ruins left of the two homesteader shanties he had burned yesterday. A lifetime of a tree's development had been hewn and then stacked as walls for living quarters. Years of growth and hours of labor reduced to burned out dust in a matter of minutes. He had ordered the destruction.

Canton had given the occupants ten minutes to clear out. Told them they were trespassers, and he had the authority to shoot them on sight. Magnanimously, he gave them ten minutes to gather their things and go. One man went for his rifle and Canton had drawn and fired within inches of his feet. The man froze in his tracks. Once stopped, the homesteader reconsidered. Good thing as the next bullet would have hit him in the chest.

The second family did not need as much coaxing. The man of that pitiful household looked relieved as if Canton had provided him with a good excuse to give up his ranching efforts. Both living abodes had been burned. They now looked like last night's fire in front of him.

Canton gazed eastward. Daylight would soon come. The sun would power the rise of the range's temperature. The heat simply cooked the grasses and scrub out here. Not unlike the panhandle of Texas, which he knew all too well. There was power in that heat. He felt the same sense of power when he scorched the homes of these trespassers.

He had checked with the title office in Reno before heading out onto the range. There was not one finalized homestead claim out here. Several were in process. Some had failed. No homestead had resulted in a clear deed with title. They were all trespassers on the licensed grazing permits. Canton smiled. Not that any legal title would have had a different result from his actions yesterday. He felt possessed of a power like the rise of the day: he could dispense a justice just as the cauldron of the sun in the desert.

One of the two men with Canton began to stretch out of his bedroll. Good men, he thought. They'd followed him through many jobs with many different employers. They had backed his every move. Both could be restrained when called for, but unrestrained when needed. They had been well paid at every stop. This job would be no different.

"Liam, it would be good to get the fire going again and start some coffee."

"Right, Mr. Canton."

He liked the deference his men showed him. Canton felt he'd earned their respect. The money flowed through him. But more than that, he held to a concrete appraisal of the law. Ranchers had spawned this new West. It was the ranchers who pushed westward from Louisiana through Texas, even when the Spanish would not. The Comanches had fought and beaten the Spanish and Mexican forces for over one hundred years. Before the determined Texans arrived, the only real settlement north of

Range War

the Rio Grande was Santa Fe. Every other settlement had been abandoned in fear of the Comanches. It took a new breed of Texas rancher, one after another to push the frontier west. As early as 1830, the Spanish had agreed to sell these newcomers land. Those original Texans were supposed to be the buffer between the Spanish and the Comanches who ruled the entire southern plains. Little did the Spanish know that those Texans would eventually win the battle with the Comanches, and later win the battle with the Spanish themselves. For Canton, the men who pushed westward raising their herds of cattle made America what it was, and what it should be. He enjoyed working for the ranchers. They had earned his respect.

"Coffee's ready."

"Thank you, Liam. We will head out today and see if we can find this Nate Crampion nester that Ferguson has such a problem with."

Liam Witherspoon looked up from the now steaming pot of dark fluid. "From what you described, our Mr. Ferguson seems to have a special problem with Crampion."

"That, he does," replied Canton. "It would be a nice start for our work here if we can solve that problem early on."

Canton noticed a look of questioning flash across Liam's face. He decided to pursue. "What is it, Liam? You look puzzled."

"Sir, just wondering what brought you to this case. Was it only the money?"

Canton smiled. "I was just thinking about that. The answer is…no. We worked for the ranchers in Texas on the same kind of problem. Ranchers were the first to take the range. It was a battle in most places with natives, rustlers, and thieves. I started off on the wrong side of the law, but working for the Texas Stockmen's group, we brought a kind of justice against people who were taking without right. It felt as if we were the ones restoring order. After my bad start in life, it felt like I was restoring my own order."

"Are we doing the same thing here?"

Canton nodded. "I think so."

His own cup of strong camp coffee in hand, Liam stood to face Canton. "Are we to use force if needed?"

Canton paused in thought. "From what little we know, I have a sense that we will *need* to use force. It would be nice to catch Crampion in the act of branding stock. He works from what Ferguson described as a remote corral out on the range. That would make it easy. If we can catch him in the act, then Crampion will meet the end he deserves. The timing will depend on how far it is to the nearest tree."

Witherspoon nodded.

"When we get to this corral, we'll pull off the safety leathers and have a round jacked in the rifles just in case."

Canton looked at his longest running hand. Witherspoon stood just under six feet tall but had broad shoulders and the shortest neck Canton had ever seen. It was if his head was connected to the straight bar running between the man's two shoulders. Lean, but hard-muscled, Witherspoon could ride all day and never get stiff. The man was a rock. Good both with horses and a gun, he was the perfect soldier on the range.

"We need to get Vern up and at 'em."

Liam smiled. "Yes, our Mr. Rivers does take his time starting out in the morning."

Canton was not smiling now. "Vern has never gotten the knack of rising before the sun. He's like an adolescent."

In something of a defense of his friend and long-time partner, Witherspoon offered, "But the man is real good with a gun."

Canton had to agree. "He is, at that. It's just a bit of a chore to get him going."

Canton knew his men. Knew their strengths and knew their weaknesses. Witherspoon would anticipate a need and step right in. Vern Rivers needed to be directed. But once directed, no one was as fearless as Rivers. Small and compact, Rivers spoke only on rare occasions and never to excess. Canton could put up with his late rising. Rivers was a solid man to have with him.

"Well, get Vern up and let's get riding. If I understand the general location of this remote corral, it could take us until midday to get to Crampion."

* * * * *

Nate Crampion looked up from the branding fire. He set down the iron and took off his gloves. Riders were coming, three of them. The leader wore a black duster and sat his horse with authority. Nate did not like the look. He did not like the feel.

"Nick, Reese, grab your guns. Riders coming, and I don't like their look."

Nick Ray strode into the lean-to and grabbed his rifle. Reese Stricker did the same. As the men moved from the fire, Nate turned his gaze away from the oncoming riders, but only momentarily. He pointed at Nick and said, "Nick, you stay near the lean-to. Reese, you move to the other side of the corral. We want to stay spread out."

Both men moved as directed. All three now focused on the approaching riders.

"That's far enough."

Crampion cradled his own rifle as he spoke the words. The riders pulled up.

The man in the black duster answered.

"My name's Frank Canton. I've been hired as the Range Detective. These are my deputies."

Unimpressed, Crampion replied with no little disdain. "What's a Range Detective? And who hired you?"

Crampion did not fail to notice a small, arrogant grin spread across the man's face. Next, Nate watched as Canton twisted slightly on his saddle, exposing a handgun strapped to his right leg. He took his time with the movement and then spoke. "I'm here to enforce the law."

"You didn't say who hired you."

Deliberate and taking his time, Canton answered. Crampion had the thought the man must be trying to convey some innate authority by taking his time to reply. "My men and I have been hired by the Nevada Stock Growers Association."

Crampion quickly retorted, "Ferguson. This must be a new attempt to harass us."

"I'm not here to harass. I'm here to enforce the law."

At this, Nate scoffed. "Then you can start by keeping Ferguson and his men from trying to run me off and take my stock. If you're here to do justice, then you can begin by doing that."

Canton narrowed his eyes. "Seems to me you need a lesson in the law. That's a branding iron over there in the fire and it's hot. It's not roundup time, and that means you're taking mavericks or other stock illegally."

"There is no law that says branding has to happen in April. Only the big ranchers make that claim."

"Maybe you should listen, then." Canton had not moved. Liam and Vern positioned their hands ready to pull weapons.

Crampion chuckled. "Then you're really here to impose the rancher's version of what they believe the law is."

Range War

"You're taking stock. I'll give you ten minutes to pack your things and leave. That stock will be returned to its rightful owners."

This time, it was Crampion who took his time to answer. "These are my cattle, my stock. You are not taking them anywhere." Crampion quickly swung his rifle to his side and leveled his aim at Canton from his waist.

Liam looked back and forth between the men out in front of them and softly said to Canton, "All three are armed, boss."

Canton nodded, but never took his eyes off Crampion. With a sneer, Canton said, "We seem to have a situation, here. You are obstructing justice. You'll have to pay for that."

Crampion was now the one sporting a grin. "You reach for that gun, and you'll be the one who pays."

Canton looked back and forth at the Crampion's companions. He then did his best to imitate Crampion's grin. "We'll be back, and soon. You might be thinkin' you've won, but you would be mistaken in that thought."

Canton turned his horse. Witherspoon and Rivers did the same. All three rode close together at a slow walk.

Crampion kept watch on the departing trio.

"Nick, you and Reese stay right where you are. Keep an eye on this bunch. Stay ready."

After ten to twenty strides of their mounts, Canton said, "Don't turn around. When I nod, we all draw and turn to ride back on them." Canton was looking straight ahead, formulating a plan as he spoke.

"You each split wide and head for the men on the sides. I'll head for Crampion. Let's see if those nesters can use that hardware they're carrying."

After the horses had taken another ten strides, Canton dipped the bill of his hat. All three men pulled hard on their reins and spurred the horses into an immediate gallop.

Rivers was the only one of the Canton trio to say anything. He bellowed, "Here comes the lead!" Riding now at a full gallop, Rivers had pulled his handgun, aimed, and took a shot at Ray. He missed.

Nick Ray had seen Rivers turn in his direction. He already had his rifle at his shoulder and squeezed his trigger about the same time Rivers fired at him. His first shot caught Rivers in his left ribcage. Rivers rocked and slumped in his saddle, his reins now going loose. No longer being urged on or directed, his horse veered away from the original path.

Canton and Witherspoon took shots with their handguns. Nate Crampion dropped to his knee and aimed his rifle at Canton. His first shot missed. Nate jacked another round into his repeater. Canton was firing shot after shot as quickly as he could thumb the rise on his hammer and pull his trigger. The lift and fall of a galloping horse made shots with a handgun difficult. Dirt erupted on both sides of Crampion, some within a matter of inches. But he was not hit.

"They shot Rivers!" yelled Witherspoon.

Canton had been focusing on Crampion, but now looked over at Rivers who was dangerously close to falling off his horse. Canton pulled at a diagonal to intercept. Witherspoon now started spraying as many shots as possible at Crampion and his hands in cover for the rescue.

Crampion took another shot at Canton. But the round left the rifle barrel just as Canton jerked to his side to assist Rivers. The bullet passed through Canton's duster, flailing just to his rear. Canton took one last shot at Crampion, reaching across his body with his right hand to aim off to his left side. The shot again missed. Crampion watched as Canton then quickly holstered his gun and reached for Rivers. With a steadying hand, he held the man upright in his saddle while moving the reins of his horse to guide Rivers's mount in a gentle turn back away from the corral and lean-to. Witherspoon pulled in behind both riders, firing over his shoulder as the group rode away.

Silence befell the scene. Gun smoke filtered away in the breeze. Nate kept watch after the departing riders and lifted-up from his knees.

"Nice shot, Nick." Crampion turned and then looked over at Ray who stood looking over the top of his rifle barrel. Blood had drained from his face. *Fear*, thought Nate. "You look a little like a ghost."

Nick didn't move, standing behind the corral fencing as if frozen. "I thought they were gonna get us. They came like a cavalry charge."

Crampion tried to settle his own nerves. He did not want his men to see how nervous he really was. He forced a smile. "But they *didn't* take us, did they?"

Nate then looked around at Reese. From the wide-eyed expression on his face, he needed no words from Reese to know he was scared, too.

Reese turned to Crampion and asked with a good dose of trepidation in his voice, "They comin' back?"

Crampion looked out at the still retreating riders. "I don't think so; at least, not today. But I'd bet a good deal on the fact we haven't seen the last of Mr. Frank Canton."

Chapter Fifteen

Spring 1878
Ferguson Ranch, Nevada

Dale Paris considered putting on his short coat for the ride to Reno. Dusk would soon settle on the prairie. This time of year, short-lived spring heat clung only to the mid-day hours. The season's daily heat lingered no longer than a spring storm. The sun's glow felt pleasant now, but by the time he reached town he would need something for warmth.

Standing on the porch of the Ferguson main house, Paris considered his just completed conversation with Angus. The man had become unquestionably obsessed with this new push to clear the range of nesters. Paris lacked the wherewithal to channel away the deep hatred Ferguson had for the people striving to make a life for themselves out on the range. In Ferguson's eyes, they were invaders, usurpers of the scarce and needed grasses. They were taking his livelihood away from him right under his very eyes. They were an affront, a challenge. To his way of thinking, Ferguson had risen to the challenge. He was ready to repel the invaders, no matter the cost, no matter the toll in lives. Dale worried that the die had been cast and, in a way, history had already been written. The only thing left was for it now to play out.

Paris stepped down off the edge of the porch onto the parched earth. He reached for the reins lightly wrapped around the single horizontal hitching post. Walking along side of his horse, he grabbed his stirrup to step up and mount. However, over the top of his saddle he saw three horsemen coming hard. Dust billowed behind the riders evidencing the effort of the horses. Paris dropped the stirrup and again wrapped his reins around the hitching post. Something told him he should stay and see what this was all about.

The sun had fallen low behind the riders. Their silhouettes were painted starkly against the pale dirt clouds lifted behind them by the animal's hooves. Normally, there would be a space between each rider. But these riders were not separated as one would expect. Two of them were riding strangely close. In fact, it looked as if one rider was supporting another. Paris stood and continued to watch the group's advance.

"Need help! Rider hurt!"

Paris recognized the voice of Frank Canton. The image of the three riders soon became more defined as they got closer. Canton held up one of the riders as he slumped across the gap between the two horses. Paris could not see any normal movement in the man. He appeared to sway at the mercy of his mount's gait.

Two cowhands came out of the bunkhouse across from the main house. Canton's plea had brought them out. The paired horses pulled up in between the two men.

"Help. Grab him. He's been shot."

The two cowhands collected the limp body and carried him into the bunkhouse. Canton and his other companion rapidly dismounted and followed. Paris moved behind the group. Canton's right hand dripped fluid that looked like a combination of dark burnt color and bright blood red. He had been holding the other rider with that hand. Paris had seen a mixture like this before. Some of the blood from the wounded man was fresh, and some was old and quite dried out. It had been sometime between whatever caused the wound and their arrival here at the ranch. That did not bode well for the injured rider.

"How far to the nearest doctor?"

Canton's voice carried a directness tinged with desperation. There was an obvious concern for his man.

The entire group had entered the bunk house, Paris bringing up the rear. They had laid the wounded rider on a bunk. One of the cowhands turned to answer Canton. "We don't have anyone who comes close to being able to help someone who's been shot. The nearest doctor is in Reno, at least an hour away."

The other cowhand who had helped carry the injured rider to the bunk placed his hand on the side of the inert man's neck. He now leaned in close as if to listen for breathing. All those around the bed went silent anticipating an assessment.

"No need to ride to Reno. This man's not going to need a doctor. He's dead."

Paris watched as Canton's face turned dark. Jaw muscles flexed as his teeth were clenched. But he did not speak. He turned on his boot heel and strode out of the room. The rider who had come in with Canton turned and followed.

Dale exchanged quizzed looks with the two cowhands left standing over the dead rider. Though clearly stunned, the cowhand who had pronounced the death looked at Paris and asked, "What should we do with the dead man?"

Paris had no good answer, but he replied, "I'll go ask Mr. Ferguson what you should do." He then headed out the door toward the main house where he could see Frank Canton just entering.

* * * * *

"We rode up and announced our intent to inspect the cattle he was branding. Crampion refused."

Canton had begun to report to Ferguson before Angus could even take his seat. While anxious, Canton spoke in measured and muted terms. His voice was not raised, not alarmed. Yet, Paris could see a suppressed determination in his delivery despite the subdued tone. Canton had started to provide a report as if he were talking about supplies to a superior military officer. However, the audible restraint did little to cover the sinister look on Canton's face. Paris watched.

"He did what?" Ferguson was incredulous. It was his first comment after Canton had relayed the complete story. The account began with Canton's observations of branding activity and then the initial conversation with Crampion. Ferguson sat riveted as Canton outlined the ride, first away, and then the charge in return. Angus blurted his question after Canton described the three men shooting rifles at Canton and his men as they approached on horseback.

"Sir, they were all armed with rifles. We were shooting handguns. I truly thought by your description that these nesters were going to be unskilled with weapons. I can now tell you that is not the case. Crampion and both his hands know how to use their repeaters. It was a bad decision on my part. It cost me a good man, a man who has ridden with me for several years."

"That's a shock," said Ferguson. "I would have done the same thing you did. I would have expected those men out there to drop their guns and run."

Canton shook his head. "They did nothing of the kind. They stood their ground, and I would have to admit, shot admirably. I will not underestimate Nate Crampion again. But he is going to pay for the loss of Vern Rivers."

Ferguson stood. "We need to respond. Respond in kind."

"Agreed," said Canton.

Ferguson turned and paced away from the other men. He moved to his oversized hearth, reached out to the mantel, then turned back. "You head out tomorrow to deal with Crampion. Take some of the men from the bunkhouse. I will collect some of the Stockgrowers and see if I can gather as many men as we can to ride out together and finish this completely."

Canton's torso lifted and rocked back with his chest extended forward. To Paris, it was a physical manifestation of agreement. "Mr. Ferguson, I am glad you see it that way, because whether you agreed or not, I would be heading out to Crampion's home tomorrow. This time we'll not be surprised as we were today."

Angus nodded. "Were you able to address any of the other nesters on your first ride out on the range?"

Canton smiled. "We were able to persuade two sets of families to leave. Their abodes were destroyed."

Angus now lifted almost in the same physical manner Canton had moments before. This news seemed to be some form of affirmation for the actions Ferguson had set in motion. "That is good to hear. If two are gone, that leaves only eight more, not including Crampion."

Canton spread his duster along his sides. Decisions were being reached. "Let me and a couple of hands take care of Crampion. In a day or two, my men from Texas will be here. If you can gather some of the Association men, then we can ride out in say, three days, and deal with the rest."

Ferguson did not reply right away. Canton continued. "We don't want to wait. We don't want Crampion to organize any of the other nesters into a collected resistance. Saw that happen in Wyoming. The quicker we can take action, now that things have begun, the better."

Ferguson crossed his arms. "The quicker the better as far as I'm concerned, too. And you must make sure Crampion's woman is removed. She must leave. Paris, here, tells me of her meetings with men regularly arriving when Crampion is gone. I am convinced she's a prostitute. We canna have that out here." The Scottish brogue belied a more emotional aspect of the prospective plan. Paris was dismayed that his earlier verbal misstep had now led to firm plans that boded poorly for Crampion and Ella.

To this point, Paris had only observed and listened. But Angus now addressed him directly.

"Paris, what are your thoughts? Do you have any suggestions?"

Caught a bit off his guard, Paris pressed to respond in a way that appeared natural, and on the surface, seemed to be some form of agreement. But he did not want anything to do with personal participation in the escalation of forced evictions. He needed to get word to Sheriff Svensson, but he did not want to say that to Ferguson.

"I've been riding for three days straight. I need to resupply. I'll head back to my office in Reno tonight, grab some items, and head out to the range tomorrow. I'll report any sightings of branding activity back here tomorrow evening if the timing works out. Otherwise, I'll stay out on the range to watch."

Ferguson considered. "That might work into the plan here. Paris can be the eyes and ears, reporting where the activity is taking place, and Mr. Canton, along with his group, can address those involved as you report it."

Paris had no intention of heading back out on the range to watch for anything. He had one thought only: he had to get word to Will Toal about his sister. He had not sent a wire yet. Now, he had to send the message as soon as he could. He would also tell Svensson about Ferguson's plans. Someone must put a stop to the coming carnage.

Chapter Sixteen

Spring 1878
Toal Ranch, Nevada

The wind was up. The normal afternoon blasts had begun already in the pre-dawn. Will Toal knew if the winds were already blowing, they would push eastward all day. Mornings were usually calm. Not today. While only a stiff breeze now, they would get stronger as the day wore on.

Will stopped at the edge of his porch. Protected here in the lee of the winds, he waited, hesitated. Once out beyond the reach of the ramada, he would no longer be protected from the gusts. He would be out amid the vagaries of nature's forces. There was something to the moment.

In a short time, he had found out that not all his family had been killed during the war. He had a sister who survived. She resided with a man in a questionable relationship while both tried to build a ranch in the middle of an open range, a range claimed by multiple legacy ranchers. But were Nate and Ella doing it legally? Whether legal or otherwise, the ranchers viewed their homestead as trespassing. As a result, his sister lived in a world of peril. Initial joy at the news of a live sibling now came with concern. He sensed that once he stepped off his porch, he would be walking into his sister's world of risk, into the whims and fancies of human forces.

He had put off this ride out of necessity. The money from the sale of his new string of horses was vital to the income for his ranch. His business with prospective horse buyers was now done. He needed to move north, and soon.

He had hoped to convince Ella to come south. He didn't want to have this newfound connection to his roots broken. While Will had to admire their grit to push forward, he also knew the type of men Nate and Ella faced. He hesitated to interfere. This was new ground. Though Ella was younger, any sense of elder sibling authority was long since gone. Will had not been able to truly re-establish their relationship. Based on his limited time with Ella, his sister appeared headstrong, an independent woman confident of her actions irrespective of their appearances. It had taken an admirable amount of effort to work her way west with Nate. She possessed remarkable qualities just to have accomplished that journey. Nevertheless, Will sensed she was afraid. He had to help. Ella was family. The decision had been an easy one. He had to do whatever he could to protect his family. Will sighed, stepped off the porch into the wind, and headed to his barn.

Once Powder was saddled, he walked the gray gelding across the compound from the barn to the hitching rail outside his porch. Though still dark, the sun would be making an appearance soon. Will grabbed his already packed saddlebags and tied them down behind his saddle. He rolled his duster and added it to the stack just behind his cantle. He might be gone for several days. With saddle bags full of ammunition, hardtack, coffee beans, and his duster, he could camp anywhere as necessary. He stepped up onto the porch and gently pushed open the front door. Already awake, Beth had fried some bacon, scrambled some eggs, and warmed some sliced potatoes. It might be his last cooked meal for days.

"Breakfast is on the table."

Will took off his coat, loosened his stampede strap and lifted his hat off his head, setting both down on an adjacent seat. "Smells good."

Beth sat across from him. There was no plate on her side of the table. She focused solely on Will. "So, what's your plan?"

Mouth full of eggs and potatoes, Will had to chew a bit before he could answer.

"Not sure I have one. Since it is on the way, I suppose I'll stop in Carson City to see if Dale Paris or Ella has left me any messages. Message or no, I'll ride north to their spread and do my best to convince Ella to come south and stay with us. We did not really try that hard to get Ella to come south when we were up there, you and I—but now things have heated up and maybe she'll listen. Even if her man Nate wants to stay, maybe I can convince them both that it would be better for her to come to Jack's Valley."

Beth nodded. "From what Dale said, there could be gunplay. Looking after your homestead is one thing, fighting groups of gunmen is another."

Will nodded his head in agreement while again chewing his breakfast before it got cold. "It definitely sounds as if things are escalating. I have had a bad feeling ever since I saw them."

Beth's face expressed her question. "Bad feeling how?"

Will set down his fork. "I'm worried I might lose her right after she comes back into my life. Something twisted about that."

Beth reached across the table with one hand to touch Will's wrist. "But fear could be the one factor that does convince them both that right now Ella should be here."

Will paused for a second as their eyes met. "I agree, fear is my best shot. It is again like having her move to Aunt Leona's during the war. Soldiers might be coming. Soldiers in cowboy garb. Strange how the war keeps returning to my life."

Beth leaned back in her chair, looked up at the ceiling and then back to Will.

"Isn't there some way to get the sheriff to control this before it gets out of hand?"

"I've thought a lot about that. Svensson is far and away more capable than Carson City's incompetent Zack Thompson. But I don't know him well. I'm hoping I can talk with him while I'm up north. Maybe Dale and I can help stir him into action." Will grabbed his napkin and dabbed at some egg yolk dripping from the side of his mouth.

"I'm impressed, you actually used a napkin instead of your sleeve." Beth smiled unabashedly while delivering the verbal jab with as much sarcasm as she could muster.

The playful sting was not lost on Will. In his best deadpan delivery, he countered, "Pretty amazing, huh? Not long ago I was dragging my knuckles and living in a rock cave."

Still smiling, Beth responded, "Marriage is finally having a positive effect."

"Depends on your point of view." Will added his own smile to make sure this comment was not taken the wrong way.

"Careful, cowboy…that front door could be locked anytime. Cold out there."

"You've displaced me to the barn before." Will referred to Beth's first visit to the ranch.

"And this lady could do it again. Best keep that in mind." Beth's smile belied any anger in her comment.

"Ah, where would you be without me?"

Her smile broadened as Beth stood and walked around the back of Will's chair. He felt her reach down on either side of his neck placing her palms open on his chest. She pulled his body into the back of his chair and closer to her.

"You're right. That door is always going to be open. You just better come back through it, Will Toal. I've worried about you riding into danger in the past. Somehow, I have the same worries here again."

"Oh, I'll be back to take some more lessons in table manners."

"Be careful, Will. Come back through that door."
"I'm plannin' on it."

* * * * *

Will guided Powder north from the ranch. Carson City sat on his route to Reno. The winds did not disappoint. They kept getting stronger. Will tilted the brim of his hat down and to the left into the oncoming gale. The sun was out, but the wind dissipated any warmth the rays brought. Wind like this knifed into a person's clothes, looking to numb the body, Will thought. He pulled his collar tight. If he kept his neck warm, he could keep the worst of the biting cold on the outside.

"Let's pull over and check the telegraph office, boy. There's probably nothing there, but best to check."

Will regularly talked to Powder on their solitary rides. They had traveled many a mile together. As with any rider and trusted mount, the non-verbal communication of reins and spurs became comfortable, understood, even anticipated. Though he knew better, Will talked to Powder as if the mustang understood the audible communication as readily as the non-verbal. To move from the non-verbal communication of contact and touch to the audible didn't seem that much of a stretch to a pair so well acquainted.

Will wrapped one of his split reins loosely around the horizontal hitching rail out in front of the telegraph office. He brushed Powder's neck with his gloved hand.

"There, hold yourself still. I should be back real soon."

The single door had no window. Will pushed through, noting the squeal of the hinges now strained against the weight of the door as it swung inward.

"Mr. Toal, I was just going to send a rider out to your ranch. Message for you just came in." The telegraph operator stood and walked to the counter holding out a single sheet of paper.

Somewhat shocked, Will asked, "From who?"

The operator unfolded the message and looked down at the small sheet to confirm his recollection.

"It's from someone named Paris."

Will took the paper. He did not look up for some time. Dale's message was short and to the point.

"Ferguson's killer Canton has been sent to get Crampion. Paris."

Chapter Seventeen

Spring 1878
Open Range, north of Reno, Nevada

Angry gusts covered the range like the devil himself was blowing a foreboding cold. The sagebrush scrub dotting the open reaches bobbed back and forth as if an invisible force combed through a head of hair. The few scattered trees did not have a chance of slowing the bursts. Too few were the standing trunks to have an impact. A forest might, but the solitary sycamore soldiers clinging to life here on the unprotected flat plains at the base of the Sierras were no impediment. The branches on those sparse spreading trees bent in submission. Newly born spring leaves were pulled from their anchors and scattered across the prairie to dry up and die amid the scrub. Canton seethed like the weather.

Liam Witherspoon rode next to Canton. After Reeves had been buried, Canton entered the Ferguson bunkhouse and asked if anyone had come across Nate Crampion. Two hands spoke of a prior minor confrontation with Crampion after he had been seen to brand cattle. Both had said the nester was a problem. Canton told them Crampion was responsible for Rivers's death and had to pay. He asked if either of them had any problem with that. Both had agreed. Canton knew them only by their first names, Bill and Trip. The two hands rode in front of Canton and Witherspoon. They knew the way to Crampion's shack.

"Sir, what is the plan?" Witherspoon raised the question tentatively.

Canton did not turn to answer. "Won't know until we get there. For starters, his home will be burned. Whether he's in it or not will depend on the circumstances."

Canton's words barely made it through his pursed lips. Once uttered, his jaw muscles clenched. Witherspoon must have noticed, as he did not pursue the conversation.

* * * * *

Ella Toal clipped wet clothes across a line strung between the back of her house and one of the two raised gateposts on their corral. Nate hated this line. Said it was dangerous. Claimed there was too much activity around a corral to string a rope. A rider might have to run after an escaped animal through this same gap and be torn off his mount. But there was no other place to hang the laundry. The only tree was much too far from the house for a single rope.

Sheets snapped in the incessant wind. Wind could be hard on the fabric, especially if it hung flapping violently for too long. But Ella also knew that clothes would dry quickly in a stiff breeze. She just had to remove them as soon as the moisture left.

Nate came home last night. He told her about the battle with Canton. He had come home to check on her. He was worried Canton or his men might have attacked the house. Ella was shocked to hear about the gun fight. Her fears had risen steadily over the last couple of months. Upon hearing of the gunplay, she almost broke down. Fear could be debilitating. She said so to Nate. He nodded and stood to take her in his arms. Ella confessed to Nate that up to now she didn't think Ferguson's men would harm her, but now that Nate had wounded one of those aggressors, they would probably come after Nate.

The pair planned their next moves. Ella brought up the idea again of moving south to stay with Will and his wife. Nate agreed that she should go. He would stay to protect the house and stock, but she should head south until this all blew over. They decided that he would ride back out to the remote corral and bring the cattle back to the house with Reese and Ray the next day. Once he got back, he would take Ella south while the boys watched their small herd.

As planned, Nate rode out early this morning. Ella did some laundry in preparation for taking some extra clothes with her to Will's ranch. She had already packed most of what she would need. She had packed her blue dress and matching hat. She did not know how long she would be gone. So, she washed all of Nate's clothes so he would have clean things to wear. It was a large load of wet fabric. It had taken her almost a half-an-hour to hang it all out. Between her focus on getting the laundry done and the noise of the wind, she had not noticed the rider's approach from her rear. Her rifle was in the house. Nate had told her to carry it with her wherever she went. But it stood inside the door as she saw the men behind her.

"I didn't think whores did laundry."

The man who spoke sat atop his horse dressed in a black duster and strange black hat with fur circled around the base. He had a gun pointed at her.

Ella began to run to the open door. The gun exploded with two shots. Both hit the dirt within inches of her feet. She stopped dead in her tracks having made little progress toward her rifle and only protection.

"That's good. No need to get back to your house. It won't be standing very long."

Ella did her best to look unfazed. But truth be known, she was panicked inside. Nate was, at this time, hours away by horse. There was no one here to protect her. This man was obviously not interested in discussion. There was anger and evil emanating from everything about him.

"My name's Frank Canton. Where's Crampion? He shot one of my men, and he's gonna pay."

Range War

Ella bared her teeth. "I'll not be intimidated. You are just here to harass. You've done that, so now be on your way."

Another shot rang out. This time the bullet hit the dirt in between her feet.

"I'll ask only one more time. Where's Crampion?"

Anger now took the place of her fear. Her ancestral Scottish roots rose to confront the assault to her world. The genes of her forefathers carried an innate hatred of tyranny.

"I wouldn't tell you what time of day it is. Why would I tell you where Nate is? It's a good thing he's not here, 'cause he'd shoot you and all your men. You all deserve it."

Canton shot her in the thigh. Ella screamed and buckled to her good knee in pain.

"I mean what I say, whore. When I say there will be consequences, there will be consequences."

"I ain't no whore!" She screamed out the words. "You and those you work for are simply evil."

Canton then shot Ella in her other leg. She screamed again and dropped to the ground.

"Tie her up. Drag her over to the tree and put her on a horse. That lady with her foul mouth is gonna hang."

Ella was now crying. But she could see through her tears that there was hesitation in the other men.

Canton turned to the other three and yelled, "Do it!"

Ella watched as the three men dismounted and approached. The pain in her legs was excruciating. She tried to roll away, but every movement only brought more pain. The men ultimately grabbed her and tied her hands. Two men each lifted her by her underarms and began pulling her to the only tree within miles. Every inch caused her to scream in agony.

Canton rode to the tree and threw a rope over the lowest branch some fifteen feet above ground. He pulled the racer end down and created a loop. He checked to see that the loop end was the right height for someone on horseback. He then dismounted and tied the butt end around the trunk of the tree.

Ella was beginning to lose consciousness. She would not last long, and she knew it. Weakened, she lifted one of her hands, now bloodied from holding her leg. She pointed at each of the men now standing around her. In a whispered voice, she said, "My husband, Nate, will come kill you all. And if he doesn't, my brother, William Toal, will hunt you down." She then fainted.

* * * * *

"She's passed out, sir." It was Witherspoon who voiced the observation.

Undeterred, Canton said, "String her up. The whore will finally get her due. We are within rights to shoot any trespasser. In addition to trespassing, Mr. Ferguson says she's been selling herself out here on his range. She deserves to swing."

Canton settled the loop around her neck as the other men propped her up in the saddle. Canton then walked to his horse's head and pulled the reins moving the animal forward. Already limp, Ella's body was held upright by the length of the rope only. After a short walk, Ella slid off the back. She hung swaying in the wind.

Canton turned around with his horse behind. He noticed Bill, Trip, and Witherspoon focused on the inert body. Canton could see in their faces a question that there was a proper justice hanging before them. Canton's blood was still up. He had ridden out this morning intending on meting out some measure of revenge upon Crampion. A measure had been delivered. The balance of his revenge would not be satisfied until Crampion was dead, himself. But he needed these men to agree with the steps now taken, to rise to the gauntlet thrown by Crampion. A war had been started. Canton had no intention of backing away. But he could tell some words were needed here in the face of action taken against a woman. He could tell that Liam, and probably the other men, too, questioned how far they should go on behalf of "restoring order", as he had called it.

"Remember, men, Crampion took the life of Vern Rivers. We rode out to make him pay. We rode out to remove both Crampion and his operation from the range. He started this war with his illegal mavericking. He upped the ante by killing Vern. Now, he must deal with a loss of his own. We'll make sure he meets the full measure of his justice soon enough."

After several moments of quiet, Witherspoon asked Canton, "Should we burn the house?"

Canton turned to the house as if to assess its worth. "No, let it stand. I want to come back here sometime after Crampion returns to see the result of his actions. We will burn it then, hopefully with him in it."

Chapter Eighteen

Spring 1878
Reno, Nevada

A soft bed with actual blankets had been welcome. Paris almost felt refreshed after a night in his own bed. He rented a small brick home on the outskirts of town. He had few neighbors. Around his humble residence there were more structures for animals than humans. He did not mind being on the fringes at all. It was only a ten-to-fifteen-minute ride into town, but here he felt miles away from the gritty, rowdy bustle of downtown Reno.

Dressed and ready, Paris walked out to his own small corral and barn. It was not much. He had only one horse and his barn consisted of a single three-sided stall that the animal could enter to get out of the weather. Saddle and tack rested in a wooden bin next to the stall. The morning air was cool, but it had a clean, crisp smell to it. Not the same smell as the air up in the Sierras, but better than the odors downtown. His plan for the day was simple. He intended to meet with Sheriff Svensson and report on the developments out on the range. From there, he had no idea how the day would go.

His horse pranced a bit after Paris mounted, making it known that his rider better be ready to go. Dale was stiff and a bit sore from the three straight days in the saddle. Obviously, his horse felt better than he did after all the miles they had covered. *Must be I'm getting old.* Paris was glad when the horse settled into a purposeful walk. He headed into town.

Reno's sheriff's office was situated sandwiched between the town post office and livery stable. No one else wanted to be all that close to the jail. Unsavory people ended up there. The structure was not impressive when viewed from the street. Wooden slats ran side by side in a vertical pattern broken only by one window and a single door. The front of the building stood removed from the main street separated by a covered walkway raised off the dirt road. But the front of the office hid a much more impressive structure to the rear. Stitched to the back was the jail. Made of brick and iron bars, it contained six cells. The walls were double-brick deep. Those walls then connected to the brick floor as an integral part of the entire edifice. Paris had toured the jail section many times, most often arriving with new prospective tenants who had committed one offense or another. It would take a serious effort most likely to include an explosive to spring anyone from this jail.

Leif Svensson sat in his chair facing the door. A simple desk with a limited number of drawers separated the sheriff from any entrant. Behind him was a larger roll top desk the table of which was stacked with several papers.

Paris assessed the sheriff. Just about six feet tall, the Norwegian-born Svensson carried a solid frame. Not an ounce of fat anywhere. He had told stories of skiing across plains of open spaces back home. Svensson was known to head up into the Sierras in the dead of winter with his long skis and poles strapped to a pack mule. He claimed skiing across new snow made him feel like he'd been transported back home. He also said it kept him fit.

Paris estimated the lawman was over forty-five years old, and while his face bore the lines of many a day in the sun, the man's arms and legs were still solid muscle. Must be the skiing. He was not overly energetic in the office, but out on a job the man was like a working mule. He pulled more than his weight, took on more than his share of responsibility, and never stopped until the job was finished.

Svensson had once informed Paris that his given name of Leif meant 'heir' or 'descendant' in his native Scandinavian language. Though still fit and outwardly attendant to his duties, he had spent a long time in the service of the law. More time than most. Paris wondered if Svensson ever bemoaned his status in life. What estate had bequeathed Svensson this job. The man was a good one. He approached his duty with conviction. But no matter what action he took, there were always two sides to the issue and Svensson invariably found himself right in the middle. Paris had seen the weight of the job in Svensson's face on multiple occasions. Today, Paris brought more competing issues which were destined to pin Svensson in the middle again. Paris stepped inside. The sheriff looked up and instantaneously expressed a measure of apprehension.

"You're not bringing me good news, are you?"

Paris could not contain a tell-tale grimace.

"Suppose so. Could you see it that quickly on my face?"

Svensson stood, walked around the front of his simple bureau, and then raised one leg as he took a partial seat on the corner. Paris sat in a chair opposite the desk. "Might as well get to it. I am sure this is about Ferguson. So, let's have it."

"Ferguson is moving forward."

Svensson winced. "Define 'moving forward'."

"While I was out on the range, I've seen members of some gang wearing a red sash. At least some of them were. They approached Nate Crampion out at his corral and lean-to on the range. There was a discussion, but I was too far away to hear. Then Crampion raised his rifle, and the gang members rode off. I told Ferguson about the encounter."

Svensson looked out his small window. "Great, that sounds like the Red Sash Gang. They are well known across three of four states. On top of that, I have Angus Ferguson going crazy against the homesteaders, now it sounds like we have a real gang of rustlers, too. I've gotten wires from Wyoming and Utah about that group. If they're out on that range, they'll be stealin' cattle, and that will only give Ferguson more justification for his war."

Paris hesitated, but then continued. "I also saw a series of wagons with men arriving at the Crampion house and met there by Ella Toal. Each set of men lifted something out of their wagon and went inside for a short while. They then exited and left. I may have made a mistake, but I told Ferguson about that, too."

"Why do you think that was a mistake?"

"Because Angus immediately jumped to the conclusion that she's a prostitute."

"Ah, and he thinks that is additional justification for him to run them off."

Paris nodded. "Exactly. But that is not the worst."

"More?"

"Ferguson's hired gun, that man Canton, apparently rode out to Crampion's range corral and there was a gun fight."

Svensson stood and strode to the door and turned back to Paris. "Are you going to tell me Nate Crampion is dead?"

Paris shook his head. "No, much the opposite. One of Canton's men was killed."

Svensson could not conceal his surprise. "I would have placed a large bet Crampion would not have come out on top against that man."

"Well, the first engagement was in his favor, but Canton collected a couple of extra men and was going to set out this morning for Crampion's home. He intends to kill Crampion."

Svensson sat back down on the corner of his desk. This time, his shoulders noticeably slumped. "Can't have that. Dealing with rustlers in the act is one thing, riding out to chase people from their lawful homes is another."

Paris now stood. Short of stature, standing, Paris was almost eye-to-eye with Svensson, though the latter was seated. "He doesn't intend to run them off. He intends to kill them."

"The woman, too?"

Paris gritted his teeth and spat the words. "I wouldn't put anything passed Canton. He's a killer and the man paying him has given him a full leash."

Svensson now stood and placed his hand on Paris's shoulder. "Thank you for bringing me the information. I know you were walking a fine line out there with Ferguson. I've said it before, and I'll say it again: I don't have any jurisdiction to intervene in land disputes between homesteaders and ranchers with grazing permits. They are all on federal land. That's a job for the U.S. marshal. But if someone is out to assault or murder citizens of this county, then I have to act."

Paris did not answer.

After a pause, Svensson continued. "I'll start collecting the men I've talked to about riding as a posse. I hope I can get a sizeable group together. Tomorrow, we'll ride out to the Crampion homestead. If necessary, we'll head to the Ferguson ranch. If Angus has authorized any assault, he's an accessory. He'll have to answer."

"I've sent a message to Will Toal telling him Canton is out after both Ella and Nate. He'll be here shortly. Bet on it."

Svensson turned to his desk and began writing on a small notepad.

"I've got to send notes to several men. The earlier I get word to them, the quicker we can ride. If you see Will Toal, tell him I'd appreciate the help, but he must stay within the bounds of the law. He is not deputized."

Paris knew that if anything happened to Ella, Will Toal would not stop to worry about being deputized. But he didn't say anything to the sheriff.

Voicing more hope than expectation, Paris then said, "Maybe if Crampion is still out on the range and only Ella is home, Canton will try to intimidate a bit but leave her alone. He really wants Crampion."

Svensson agreed.

"I cannot imagine even someone like Canton would go out of their way to harm a defenseless woman. If Crampion is out on the range, she should be safe."

Paris lifted both hands extending them outward from his sides.

"Hope you're right, but I am not so sure about Canton. He doesn't yell, scream, or get emotional. Even when his man died right in front of him, there was no overt reaction. But I could sense a vast well of anger. I don't know that we've seen the lengths that man will go to."

"I'll telegraph the U.S. marshal, but the nearest one is in Sacramento. He's two or three days away, and that assumes he's not out riding on some investigation or scout."

Paris headed to the doorway. "I'll ride out to the Crampion home. If anything untoward has happened, I'll get word to you."

Svensson nodded. "Best stay in touch. If you're still out on the range late tomorrow, plan to meet me and the posse either at Crampion's or Ferguson's ranch."

Paris pulled his bowler hat down to shade his eyes. "See you then."

Chapter Nineteen

Spring 1878
Crampion Homestead

The wind had been blowing all day. When they started early in the morning, the gusts stuck to a pattern of howling dawn to dusk. Not to disappoint or diverge from historical custom, the force of the afternoon blows had only gotten stronger. Nate Crampion checked the stampede strap on his hat. Strung below his chin, that strap was the only thing holding his hat on his head right now. The wind felt far stronger than any breeze developed if galloping a horse with a stampede. That's what gave the strap its name. It came in handy to keep the hat in place if a cowboy had to take off at a run. But today, Nate thought the name might be changed to a 'wind strap.' Out here on this range, they provided stability far more often in the wind rather than any stampedes. He was heading to his home, riding east. The wind was at his back coming down the slopes of the Sierras. Nate pulled the front of his hat down. His horse knew the way home from the range corral. He let his mount navigate the route as he looked down over the top of the animal's neck trying to keep his eyes free from being hit by flying debris.

Nate had almost reached home before he looked up. One hundred yards away he saw a figure hanging from the lone tree near his house. He immediately recognized the clothes. The body was swaying in a twisted motion in the firm gusts. He knew instantly what he was looking at.

"*Ella!*"

Nate rake his spurs violently over the sides of his horse's flanks. He gave no thought to the animal's well-being. Ella was hanging from the tree. His only thought was to get to her as quickly as he could.

At the base of the tree, he pulled up to a sliding stop. In one look he could tell she was gone. In that momentous instant, a singular thought pulsed in his brain: Ella and everything she had been to him was gone. Life had vanished from this vibrant woman who had followed him as he chased his distant dream of becoming a rancher. Gone was the smile, the welcome home each day, the one person who had supported him with no questions asked. Gone was his chance to propose. He had waited, intending to bend his knee after a good year's sales from the herd. This year would have seen good sales. Tears welled across his bottom eyelids and dripped down each cheek. He stepped off his horse in a subdued gloom. Grief felt heavy. It was hard to lift his feet as he walked to the trunk of the tree and cut the rope. He kept a tight hold on the rope as he lowered the body gently into his arms. He could not escape the reality there in his hands: Ella was gone.

* * * * *

Will Toal rode up to the Crampion home. It had been a long day's ride in the unrelenting wind. He had thought about stopping in Reno first to see if he could find Dale Paris and get more information. But as he rode, he decided he should get to Ella's place as soon as he could.

Along the way, he imagined the conversation he needed to have with Ella. He imagined that conversation with Nate present, and Nate absent. He sifted through these conversations time and time again trying to find the right words, words that would convince Ella to ride south. He did this often before heading into a meeting of importance. He was always able to develop what he considered a good plan. But he knew the real conversations never followed the imaginary design. Life had its own plan.

From a half-mile out from the Crampion ranch, things looked strange. A saddled horse wandered around the yard. Its reins were unattached to any fence or hitching post. As he got closer, he saw a man sitting out in front of the main door next to a body. The body was wearing a blue dress, a dress Will knew well. He squeezed his spurs into Powder's flanks and ran the last quarter- mile. Will instinctively scanned the plains for signs of other men. He saw none. He loosened the leather safety strap on his side arm just in case. Something was seriously wrong. He pulled up at the door and slid off. It was Nate sitting next to a prone Ella. Nate looked up with eyes red from tears.

"They hung her. They hung Ella."

Will knew something had been wrong, very wrong as he rushed up to the door. Ella was lying flat and the whole scene seemed out of place.

But Nate's words stopped him dead. He knelt on one knee and reached out to Ella. He gently pulled down the raised collar of her dress and saw the angry colored scar circling her neck. Her face displayed a distortion born from a painful demise. He didn't want to believe the words. But the truth stared at him from the pale face below. Will dipped his head. His sister just recently found had been taken. Anger stirred. A heat from deep within rose to his neck and throbbed at his temples in intermediate beats of pressure against his hatband. He lifted his hat off his head and looked at Nate.

Nate spoke, but he didn't look at Will. Pain spread across his face. It was the hollow look of a man whose soul had been carved in two. Part of Nate lay dead with Ella.

"She was doing laundry. She was going to pack. We had agreed she should go with you to your ranch. She wasn't wearing her blue dress and hat when they did it. She loved this silly thing. I put it on her not only because she loved it, but to cover up the scar. I didn't want to bury her with that scar around her neck showing. Stupid, but I did it."

"They will pay."

Crampion's face changed from defeat covered in dried tears stained with wind dust to a face of anger to match Will's. "Damn right. The bastards will pay."

"Know who did it?"

Will watched as Nate seemed to continue his temporary path from grief to anger. Nate collected his thoughts and then answered, "I have a pretty good idea who it was."

Will then listened as Nate gave him a brief description of the events over the last couple of days. Nate told him of the gunfight at the range corral. He further explained their plan that Ella would come south to live with Will and Beth while Nate tried to protect the herd and get it out for sale. They planned for the hands to watch the herd here by the house as Nate rode south to drop off Ella. The money from the sale was important. It would be the first step toward realizing the dream and making it a reality. He then told Will of his intent to propose as soon as they had the money. Tears streamed down his face as he recounted this last part.

Then, a voice sounded in the distance.

"Will Toal. It's Dale Paris. I see Powder and I know you are there. Don't want to startle."

Will turned and saw Paris approaching in the distance. The wind carried Dale's voice, making it seem he was further away than he was. Will waved him to come on.

Dale dismounted and walked to the pair still in their same positions over Ella. "What happened?"

"They killed Ella, Dale. They hung her. They hung my sister. They hung her for no damn reason at all."

The words erupted from Will. He stood as if the volcanic tirade lifted him from his kneeling position through some invisible force.

"Oh, Will. I am so sorry."

Will watched as Paris then bent at the waist and braced his hands on his knees.

"I did this. I made this happen." Paris then looked up distraught. "You have a right to kill me, both of you. I made this happen."

Will was astonished. "How in the hell did *you* make this happen? Nate thinks Canton did this in revenge for wounding one of Canton's men in a gunfight."

Paris nodded. "Oh, I'm sure that is part of it. Nate, that man you shot died. But that was not all. In my last report to Ferguson, I told him I'd seen men coming here to the house in wagons. I told Ferguson it looked like they were dropping something off. It was my last report to the man before I decided I had to quit his employment."

Nate spoke up. "She would do sewing and mending for folks around here. Other homesteaders. Word had gotten out that she could mend, and they would bring clothes and other things to her to be fixed. It kept her busy while I was away."

Paris responded, "I thought so. I told Ferguson it looked like it was something she was doing for money, a fee."

Will now looked puzzled. "So, how do you figure that has anything to do with Ella's death?"

Paris lifted from his bent position. "Because Ferguson immediately jumped to the conclusion that Ella was a prostitute. I told him there would be no need for people to drop off items in wagons. They'd just ride up, if she was a prostitute. But Ferguson went almost crazy. Said it was an offense to his dead wife for prostitution to happen out on his land. When Canton came in and told him about the shooting with Nate,

Ferguson told Canton to do whatever he needed to do, but get rid of the Crampions."

Will took a moment to process what he had just been told. He then reached out to Dale's shoulder. "You didn't kill Ella. Ferguson and Canton did. Dale, you and I have been through a lot, and I know you would never intentionally do anything to hurt me or my family."

The relief on Paris's face was almost palpable. Will could sense how hard it had been for Paris to tell him what he had. Will and Paris started off on opposite sides of a gunfight themselves and for a long time Will distrusted anything Paris said or did. But they had worked on multiple chases of outlaws, and each had saved the other's life at least once. Will came to trust this man. He hoped his words put his mind at rest that all their history led to a clear understanding they both acted in each other's interest.

"You have no idea how hard that was to tell you."

Will gave a slight smile. "Oh, based on our history, I imagine I could tell. Were you watching to see if I went for my gun?"

Paris nodded. "I supposed a thought along those lines crept into the back of my mind."

"Well, if I had, you'd have lost."

"Never doubted. By the way, I met with Sheriff Svensson earlier today. Told him what I just told you. He is collecting a posse just in case something happened to Nate or Ella. The posse will be riding out here tomorrow."

Will then turned to Nate. Any smile immediately dissipated. A stern frown descended from his hairline to eyebrow.

"Well, that about confirms it."

Nate nodded. "But we have no witness. Even if we go to the law, Ferguson will beat any conviction."

Will considered, then answered. "Let's see if we can develop something that will stick. Let's first see to a proper burial for Ella. Then Dale and I will look around to see if we can find any tracks we can follow. They just might lead us to Ferguson's."

Nate shook his head. "Wind's blown away any tracks."

Will looked in the direction of the Ferguson ranch. Behind the house was a creek, the main reason Nate and Ella had planted roots here. Will turned back to Nate. "Let's see to Ella and then Dale and I will take a look at the creek. If the riders headed back to the Ferguson ranch directly, they would have crossed the creek. Muddied tracks would last, even in this wind."

* * * * *

They buried Ella. Will and Nate had jointly dug the grave. Nate then did his best to deliver words that conveyed what he felt inside. Will and Dale stood with hats in hand.

Nate spoke through the pain. He spoke to Ella as if no one else was around. He told her he loved her. He told her he was sorry he was not here. He tried to imagine what it must have been in those last moments. He apologized for failing her.

When he was done Nate said, "I've got to sit down." Defeat hung from the man's shoulders.

"Understood," said Will. "You go inside. It'll be dark soon; Dale and I will walk over and look at the creek. We'll meet you back here after we've taken a look."

Nate walked to the house while Will tipped his hat in the direction of the creek to signal Paris he should follow.

Dale watched Nate go. He kept he eyes on the young man. "Should one of us stay with him? You don't think he'll do something stupid to himself, do you?"

Will looked in Nate's direction. "No. He's dealing with a horrible loss right now. So am I. But I think Nate's got a reservoir down deep and he'll start to draw from it. The anger will take over. It already has for me."

They walked to the water's edge. Will knelt and pointed to several sets of tracks in the soft mud, now dried in the incessant wind. It was if molds had been created and set on the border of the waterway.

"Looks like four horses," said Will pointing to the impressions.

Paris agreed and added, "And they are headed to Ferguson's."

Will stood and spoke directly to Paris. "Got an idea. Let's head back to the house and talk to Nate."

As they walked, two cowhands driving about fifty to a hundred head of cattle pulled up, herding the group into the large corral by the house. The two men dismounted and approached Will.

"Who are you?"

"I'm Will Toal. I was Ella's brother."

One of the hands tipped up the front bill of his hat. "What do you mean *was* Ella's brother? I don't understand."

Will lifted his own hat and wiped his brow. "Ella's been killed. She was hung before Nate got home."

"My God. They hung her?"

"Yep."

The same hand then said, "Must've been 'cause we shot one of their men. But hanging a defenseless woman... Anyone who'd do that is plumb evil."

Will nodded in agreement. "No argument there."

"My name is Reese Stricker. This here's Nick Ray. We work for Nate off and on as he needs. We met up with some other homesteaders on our way here. They plan to hold a meeting. Folks have heard about Ferguson's men forcing two sets of families out of the county. Ran them straight off. People are mad, afraid mad. They want to collect up for defense and they want Nate to lead them."

Will nodded. "That might work into a plan I am developing. Let's head over to the house. Nate's inside. He's pretty beat up with the loss of Ella. Working with other folks would be a good diversion from any ideas he might have of starting a personal vendetta."

The group got to the house. Will stopped at the opening. "Nate. Okay if we come inside? Your hands are with us."

"Sure. Come in."

When everyone collected inside, Will waved his hat in a circular motion to the group.

"I got an idea as to how we might move forward."

Everyone waited. Will continued. "Reese and Nick said they met some other homesteaders who are worried that Ferguson's men are going to come for them soon. They are going to meet tomorrow. They want you, Nate, to lead them. I think that would be a good idea. I would suggest that you ride to the meeting tomorrow and see if you can organize the group rather than have some rag tag collection that will only get hurt. Then, Dale, you ride back to Reno and find Sheriff Svensson. Tell him what happened here and get both him and his posse out to Ferguson's. I'll meet you there."

Nate questioned, "You're going to Ferguson's alone?"

"Yep. I think I'll try to bait Ferguson into admitting what he's done. He might not even know what happened to Ella. Canton may or may not have told him. If he doesn't know, it would be good to see his expression when I tell him. And who better to approach him than another rancher with holdings equal to his and the brother of the woman killed?"

Dale then interjected, "What if you meet up with Canton?"

"I'll try to bait him too, only in a different way."

Paris objected. "Will, your plan sounds crazy. That ranch is full of hands ready to ride out and shoot up homesteaders. You take the opposite side, and you might not ride out of there."

Will shook his head.

"I'll watch my step. I intend to instill a bit of doubt in his troops. Do they want to be associated with men who kill innocent unarmed women? And I'm not worried about Ferguson. He's a bag of emotions, but he won't attack me."

Paris did not give up the argument. "And what about Canton?"

"Oh, I hope he's up for a fight. I'll be happy to give him what he deserves."

"All by yourself?"

"Partially. But I'll also be counting on you, Dale, to get Svensson and his group out there as soon as you can."

Chapter Twenty

Spring 1878
Ferguson Ranch

As if in observance of a life lost, the winds in the morning were calm.

Will had left Nate's house early. Powder had been ridden hard the day before. There was little forage around the immediate area of the Crampion abode. Last night, Will put Powder in one of the corrals where he shared hay along with the cattle. But he probably had not gotten much to eat. As a result, Will was taking it slower than usual.

Thoughts, hard thoughts, kept surfacing as he rode. He had tried to put on a strong face in front of Nate. He could see the poor man struggled to find motivation to move forward. Will had assisted taking care of Ella and dealing with the hands. But now, he was left to his own thoughts as he rode his gray mustang.

The loss of Ella ripped open old wounds. He had not seen the chance arrival of a sibling he'd thought long since dead. Then, she was gone, taken from him. But what about Ella? As hard as it may be to deal with his own loss, Will struggled to push thoughts of Ella away: the terror she must have felt as they placed the rope around her neck; the panic of complete helplessness, of absolute absurdity. She had left home so young. It must have taken a form of strength, a determination not found in most. Even though a young woman, she'd forged a life here on a stark plain trying to build something out of nothing. How awful it must have been to look for help and have no one near. Then, it was done.

A life lost.

Powder's hooves moved forward in a rhythmic constant. Will knew he had to move forward as a constant himself. Beth and the children needed him to do that. But forcing thoughts of Ella back down the well he'd dug long ago was going to be hard.

Will knew Nate had planned to let his small herd graze within proximity of his house with Reese and Nick watching, and then collect the group at night. They hoped to push the mature steers to Reno for an early sale. Keeping them close to the house was the key to making sure they were not run off or taken from the open range. Nate and his hands knew that any attempt to beat the other ranchers to market would not go over well. But Nate needed the money.

Will had other plans. His focus was Canton. He wanted to get confirmation Canton had been the one to kill Ella. If he got that confirmation, there was no doubt in his mind that he and Canton would face off at some point.

Will headed southwest, skirting Pyramid Lake. Ferguson Ranch was west of Pyramid, up off the flat plains and further into the foothills of the Sierras. Will knew from past dealings with Angus that a portion of his holdings included deeded acres that bordered the Truckee River. The Truckee flowed east from Lake Tahoe and pierced Ferguson's property as it hit the flatlands. The river then flowed through the town of Reno on the way back out to the range and its terminus at Pyramid Lake. Though Ferguson's property bordered the Truckee at the base of the mountains, Ferguson turned his herd out on the western portion of the open range in addition to having them graze on his deeded property. Angus claimed he had a grazing permit which covered some thirty thousand acres. Will thought that claim was questionable. He'd heard from ranch owners in the south that Ferguson had been one of the early settlers to the north and had simply claimed the land. No one had ever seen any actual permit.

As he rode, Will remembered Ferguson's flawed plan to dynamite the Truckee River Dam at its source on the borders of Lake Tahoe. The plan was ill advised from the start, and ultimately cost Ferguson his only son, Dirk. Ferguson had pushed other ranchers to assist in the faulty pursuit of the dam's destruction, thinking they could lift the restriction of the Truckee's flow. A drought of more than two years had put the cattle herds both in the north and south in severe jeopardy. Ferguson intended to open the dam and let the river flow to succor his herd. But the plan failed. Good thing, too. If he had blown up the dam, the result would have undoubtedly been a flood, and then, even less of a flow out of Lake Tahoe. Rational minds could see the fault in the idea, but Angus did not. Ferguson had pushed that specious plan back then and he was doing it again here with the homesteaders. Problem was, he had even more support among the large ranchers to the north and their political lackeys when it came to the homesteaders.

The Ferguson ranch headquarters came into view. Will pulled up Powder. As was his custom, Will started a quick conversation with the mustang.

"So, Dale thinks I'm crazy for heading into this ranch alone. You agree?"

The horse did not move.

"Ah, thinking of a good response, are you? Playing it close to the vest?"

Again, no answer, despite Will's expectation. So, he continued. "I just want to look the man eye-to-eye and see his reaction when I accuse him of killing Ella."

Powder lowered his head and rubbed his nose and forehead on his lower leg. It was an equine version of wiping his brow.

"I take that as an indication of disgust with my plan. Well, let's just see what develops. Whether it's a good idea or not, I would definitely agree we should be ready to ride and ride hard if things don't work out."

Will gently squeezed the flanks of the mustang and continued into the main compound. Several men were walking from one building to another. One asked, "Can I help you?"

Will responded, "Looking for Angus Ferguson."

"And who are you?"

"Name's Will Toal. He'll know me. I ranch in Jack's Valley to the south."

"I'll see if I can find him. Why don't you tie-up?"

Will smiled. "Much obliged."

Will wrapped one of the split reins over the hitching rail. He stood by Powder waiting for the man to return. The ranch compound was auspicious, the biggest Will had ever seen. The main house was huge. Across from the main home was a simple bunkhouse Will estimated could house maybe fourteen or fifteen men. Behind the main house, he could see the roof of a wooden barn. The color of the unpainted walls had become a dark brown, almost black. Exposed wood revealed the age of a building unprotected from the weather. It was probably one of the first structures Angus had constructed. Sun, air, and wind had left the wood aged, at a loss of its original vibrant color. It now looked fragile, old. When Will last saw its owner, he, too, looked old and frail. He had been near broken at the then recent loss of his only son.

"Will Toal, what brings you here?"

It was Angus who had just stepped out of his front door. The man no longer looked frail. He had a strident purpose to his stance. Will found the tone obtuse, knowing, and a bit condescending all at the same time. He figured that Angus had already heard about what took place at Crampion's and had no intention of assuming a defensive stance. Angus opted for the offensive. So be it. Will decided if he wanted to be direct, then let's be direct.

"Did you order the death of my sister, Ella Toal?"

"You mean the trespasser who's been rustling my cattle? The one who lives with that Crampion fellow?" An insidious grin crept across Angus's lips. Will found it hard to keep his emotions under control. He had a strong urge to wipe that smile off Ferguson's lips on a permanent basis.

"She was not trespassing nor rustling, and you know it. You murdered an innocent girl, Angus. An innocent girl. You have gone amok, Ferguson. You've sunk into an evil hole after you killed your own son with your crazy plan to blow up that dam. Now you want to take out your frustration, your own guilt, on the rest of the world."

Will had planned to use the death of Ferguson's son as a trigger, hoping to push Angus to reveal the truth about Ella in a raged response. The conversation had only started, and he just played his best card.

"You doona have any idea how my son died!" The words were screamed.

It was Will who now smiled. *Got him, now a little push further.* The thickness of the Scottish brogue rising in the heat of emotion reminded him of his own father, whose roots also hailed from the land of glens and heather. When he'd argued with his father as a boy, he knew he'd won when the brogue became stronger.

"I was there. I know *exactly* how Dirk died. I watched it. He rode into a volley of gunfire for you, Angus; for your ridiculous plan to blow up the dam. He died for your mistake."

"The boy was courageous."

Will noted a slight quiver in Ferguson's voice. Whether grief or rage, he could not tell. It didn't matter. Will hoped his simple plan might work in response to either of those two emotions.

"Oh, he was courageous. He rode to his death, probably knowing what a stupid effort it was. He probably hoped to keep you from killing yourself with your reckless idea."

Will watched as Angus clenched his hands at his sides. He was unarmed, but a small crowd of cowhands had gathered drawn by the raised voices. They *were* armed. Angus had not responded. Maybe the jabs were hitting home. Will pushed further, he was close. He had to know if Angus was behind Ella's death.

"And you are doing it again, Angus. You are out killing people for no reason. You'll have to pay. Those who did this will pay."

"There is no law against killing a trespasser, a rustler!"

Again, the comment was loud enough to be heard throughout the compound. Will could sense the tension mounting in those now watching the argument. A casual glance to his right netted a look at two hands, both of whom seemed confused. Uncertainty in those observing might be the best he could expect, at the moment. If he pushed too far and these hands reached a point of thinking they should defend their boss, then Will would not ride out in one piece. He knew he had to end this, and soon.

"Angus, you just admitted it. I thought so. Tracks of those who did it led here."

Ferguson threw up his hands. "There could be no tracks in yesterday's winds."

"There were tracks enough if you knew what to look for." Will's anger was not barely contained.

"You have no proof a'tall."

"Got all I needed, right here. It's in your voice and in your face. You killed Ella. I'll be back with the sheriff."

"Toal, you have no proof. You bring any charge, and a jury will laugh you out of court."

Will decided he'd gone as far as he could under the circumstances. But he chose to make one more stab at uncovering what really happened.

"Where's Canton? I'm sure he was the one to carry out your orders."

"Ha. Canton's not here now. No need to be. But I'm sure you will meet up with him sometime soon."

Will grabbed his reins, stepped into his stirrup, and swung up atop Powder. He sat still and looked directly at Ferguson.

"Tell Canton I look forward to it."

Will pulled the reins sideways and walked Powder from the compound. He did not look back.

Chapter Twenty-One

Spring 1878
Ferguson Ranch

The sun hung directly overhead trying to burn a hole in the umbrella of the blue horizon. There was an intense clarity beneath the cloudless spring sky. To the west, the Sierras stood at what seemed no more than arm's length. Despite the distance, every outcropping, every pine tree near the crests, every canyon crevasse, seemed to stretch closer in the limpid brilliance of the day.

Will had ridden for an hour away from the Ferguson Ranch. He attempted to focus on the stunning picture before him. He tried to absorb the unrivaled uniqueness of his surroundings. He struggled to let the vision of the geography distract the emotion boiling within. This geography caused him to stop his migration west some ten years ago. But even the spectacular beauty of the open range and majestic stand of mountains could not conquer the anger inside. Try as he might, he knew he was not thinking clearly. The startling joy in discovering Ella lived through the war had now been crushed. In a matter of a month, he had gone from a family rejuvenated to a history again extinguished. And for what? At best, she had been killed based on a tenuous land claim. At worst, she had been killed because of some prejudice she was living with someone and not married. She had been poorly judged. Maybe a similar short-sighted judgment should be applied to those who killed her.

He had just left Angus Ferguson, the man responsible for the murder of his sister. He should have shot him on sight.

Will stopped. He'd been heading west. Why? He didn't know. Will owned property to the west up along the Truckee River. He had always called it the Purcell Ranch, his wife Beth's ranch. Maybe he had headed in that direction by instinct. Maybe a deep survival surge to reach home. The anger had blindfolded him, obscured his purpose. He sighed.

"Well, Powder, I suppose you were right. That did not go so well, did it?"

The gray mustang bent left at the neck as if to look up at his rider.

"What? You got something to say? You wanna let me know you told me so?"

The horse turned the upper portion of his head at an angle right and shook his large head back around to the opposite side of his body. More than likely, the extended movement displayed nothing more than an equine question as to why they had stopped. Will attributed something further to the large shake of the head.

"Disgusted, huh? Yeah, you're probably right. I should have waited for Paris. Speaking of Paris, he's supposed to be headed out here. We probably should turn south toward Reno if we're gonna connect with him. Shouldn't be traveling up to the Truckee Ranch. Not sure why I was pushing in that direction."

Will pulled the reins to his left. As he did, he saw a flaw in the day's perfect visage over the range. Dust.

"Well, what do we have here? That looks like a sizable group on the move. Should we wait and see who it is, or make a run for it?"

No answer came from his equine partner.

The cloud of dust seemed to change direction, now headed directly at Will.

"Well, they've seen us. No sense in scurrying for it. If that's Frank Canton and his bunch, I might not make it home. But I'll do my best to make sure he goes before I do."

Will squinted under the glaring daylight doing his best to make out the identity of the riders approaching.

"I do believe that is Dale Paris and his short-legged horse out in front. Don't recognize the mounts for the rest of the group, but it's hard to miss the choppy gait of that stout little thing Paris rides."

As they got closer, Will could identify Sheriff Svensson riding next to Paris. He leaned forward resting his elbow on his saddle horn.

"Well, Powder, I guess Paris convinced the sheriff to gather a posse. The day is only half done, but it could get real interesting before the sun sets."

Svensson raised his hand, and the group came to a stop collecting around Will. Svensson was the first to speak. "Will Toal, we've just been to the Crampion ranch and know what happened to your sister." After a short pause, Svensson added, "My condolences."

Will looked back to his right at the towering mountains. After a moment, he returned his gaze to Svensson. "Sheriff, signs were clear that things were going to get out of hand."

Svensson did not hesitate. "No one could have anticipated that any man hereabouts would hang a woman. They had no legal cause. When word gets out as to what they've done, there'll be a lot of people good and upset. They've gone too far. Those responsible need to stand for their deeds."

With the anger and emotion barely curtailed below the surface of his stare, Will responded. "Those who did this should be treated in the same manner as my sister. But those are not the only ones who share blame. Those who gave the order need to face justice as well."

"Agreed," said Svensson.

Dale Paris leaned forward in his saddle. "You said yesterday you'd be riding to Ferguson's. I had hoped you would change your mind. I left before you to head for Reno. Nate said you intended to follow the tracks. He said you convinced him they lead to the Ferguson Ranch, just as you and I talked about yesterday."

Will nodded. "They did."

Paris pursued. "Will, you didn't ride all the way into the ranch compound there alone, did you?"

"I did. Probably not the smartest thing I've ever done, but I had to look straight into Angus's eye and ask him directly if he ordered Ella's death."

Paris shook his head. "I'm surprised you're alive to tell what happened. What did he say?"

"He didn't deny it. He did his best to provide justification. Said there was no law preventing the killing of a rustler or trespasser." Will hesitated as the emotion hit him back deep in his throat. "No, he didn't deny it, and in trying to justify himself, he plainly admitted it."

Svensson now spoke. "And he will pay. I intend to ride to Ferguson's ranch and arrest him."

Will surveyed the group of men surrounding his horse. By quick count they numbered about six, not including Svensson and Paris. "Not sure you have enough men here to do that. Angus probably has twice this number lazing about in his bunk house."

"No matter. Based on what I've heard from both you and Nate, he should be arrested and stand trial. Might not stick, but that's how I see it. Like you to ride with us, if you're willing."

"I'm willing. I'm sure you know I've a keen interest in seeing Angus get what's coming to him. Actually, I'm glad there are lawmen who are inclined to do what's called for. We don't see a whole lot of that in Carson City."

Svensson now shook his head.

"Not sure what you see or don't see in Carson City, but I know my job, and these men have been deputized to assist. If you're agreeable to come along and help, consider yourself deputized as well."

Will drew down the bill of his hat. "I'm in."

Range War

* * * * *

Leif Svensson scanned the fields of short nascent grasses bathed in springtime green. He knew the color and the height of the stiff-bladed weed would not last long. Here, north of the Truckee, there was little water. Despite the looming Sierras not far to the west, little moisture found its way to acres pleading for water. By June it would be thin and brown, coming close to the color of the dirt underneath. But the span was green this time of year. That must have been why Angus Ferguson stopped here to plant his roots.

Svensson shifted his six-foot body in his saddle. Today's ride had been the longest he'd made in some time. His backside was feeling it. He was a big man, wide and firmly muscled just as his father. He'd heard stories of his ancestors sailing the world raiding and spreading terror. Vikings raided out of necessity. There were no fields like this in Scandinavia. As a boy he had heard stories of Viking bravery. It was in the blood. These open acres would have looked like paradise to a Viking running from the depth of an arctic winter. Now that he thought of it, Angus's lineage was from Scotland. As dried out and paltry as the plain could be in September here north of Reno, it probably looked fine to Ferguson here in spring compared to the barren hills of the Highlands.

Riding at the head of the posse, Svensson pulled up as the Ferguson Ranch came into view. He looked to Will riding next to him. "Was Frank Canton and his group of Texans at the ranch when you were there?"

Will shook his head in the negative. "No. If they were, I'm not sure I'd have made it out of there."

"How long would you say it's been since you left earlier?"

Will shrugged. "No more than an hour."

Svensson scanned the horizon. Except for the stand of trees surrounding the immediate ranch compound, there was nothing but acres of flat ground. Anyone approaching could be seen for miles. "Don't see any riders anywhere on the horizon. Let's hope Canton is still out on the range. He's probably creating more havoc, but right now, I think we have a better chance of taking Ferguson into custody without bloodshed if Canton is not around."

"Probably right," said Will, who had not taken his eyes off the ranch.

Svensson then turned to Paris. "Dale, I'd like it if you and Will rode into the ranch with me to confront Ferguson."

Paris lifted his ever-present bowler hat and wiped his brow. "Could be interesting. Wonder if Angus is gonna blow a gusset at seeing me involved, figuring as how I was quite recently in his employ." The sheriff noticed a confident smile spreading on Paris's face as he spoke.

Svensson then swiveled in his saddle to face the men behind. "Rest of you men take positions surrounding the compound. Make sure two of you are positioned at either end of the road through the ranch so you can watch and make sure we get Ferguson. The rest spread out, but make sure you can see the men at the entrance and exit. Those men can signal the rest if anyone tries to make a break for it. Any questions?"

No one said anything at first. Then, Will responded, "I like the strategy. I doubt Angus would try to make a run for it. If anything, he might just call for his hands to open fire. If he does, I hope the rest of you will come in guns blazing as we try to make our exit. We all should stay mounted."

"Absolutely," said Svensson. "Everyone ready?"

Hearing no objections, the sheriff then said, "Let's go."

Svensson led the way with Paris and Will right behind. The six deputies rode fast to encircle the compound and spread out. Svensson looked at Will as they rode in at a slow trot.

"I'll do the talking. I might look to you to confirm the basis for the arrest, but I think it best if I do the talking."

Will nodded. "Only right. You are the law, not me."

Svensson watched ahead as several cowhands stepped out into the road. The posse had been seen long before they got close. All wore sidearms. Two carried rifles. "No secret in our arrival."

Will smiled. "No. When they see you, there's probably no secret as to why you're here, either."

Nearing the outer buildings Paris said under his breath, "I'll keep a close watch on those two with the rifles. Cowhands are not usually exceptional with handguns, but rifles are another matter. If any shooting starts, Will, you and I should focus on those two with the rifles."

Will nodded. "I'll take the one on the right, you watch the one on the left."

As the trio reached the compound, they settled their horses to a walk.

One of the men carrying a rifle called out, "What do you want?" He stood in the middle of the road entrance cradling his rifle, resting it across the thick flannel shirt he wore. There was an arrogance in the man's demeanor, a challenge issued as one not in control but trying to impress.

Svensson answered, "I'm here on official business to see Angus Ferguson. Go ask him to show himself."

The man holding the rifle did not move, but he did nod his head in the direction of another cowhand standing at the entrance to the main house. In response to what must have been an unspoken command, the second cowboy turned and entered the house. Not long after, Angus Ferguson emerged wearing a tan, small-brimmed Stetson, thick woolen shirt, and slacks. He was not armed.

"What's the meaning of this, Svensson?"

Still astride his horse, Svensson looked down with a stern eye. Though he had seen Ferguson many times, he marveled at the stout Celtic stature of the man. He had to be in his sixties, but one could still see the brick hard muscles of his upper leg flex against his pants as he walked. That solid stature fit the man's personality: hard, unbending, and lacking in flexibility both physically and intellectually.

Svensson answered, "Angus Ferguson, you're under arrest as an accomplice and accessory to the murder of Ella Toal. Get your coat and horse and be ready to ride."

"You can't be serious. You have no proof, Svensson. I have never been near that woman. And you are never going to prove I ordered anything. If you put me in jail, I'll be released within an hour."

"Could be, Angus, but that's not going to stop me from putting you under arrest. You know what you've done. You must answer for that. God willing, there'll be a trial, and a jury will decide what to do with you."

"Svensson, you think you can come in here onto my land and take me from it like some Viking of old?"

Svensson responded without emotion. "Vikings sent any Scot before them running for their heather."

"There's nae a Scot afraid of any Viking." The brogue became thick.

Svensson shook his head. "Beg to differ, Angus. History tells a different story."

Ferguson lifted his head backward as his lips broke into a grin that was half-smile and half-sneer.

"You only have three men here. You think your authority can overcome those standing around you?" An air of haughty ego dripped from every word.

Undeterred, Svensson smiled right back.

"There are men surrounding your compound, Angus. The odds are not exactly what you think they might be at first sight. You'll not find any escape to the heather today."

"And what if I just order my hands to start shooting at you three?"

Will was the one who answered that challenge. "Then Angus, you'll be the first one to die, 'cause I'll make sure that happens right quick."

"Will Toal, you haven't even drawn your pistol."

"No matter. You won't get the order to shoot out of your mouth before you'll hit the ground."

"You'd shoot an unarmed man down in cold blood?"

"You're gettin' more of a chance than you gave my sister. All you must do is get up on your horse, ride into town, and get a fair trial. Ella got none of that. But if you want to start a gun battle, well, you'll just have to face the consequences here and now."

Svensson took note that Will uttered the words in a cool confidence. They had the ring of not caring about his own death, but sure he was going to make certain Angus went first. The tenor of the delivery left little doubt as to the sincerity of Will's intent. Svensson could see a change in Ferguson's face. The smile had left. It appeared that Ferguson had begun to weigh his options with additional care. Svensson didn't have to look around at every cowhand. By the look of the two hands in front of him, the sheriff knew all were on edge as to the next move. Guns could start blazing in an instant.

Ferguson lifted his chin and yelled at one of the hands across the road and behind the sheriff. "Saddle my horse and bring it out front here. I might as well go with these men. I'll not be in jail long. The lawyers will see to that. No need for bloodshed here."

Svensson was now the one to smile. Ferguson had blinked. They might just make it out of here in one piece.

"Svensson, I'll get my coat and return."

"Stay where you are Ferguson. You'll not leave my sight. Have your man there behind you go get your coat."

Ferguson's eyes squinted in an angry frown. Without looking away from Svensson he called over his shoulder to the man at his back. "Go get my heavy coat. No tellin' what kind of accommodations our good sheriff has in store for me tonight."

The man went inside and returned about the time another cowhand walked Ferguson's saddle horse out to the group. Ferguson shoved his arms into his coat sleeves, stepped into his stirrup and swung up onto his saddle. Now mounted, he turned and looked directly at the sheriff.

"You'll regret this, Svensson."

"No, Angus, I don't think I will. Let's ride."

Chapter Twenty-Two

Spring 1878
Nevada Stockman's Association in Reno, Nevada

Wide leather chairs spread throughout a large extended room. Wood paneled walls carried a wax and sheen reflecting light as though they were timbered mirrors. A blaze burned in an oversized fireplace; a huge hearth meant to impress. In fact, everything in the room was meant to impress. From the carpets to the wall hanging portraits of ranches and cattle in open spaces, the room spoke of wealth and privilege. There were no windows in this chamber. Those of lesser status were removed from the reality of those fortunate to be allowed within. Oil lanterns flickered on tables placed next to chairs which provided a subdued secretive illumination. Libations were sipped slowly in hushed reserve.

The men scattered among the chairs were quiet. A diffuse cloud of pipe and cigar smoke clung to the ceiling. Born of nervous tobacco infused respiration, the vaporous haze blanketed a stillness, a saturated forced silence. Angus Ferguson had been arrested. If he were to be bound for trial, the consequences could get complicated for those of the Stockman's group supporting the effort to deal with the homesteaders and rustlers.

Gentry MacDonald stood by the hearth. He was the only man standing. Tall and lean, possessed of erect posture, MacDonald was the quintessential politician. Trained as a lawyer, hardened by successful courtroom battles, he tendered an air of handshake interest in every potential voter he met. But any apparent attention, particularly of those MacDonald believed to be of lesser social standing, was the superficial interest of a narcissist. There was only one thing MacDonald cared about: the governor's office. Currently the State Attorney General, MacDonald cultivated those in the club where he stood as steppingstones to that focal interest. Power pervaded this room and its members like the smoke perpetually captured below the ceiling.

MacDonald wore a tailored black coat that extended to thigh level. Beneath was a dark gray silk vest which smartly contrasted to his light gray pinstriped wool slacks. The pants possessed a sharp pleat to both front and back. The slender slacks tapered in tailored perfection as they perfectly reached the top of high polished black boots. He could have been the bridegroom at a wedding. MacDonald's future political plans had a good deal riding on the results of the next few minutes. He heard men entering the front of the Club. Resolution approached.

"MacDonald, you did well. You did well by another of the clans."

Gentry watched as Angus Ferguson entered the room. Ferguson was the opposite of MacDonald's sartorial presence. Short, wide, supported by thick, bandy-legged pillars, the man eschewed force. Ferguson shouted the words before he even came into view. MacDonald knew instantaneously that his efforts behind the scenes to block any indictment of Angus had been successful.

"There'll be no jail time for this Scot!"

Ferguson made sure every man both in the room and those following his entrance could clearly hear his statement.

Angus was followed by Carter McKinnon, State Senator Ronald Tisdale, State Water Commissioner W.J. Clarke, and ranchers William C. Irvine and Hubert Teshemacher. All had appeared and supported the district attorney's decision to have Angus Ferguson released forthwith. The group was in high spirits as they entered the room.

"Gentry, thank you for speaking to our local district attorney," said Ferguson.

"My pleasure, Angus. Based on the paltry set of facts as relayed to me, I did not think there could ever be any conviction."

"That's exactly what I told our crazy sheriff, Svensson, when he came out to arrest me. Gentlemen, we are going to have to deal with that man."

Having already anticipated such a comment, MacDonald answered, "Angus, it is not long before the next election. We can deal with Leif Svensson then. There is no reason to push something like a recall now."

"I'm not thinking of a *recall*, Gentry. I'm thinking of a different kind of elimination."

MacDonald did not answer, choosing to avoid comments that might come back to haunt the ambitious politician later.

But Ferguson did not stop there. Riding the emotion of his recent victorious release at the hands of the well-controlled local legal system, he pushed forward with swelling momentum. "I have said it before, we need to bring this to an end. The nesters need to be eliminated. They violate the law, they trespass, and they rustle our cattle. It's high time to put an end to it."

Another group of men entered the room. Frank Canton with five of his Texas gunmen stood just inside the doorway as if waiting for invitation or instruction.

Ferguson looked at Canton and then back to the group of club members. "The answer rests with Mr. Canton there and his deputies. We need to give him a specific list of those people out on the range who need to be removed."

Carter McKinnon sunk his hands into his jacket pockets as he formed a question. "But Angus, we are talking about maybe seventy people."

Undeterred, Ferguson responded. "Then let the list include seventy people. They all need to be removed."

William Irvine then asked, "And when do you think we should compile this list?"

"Right now. I suggest we each grab a glass of whiskey, sit down, and give Mr. Canton the names each of us can think of. There is no better time than now."

Ronald Tisdale inquired, "And when should Mr. Canton start with these eliminations?"

Angus answered without hesitation. "Tomorrow."

* * * * *

Will Toal stood across from the Reno Stockman's Club. It was the end of a long day. After assisting Sheriff Svensson to fill out a lengthy report of the day's events and the arrest of Angus Ferguson, he intended to ride back home. Sable colored clouds breached the crest of the Sierras to the west following their climb up and over the range. They were textured, just like the fur which gave them their color. The mountains often stood as a barrier to the storms which perennially came from the Pacific Ocean further west. Any spread of thick dark clouds that survived the climb over the peaks did so having been pushed up and over by a strong weather system.

Dale Paris stood by Will's side as they stepped across the covered boardwalk in front of the sheriff's office. The pair stopped at the edge of the wooden platform just as a large group of men exited the Stockman's building up the street. Will watched as Angus Ferguson led the men out onto the dirt roadway where they gathered, briefly spoke, and began to disperse. Ferguson looked up and caught Will's eye. The short, stocky Highlander sneered across the dirt avenue in confident arrogance.

Paris tipped the front of his bowler hat up as he took in the scene.

"Sheriff said it wouldn't be long before Ferguson was released. The man didn't waste time gathering up the other ranchers so he could gloat. Wonder what they talked about in their shiny little club?"

Will added in disgust, "Leif says that based on how the Attorney General reacted, he thinks the local district attorney is not even going to file charges. Angus is going to walk."

A man dressed completely in black strode up next to Ferguson. Several other well-armed men collected around the pair. Will watched as Ferguson nodded in his direction. Now the man in black stared at Will, along with Angus.

Without moving his head, Will asked, "That Canton?"

"It is," said Paris.

"Maybe I should walk over right now and set this straight before it goes any further."

Dale grabbed Will's elbow just as he'd started to lean forward setting his body in motion to move off the boardwalk and into the street. "Not a good idea. Several of those standing around him are Canton's men from Texas. Even if you were to call out Canton and get the best of him, it would only start a six-shooter free-for-all right here in the street. Your chances of walking away from that would not be good."

Will hesitated, regained his balance just at the edge of the boardwalk. His gaze still locked on Canton. "Dale, it's going to come down to that at some point, mark my words."

"It just might, but you gotta pick a better time and a better place."

Muscles bulged at the edge of Will's jaw as his teeth clenched tighter. Canton and Ferguson walked to their horses, mounted, and rode slowly in front of the spot where Paris and Will stood. Ferguson did not look down, but Will could not miss the triumphant smile lifting his mouth. Canton glared at Will until he was past, and he had to pull his head back forward. Will held the man's eyes the entire way.

"Dale, something's very wrong here. People expect to live and work in peace, move forward in life. Things might not always be easy, but that's what they expect. Angus has upset that order. It's moving in the wrong direction, and if it doesn't change quick, it's only going to get worse." The words came flat, without emotion, not quite a statement and more as a question.

"Sure seems so. Angus is pushing to make the world look like he thinks it should, no matter who might stand in his way."

Will could sense Paris watching him for a reaction, but he did not respond.

Dale added to his thought. "Yep, Angus probably thinks he is on his way to seeing his vision done. And he's got his gun riding right next to him ready to make it happen. Chances are, regular people would be able to deal with Angus at some point. But there is only one person hereabouts who can deal with Canton—and that is you."

"So be it." As he answered, Will kept his eyes on the riders leaving town.

The vapors blowing over the mountains blocked the sun to cut short the day. Clouds and shadows deposited an early evening gray gloom. Darkened veins lined the random folds in the ever-thickening reservoirs of floating water. Again, the Confederate gray hung from the sky and invaded Will's heart. Another defeat. Another unexplained stab in the flank of life that challenged motivation to move forward. Were it not for Beth and the kids, Will knew he'd have probably stepped down into the street and headed for Canton. Too much of his life and his family had been destroyed by men like Canton and Ferguson. His parents were gone. His family farm was gone. Now, Ella was gone. She'd been back in his life for only a short time. Another loss.

Will looked to the sky. Rain would come. It was going to be a wet ride home.

Chapter Twenty-Three

Spring 1878
Toal Ranch, Nevada

Will quietly stepped up onto the porch under his ramada as it reached beyond the front roof. It was late. The kids would be in bed and did not need to be awakened by the sound of heavy boots. He stood still as droplets continued to stream down his slicker, even though he now had a cover over his head. He looked down at his boots and chaps. All wet. *Soaked* would be a better word, he thought. The darkness behind him carried the incessant sound of raindrops hitting small puddles left by a footstep or horseshoe imprint in the now water-soaked dirt. He'd been listening to that same sound and watching the constant flow down his slicker for the last four hours. The weather fit his mood. It was if the world did his crying for him. The tears came from the sky.

A soft glow of light filtered its way through the curtains covering the front windows. Will could tell all lanterns were doused. He had instructed the family never to leave a lantern on late at night. If riders came, any lanterns would be extinguished until the identity of those approaching could be determined. But Will hoped the glow through the window meant Beth had left a fire going so he could warm up a bit before heading to bed. Then, the glow spread as the door opened.

"Wet?"

Beth filled the doorway standing there in her nightclothes. A thick shawl covered her shoulders. Long strands of blonde hair had been set free and now fluttered in the cold breezes rushing to invade the warm innards of the house. Will tried to smile. It was a perfect image of home. But the smile was forced.

"You could say that. Figured I'd stand here a bit to just drip outside."

Beth reached out. "Give me your slicker. We can hang it here outside for the time being. Pull off your chaps and we'll hang those, too. Let's sit a short while here on our bench and you can tell me about the day. We can keep the drip time short and continue inside in front of the fire. I'm not dressed to stay outside in this weather much longer, and you must be as cold as you are wet."

Will unhooked the buckle on his chaps and slumped onto the bench. He knew Beth watched. He could not disguise his current emotional state—it was evident in every line of his body.

Beth hung the slicker on the outside wall and stood in front of Will. She pulled off his hat and ran her fingers through his wet hair. "Tell me. It's bad. I can see it in you before you speak."

"Ella's dead. They hung her."

The words did not rise or float as did most conversation. The simple statement seemed to exit his mouth and then sink like the raindrops beyond the porch falling into the sodden earth.

"Oh, Will, they couldn't." Beth reached out with both hands and cupped each side of her husband's face. She leaned forward to kiss his forehead, lingering there in sympathetic emphasis.

Will did not answer. His eyes closed. He reveled in the closeness, the connection. Here stood his foundation, his reason to move through the gloom.

Beth spun to the side to sit next to Will but never let go of his face. She virtually pulled his head sideways to maintain eye-to-eye contact.

"I don't know where to even start, or what to say. She just came back into your life and now she's gone. How? What happened? Why would anyone do such a thing?"

Will did not respond at first. He had only barely begun to deal with his emotions to reconnect with his sister, to re-establish any bond created before he left for the war. Now, that had ended almost before it began. He took a breath and exhaled a long, deep sigh.

"There was a gunfight out at Nate's remote corral the day before I arrived. One of Angus's new range detectives got shot. Nate was worried about Ella and came back to check on her. He told me they had decided Ella should come here. But he was worried about his cattle now all branded and ready for sale.

Paris was at Ferguson's when the detectives brought in a man shot during the gun battle with Nate. Apparently, the man died soon after arrival. Ferguson then ordered this man named Frank Canton to deal with the situation. The dead detective was one of Canton's hired guns from Texas. Canton's a killer, but Angus has set him up as head of the Stock Grower's range detectives.

"The next day, the day I got there, Ella was to get set to leave while Nate went back out to his line house on the range to get the rest of his stock. He intended to keep them under close watch. There were no witnesses, but Dale and I think this man Canton was the one who rode to Nate's and hung Ella. Though he didn't outright admit it, Angus saw no fault in the killing. Canton and his gun hands came back and…and hung her right there in her own yard. Nate returned and found her just before I arrived."

"How do you know Angus Ferguson saw no fault in hanging a woman?"

"Because I followed the tracks of the killers back to his ranch and confronted him."

"Oh, Will. You could have been killed."

Will nodded. "Probably not the best of plans. But I had to see the man's eyes when I accused him. He ordered it; I could tell."

"Then what did you do?"

"I headed back to Nate's but met up with Dale Paris and Sheriff Svensson who had collected a small posse. We went back to Ferguson's ranch and arrested Angus."

"Arrested him?"

"Yep. Svensson called it an accessory to murder."

Beth now let go of Will's face but held his eyes.

"That took courage, and I imagine you were again in a position where guns might have come into play."

Will looked out into the rain invaded darkness. "There were several moments where it could have gone either way. But ultimately, Angus agreed to come into town and be bound for trial."

"The sheriff took him to jail?"

"He did. But it didn't last long. Angus and his cronies in the Stock Grower's Association spoke to the District Attorney who refused to file charges. Angus was immediately released."

"Why?"

"Lack of witnesses. No one was there when Ella was killed. No one could testify that Angus ordered it. Sheriff knew it would never stick."

Beth now reached out to slip her hand under Will's arm and pull herself close. "But he is to be commended for taking action. Zack Thompson in Carson City would never have done that."

"Agreed. But I stood outside the sheriff's office and watched Angus and Frank Canton ride off. I watched the man who hung my sister ride out of town like he was some kind of king who'd just ordered the death of an insignificant serf."

"What's Svensson going to do now?"

"Word in Reno got around real quick after we all rode in and pushed Angus into the jail lockup. Lots of folks were pretty upset. Almost all who heard thought hanging a woman without any trial was outrageous. Svensson said he'd make sure the local newspaper got the full report and would do his best to make it look bad for Ferguson and the Stock Growers."

"The man has guts."

"Dale says that Ferguson has already threatened Svensson. Says he has to step down or he might get killed. Svensson knows he's up for re-election in five or six months and the Stock Growers will see to it he's replaced. But he's not cowed."

Beth sighed. "It takes even more courage to act as he has knowing he has only a short time in office."

Will looked up and then back down to Beth.

"But it won't do much in the end. Ferguson and his Association control all the power in Reno. They control the legislature and the courts. He'll not go to jail. Knowing Angus even as little as I do, the fact he got released without even spending one night in jail will probably just embolden him to push for more killings. It's going to be a war out there."

"What about Nate?"

"He knows it's coming. From what I can tell, he hopes it does. Nate's good with his gun. He won't have to go looking for Canton. He'll get his chance to deal with that killer. Canton will come to him."

"Is that wise? Sounds like Canton has numbers."

"He does. But there is no convincing Nate to leave his spread. He and I buried Ella there. To him, it is now sacred ground. He'll fight."

"Will, it's such a loss for you. It's cruel."

"What they did to Ella was cruel. Not sure Nate can survive a meeting with Canton. But I intend to make sure Frank Canton pays."

"And how do you plan to do that?"

Will smiled for the first time since he'd arrived. "Figured I'd talk to you. You always have good ideas."

Beth twisted to stare at the darkness. Without turning back to look at Will, she said, "It's your sister. I know it would be useless to think you'd let it go."

"You know me better than that."

Beth nodded.

"Yes, I know you better than that. So, here's what I'd suggest: Get men. Plenty of them, 'cause if there is a war, you're going to need troops."

"Svensson says he has over fifty men in town who would ride with him to confront Ferguson and his killers."

"Get more."

Beth stared at Will with a face he could see carried the weight of a wife and mother of three children who did not want to become a widow.

"Get more. And get Canton. He goes, and Ferguson won't take another step."

Will smiled.

"Had the same exact thought. Let's go inside and get warm."

Chapter Twenty-Four

Spring 1878
Ferguson Ranch

Angus Ferguson marveled at the simple scene before him. How was it a transparent glow could be changed into a diverse light show just by passing through a clear glass tumbler? God created the light. Man created the cuts in the glass. The yellow hues of the muted firelight transformed into multiple colors as it prismed through the cuts of the crystal cup. The jeweled patterns carved into the hardened glass created a gemlike quality to the vessel resting on the small table next to his leather chair. Bronze whiskey languished in the bottom half of the short, clear chalice, it, too, transforming the hearth's glimmer into shades of amber with mottled yellow striations. The kaleidoscope of colors was magnificent if you focused on the quiet transformation. He sat in silence, thinking one could argue man had thus changed something heaven sent for the better.

Somehow, clearing the range felt like a similar improvement of another of God's gifts. Maybe it was the result of sipping on his third glass of bourbon, but Angus checked his own resolve for the removal of the nesters. The open range was, itself, the product of omniscient handiwork. Only the good Lord could have created the open plain at the base of the monumental snow-capped Sierras. By taking control over the flat expanses, the large ranch owners grew beef that supported the burgeoning populations from Virginia City to Reno and San Francisco. Wasn't that the same as man's efforts to modify the light flowing through his glass? Wasn't the rainbow generated by man's hands on the sides of his cup the same as his own efforts to improve the use of the land to feed more of God's creatures?

But the nesters would ruin what He'd done. If the influx was not checked, these interlopers would chop up the range making it impossible for cattle to forage across the spaces needed here on the semi-barren scrub. If these squatters continued to proliferate, all the cattle would end up dead. Couldn't the people of Reno see that? Could they not see that what was being done about these nesters was not only necessary, but also vital?

Angus twirled the whiskey using his finger as a human swizzle stick. Many were going to hate him for what was about to happen. But those thoughts would be short-lived. Everyone would eventually see that the order of the ranching world benefited the larger good, remaining just as it stood right now. *For goodness' sake, they eat our beef! Without us, they would starve.*

Angus took a sip and smiled. No, he would like to think his motives centered around the enhancement of God's creation. But he had to admit to himself the real reason was much simpler. He had been here first. He had built this ranch just like the other owners. Without their efforts, none of these nesters would have the ability to blithely ride out onto the range and set up some shack and collect steers. Ferguson and his fellow ranchers had opened the land. They'd fought Paiutes, battled through droughts, and pushed the natural game away so that the beef cattle had unfettered access to the limited grasses. They had created the clean slate upon which these nesters intended to chalk their futures. *Well, it took a great deal more than chalk and a rolling wagon full of furniture. We didn't have that. We created everything we have by hand—our own hands.*

He recrossed his legs. The movement led him to another thought, another maybe even more fundamental justification: *We ranchers are backed by the law. We had the original claims on the land. These interlopers are trespassers. We have every right to give them a simple option: either leave immediately or die. It boiled down to that.*

To many, it would seem cruel. But those who think that way are weak. Popular opinion will surely be averse. So be it. Someday, that popular opinion will come around to acknowledge what we are doing is right.

Right versus wrong. That was all he had to live for. His wife had died. She'd tried to give him children, but lost several before childbirth. Lost all but Dirk. And now, he was gone, too. He had no one to pass his legacy on to. But clearing the range would be his legacy. He'd make sure the range would remain open to support even more people as they arrived in Reno. Someday, they'd understand and agree.

"Mr. Ferguson, you wanted to see me?"

Angus turned. Frank Canton stood in the doorway. "Frank, yes, I wanted to make sure the arrangements for tomorrow are set. Come, have a seat."

Ferguson watched as the man from Texas strode across the room and stood in front of the fire.

"Mind if I stand here for a moment? Cold outside, and the fire looks to be good and hot."

"Not at all. Don't they have the stove going in the bunkhouse?"

Canton pulled off his hat and brushed back the hair at the top of his forehead. "They do, but I've been outside checking over the preparations for tomorrow. Wanted to make sure the stock we need is identified, and the supplies are ready to be packed in the morning. There's a bite of cold this late."

Angus did not hide his approval of the man's diligence. "Frank, the way you go about your job gives me great confidence that I've hired the right man."

Canton touched the top of his fur skin hat. He wore a more common wide brimmed hat during the summer months. But in winter and into spring, he wore a fur capped hat with a small bill. Kept his head warmer.

"All jobs take planning. We are looking at over forty men riding out tomorrow. Supplies, ammunition, and animals all must be in place. Getting those items ready is what you pay me for."

"How many days do you think this will take?"

Canton shrugged. "Hard to tell. Could be as little as three days or as long as seven. I don't see it lasting beyond that. But I've made sure we'll have enough food and shelter on hand."

"Do you have the large roundup tent coming? The ranch owners can use that for shelter wherever we camp."

"I do."

Canton moved to sit in the adjacent leather chair also positioned to face the fire. Angus took another sip of his whiskey. "Would you like a drink?"

"A drink would go down well. The outside feels a bit warmer now. With a glass of whiskey, maybe the insides will heat up to match."

Angus turned in his seat to wave at the ever-present Chinese butler on the other side of the room. Raising his own glass as an example, he said, "Please, get Mr. Canton one of these." The Asian attendant nodded, lifting the braided strand of hair reaching down his back, turned, and left on his instructed mission.

"Alright, Frank, tell me what you have planned."

"It's been four days since we dealt with the Toal woman. From the earlier gunfight out at his range corral, I'm guessing Crampion will now be armed and ready. The loss of his woman will be like a wound. A wounded animal will fight. I 'spect that'll be true of Crampion."

"But we should have substantial numbers."

"Yes, we will have very substantial numbers. The additional men from Texas arrived yesterday, as you know. That means I have twelve men in my group counting myself and Liam Witherspoon. You have five men coming from your ranch. That means six from Ferguson Ranch, with you. Carter McKinnon has five, in addition to himself, for another six. The other ranchers are bringing a total of twenty men. Further, Mr. Reiker, Mr. MacDonald, and Mr. Tisdale have also said they intend to come along. If you add that all up, you get forty-nine riders. There is even talk that once we get moving, some additional ranchers might join. All will be armed."

"And how many men does Crampion have? We have to get there first."

"Himself and two others."

Angus let his upper body slump into the upright portion of his seat. He let a look of confidence spread further enhancing the arrogance of the body movement. He barely acknowledged his butler as the man arrived with Canton's glass of whiskey. "Crampion is not a match for us."

Canton subtly raised his glass in subdued salute to his employer and then took his first sip. The motion and the initial savoring of the liquor took an extra moment before he replied. Ferguson did not fail to notice the obvious approval as to the quality of the drink.

"Very nice," said Canton. "Very nice, indeed."

"Should be. Comes all the way from Kentucky. They know how to distill good whiskey there. The only place to do it better is in Scotland where I come from."

"Yes, Crampion will be outnumbered. But having engaged him once, I can tell you he and his hands all know how to use their guns. They had repeater rifles. I can speak for my twelve men. They can all shoot. But we don't really know how all these other men will do when under fire. I fear they might think this is some kind of pleasure hunt. Crampion cannot be underestimated."

"What is your plan to take Crampion?"

Canton swallowed a second sip. "Pretty simple. We surround his place and start shooting. We set the men at rifle distance all in a circle. That way those opposing lines cannot hit each other as their rounds all fire only to the center, Crampion's shack."

Angus nodded. "Sooner or later, if we fill the place with enough lead, Crampion and his hands will get hit and we're done."

"Exactly. Just must be patient. My idea is to wait him out but keep up the shooting. No one needs to play hero. Everyone is to stay on the perimeter and fire away."

"I like the plan."

Canton set his glass down on the table in between the men. "But will this group all agree to follow my instructions? I am counting on you to impress on the entire group that I will be calling the shots."

"I'll make that very clear. Not to worry. Now, you know there will also be two reporters coming, correct?"

"I heard something about that. Can't say I like the idea, but yes, I heard."

Angus smiled. "My idea was that the rest of the world should know exactly what we do and why we are doing it. We can control the story if we have the reporters there with us while we indicate what is happening and why. One will be from the Reno Gazette and the other will be coming from Chicago."

Canton acknowledged the comments. "I hear you, but again, I am going to leave it to you to impress on these men, especially a pair of city dwellers like these reporters, that they have to follow my instructions."

"I'll take care of it. Now, once we take care of Crampion, what is your plan from there?"

Canton reached into his jacket and pulled out a folded piece of paper. Without looking at it, he waved it in Ferguson's direction. "The names we were given by all the ranchers four days ago add up to a total of seventy nesters. They make up about twenty-five different homesteads. I have listed them here along with their locations. I have gone over the list with your head wrangler, and he has described each setting. I think I have a pretty good idea on how to approach them as we move down the list. My idea is that after we deal with Crampion, we go to the nearest location and spread outward from that spot until we have handled each. We can pick camping grounds as we go."

It was now Angus who lifted his glass for a sip.

"And what if something goes wrong? Is there a backup plan?"

Canton nodded. "At the Stockman's meeting, Tisdale pulled me aside and said we could collect at his ranch after we completed the sweep of the nesters. He suggested that we all stay there for at least a couple of days to see if there is going to be any reaction from the sheriff and townspeople."

"That fits Tisdale. He thinks ahead."

"I thought so, too. So, I rode over there to check out his place. It could be quickly and easily fortified. He can accommodate our entire group under roof if we use his barn and bunkhouses. He also has some large corrals surrounding the main compound. The corrals will be sufficient to hold our riding and supply stock."

"Sounds like you thought of just about everything."

Canton shook his head. "You never know what might happen. You cannot plan for everything. But this operation is not all that complicated. If the men follow what I tell them, it should work fine."

"When should we leave?"

"By the time we get everyone here at your ranch tomorrow and pack up the mules, it'll probably be close to noon. I don't want to ride into

Crampion's in broad daylight. I think we ride out to about two miles away and camp. It'll be an easy ride for day one. We then get up early the next morning before daybreak and surround Crampion's place. The shooting will start at dawn."

Angus Ferguson sat looking at the fire. He was on the brink of his legacy. He would bring a clear and open range to Nevada. Some day they would thank him. He raised his glass and held it out to Canton.

"Then, here's to tomorrow. To the return of the open range."

Ferguson tilted his glass almost upside down and finished off the last of his whiskey. He then rammed it down on the table as if in emphasis as he stood.

"To tomorrow."

Chapter Twenty-Five

Spring 1878
KC Ranch, Open Range

Darkness. Motionless, he tried to force his hearing to reach into the infinite black obscurity as if his ears could see what his eyes could not. He heard something; he knew it. Maybe the crack of a small branch, an equine nicker, or the click of an iron horseshoe on a rock. It woke him. Yet, the canopy of dark, the umbrella of color's absence, did not reveal any sound. It was as if the world had lost its ability to trigger the senses. Ella was gone. Maybe her passing just left him deaf and blind. No, it was a sound. They would come for him. He knew it.

Whether a sound or an impulse jabbing him in the depths of sleep, he awoke. No cobwebs clouded his mind. A sense rose from deep within. It was not fear, maybe apprehension. Any fear of his own death had diminished with Ella being gone. Care of this life was not the same. But blood pumped vigorously through his veins. There was no way sleep would return. He rose as quietly as he could. He had to check what he could outside.

Nate Crampion stood in his doorway looking out into the shadow on the plains. It spread over the flat expanse that ran east all the way to Utah. There were mountains, small mountains that interrupted the flat expanse to the west as the Sierras descended from on high. But his door faced east like every other door on this side of the Sierras. It was a small attempt to avoid the near constant winds that came out of the west down the slopes of those very same mountains. Morning would soon arrive, but not yet. If they were to come, they'd probably come from the west.

Ferguson's ranch was to the west, opposite from where he was looking now. Maybe he should take a look out of the back door.

Nate turned and headed back into his small abode. Nick Ray and Reese Stricker, his only two hands, had bunked inside the house. They sprawled across the floor in their bed rolls. With Ella gone, there was no need for them to bunk outside. More important, while the walls were not thick, they did provide some measure of protection.

Two strangers had come up to the house late yesterday afternoon. Said they were looking to homestead but needed shelter. Nate had offered to let them stay the night. There had been lots of talk over dinner as to the current situation here on the open range. By the time they had ended the discussion, both men indicated they would probably pass on settling here and head further north as the current battle with the large ranch owners did not sound inviting. They said their names were Bo Richardson and Tom Meyer.

Meyer awoke and sat up as Nate came in the door. "Daybreak yet?"

Nate shook his head. "No, not yet. Just up early. It's a habit."

He did not want to say anything about the sound that woke him. Figured the discussion last night struck both the visitors with enough fear and no need to add to it.

Meyer rolled out of his blanket and pulled on his boots. Richardson began to stir with the movement. "What's going on?"

Meyer turned to his traveling companion and said, "Come on. Let's go out to the creek and get some water for coffee and breakfast. It's the least we can do as guests."

Richardson rolled over and looked out the door. "It's still dark."

Meyer chuckled. "Yep. It's still dark. Perfect time to start the coffee. Get movin'."

Both men stood. One grabbed a bucket and the other a large pan. Never had enough water in the kitchen. Meyer turned to Nate before he left. "Be right back."

Crampion smiled as he sat at the only table in the dwelling. "No rush. Thanks for getting the water. As soon as you fill those, I'll start making breakfast and you both can either stay or continue on your travels."

Nate grabbed a pencil and opened a small hard covered book. It was a journal. After Ella's death he had started writing entries of the places he and Ella had been and the highlights of their journey west. He never wanted to forget the time they'd spent together. He lit the oil lamp and started to write.

* * * * *

As Tom Meyers and Bo Richardson bent down to fill the buckets, they heard the triggers of two guns click behind them.

"Drop the buckets slow and real quiet. You reach for any guns, you're dead."

Meyer let go of his bucket and raised his hands. Richardson did the same.

"Mister, we're just travelin' through. Got no issue with anyone in these parts."

Frank Canton moved silently around to the front of the two men.

"Who are you?"

Meyer tilted his head in the direction of Bo and responded. "Name's Tom Meyer and this here's Bo Richardson. We were thinking of homesteading and was looking for a place to stay. This fella Nate Crampion offered us a roof but told us how things are for homesteaders hereabouts. We're plannin' on riding out this morning to head north to Oregon."

Canton lifted each man's jacket. He found no guns. Neither were armed.

"You men need to leave. Leave quiet."

"But we got gear inside."

"Leave it. Get your horses, saddle them as quiet as you can and leave. You do anything to warn those inside and you're both dead men. Do I make myself clear?"

Meyer and Richardson backed up a few steps, turned, and headed for the corral. Their saddles rested on the fence. Each grabbed their bridles and headed into the enclosure to catch their mounts.

* * * * *

Nick Ray stood and stretched. "Sun's comin' up. What's the plan for the day?"

Nate was still writing. He looked up. "Not sure. We've brought all the mavericks here to the house. I think we should head down to Reno as soon as we can to see if we can find a broker who will buy this early before the roundup."

Nick looked at Nate. "That's gonna cause some people to talk; talk that's goin' to get back to Ferguson."

"Probably. But we don't have much choice. If we keep them here, Ferguson and his men will come riding down and try to take them. Our best chance is to sell them as soon as we can. So, either today or tomorrow, you, me, and Reese gotta get our rigs ready for a quick drive."

Nick raised his arms in a stretch. "Shouldn't be that hard. It's not far. Could probably make the trip in one day. Two days, at most."

Ray now walked to the door. "Where's our two guests?"

"They went out for water. Didn't notice as I'm writing, but they went out a while ago now. Should be back."

"Been gone for a long time if they were just gonna get water. Hey, that's the sound of horses. What the—"

Just then, a shot rang out. Nick Ray's body flew backward into the room. Nate dropped his pencil and jumped to where Nick sprawled on the floor. Blood oozed from his chest.

"Damn. Nate, it hurts."

Nate squeezed his hands under both Nick's armpits and pulled him toward the center of the room. As he did, bullets started hitting the walls and all around the doorway by the dozens. Nate immediately knew there were multiple gunmen shooting. There were just too many bullets to be coming from less than a dozen guns. Reese was on his knees and wiped the sleep from his eyes. Those eyes were suddenly spread wide open and looked for understanding.

"What the hell is going on?"

Nate answered as he sucked in his breath in effort to drag Nick away from the door.

"Reese, crawl over along the wall and shut the door. Grab your rifle and start shootin' back. As soon as I get Nick into the bed, I'll do the same."

Bullets ripped through the wooden walls. Most were slowed by the passage through the rough-cut slabs, but many zipped in as if moving through paper. Nate had the fleeting thought that it was random death. You wouldn't know which hunk of wood would protect you or which one would become the pathway for your demise.

Nate lifted Nick Ray onto his bed. Blood was streaming from his chest.

"Here, I'm gonna pull up your shirt to see exactly where the blood is coming from." He pulled off his own scarf with one hand as he separated Nick's shirt with the other. Just as he did, a bullet whisked his hat off his head.

"Damn!" said Nate. "There has to be way more than a dozen guns out there."

Nick grimaced. "Seem like bullets are coming from everywhere. They haven't stopped."

"Quit talking. Hold this. I plugged my scarf into the hole in your chest. Don't look good, but it's the best I can do for the moment. I've got to get my rifle and start helping Reese before they storm the place."

"Go. Get one or two for me."

"Oh, I'll get more than that."

Nate picked up his rifle and jacked a round into the chamber. Just as the finger loop hit the stock completing the load, he saw a man run from behind the corral heading to the one-sided wall where they normally tied up the horses to keep them out of the wind. Nate instinctively aimed and shot through his window. The man convulsed, lifted, and then dropped to the ground and didn't move.

Reese said over his shoulder, "Glad you're up and firing. Just got me one out there. Did you hit that one?"

Nate dropped and slid across the floor as more bullets hit the wall near the window he shot from. He rolled over on his back.

"Yep, I got one, too. But I gotta feelin' there are way too many out there for this to last too long."

Reese fired. "Ha! Got another. Whoever is out there must think this was going to be some kind of turkey shoot. They're not doin' that much to stay protected."

Nate lifted and looked out another window opposite from the wall he'd used on his last shot. As soon as he peeked over the windowsill, five shots hit the wall and he rolled immediately back to the ground. After that barrage ended, Nate sat back up and aimed out the window. He could see the heads of two men lying in the creek behind the house but looking over the rise of the bank. Nate fired, jacked another round, and fired again. The face of the man on the left was obliterated. The hat came off the one to the right, but he ducked too quickly to be hit.

"Got another."

Reese looked across the room as he sank to his back and started reloading his rifle.

"How many do you think we have to kill before they leave us alone?"

Nate again peeked over the sill. There was a lull in the shooting. He turned to face Reese.

"We've just killed four of them. This ain't normal. This group won't run. My guess is that we've got to kill them all before they leave us alone."

Reese slumped further on his back in resignation. "Thought you were goin' to say that. We got enough ammo?"

"Probably not."

"Then, this don't look good."

Nate nodded. "Nope. The picture is not a good one. Our best chance is to make every shot count and take out as many as we can. Maybe, just maybe they'll get tired of losing men."

Reese grinned. "Well, then let's get as many as we can." He flipped over onto his stomach and pushed open the front door. He fired three shots in quick succession.

Nate crawled to the back door. He cracked it open. Bullets immediately hit the door about waist level. The wooden latch was left in splinters.

"They're even around the back. The whole place is surrounded," said Nate.

There was a pause in the hail of bullets striking the back door. Nate waited just a moment, then pushed the door open and rolled further into the opening coming to rest with his gun aimed and propped by his elbows on the ground. He saw three men sitting on another portion of the creek out back. He fired twice and hit two more. As soon as he fired, he rolled to the opposite side of the door just as another hailstorm of lead flew into the house. It came through the open door this time at floor level where he'd just taken his shots.

"Augh!"

Nate looked over at Reese, who was shaking his foot. "They shot my foot." Blood began to stream out of the man's boot. Reese again rolled onto his back.

"Can you pull the boot off? I'll get a rag to tie around it."

Reese answered with a face contorted in pain. "Naw, the boot is probably the best way to keep pressure on it for the time being. It just hurts like hell."

Nate crawled back to the broken window where he'd taken his first shot. He peeked over the windowsill but saw nothing. The shooting had stopped.

Still on his back, Reese asked, "Think they're considerin' movin' on?"

Nate chuckled. "No such luck. Probably just counting their dead and coming up with a better plan than shootin' wildly at the house."

Nate then crawled on his belly to check on Nick. He reached up and touched the prone man's arm. There was no response. Nate kneeled and saw that Nick's eyes were staring motionless at the ceiling. He touched his neck. No pulse. Nate then glanced down the length of the prone man and saw several new gunshot wounds. "Ah, hell. Nick took more shots layin' here on the bed. He's dead."

Reese winced. "Remind me if we make it to nighttime not to get into the bed. Appears it's not safe."

Nate then moved to the table in the middle of the room. He turned it on its side and pushed the thick wooden tabletop to the wall below the window.

"Now might have a bit more protection with another layer of wood as I'm lookin' out the window tryin' to get a shot. How's the foot?"

"Must be goin' numb. Don't feel as bad right now. How long do you think they'll wait before the next round of bullets start flyin' our way?"

Nate curled next to the overturned table and began to reload his rifle. "No tellin'. They haven't said anything like they want to negotiate. I figure that means no deals. Either we die, or they do."

"Thanks for giving me some hope."

Nate laughed. "Hope. Reese, we got no hope. Best send up some prayers."

* * * * *

The morning passed without any further shooting. Nate held his position behind the table periodically lifting for a look out the window in hopes of seeing movement. At one point, he'd seen riders move away from the building. One rider wore black. *Had to be Frank Canton. It figured.* The group stopped far out of rifle range, dismounted, and looked as if they talked. Nate sat back down.

"Looks like Frank Canton out there. He and some others just rode out of rifle range and look like they're talkin'. Probably coming up with some new strategy."

Nate rose again to take a look. He saw a horse and wagon approaching the long road to his house and recognized the rig.

"Reese, Jack Flagg is rolling up."

Just as he uttered these words, Canton and two others who had been part of the far-off open ground strategy meeting pulled their revolvers, aimed, and took shots at Flagg.

"They're shootin' at Jack!"

Reese looked across to Nate. "Why would they do that?"

"No witnesses. They don't want any witnesses."

"What's Jack doin' now?"

"Turned and running like hell towards Reno."

"Does it look like he's going to make it?"

Nate ducked not wanting to be exposed for longer than needed. He lifted again, glanced over the sill quickly and flopped back down. He then responded to Reese.

"I can't be sure, but it looks like Jack's got a good head start. Two riders set off after him. He usually carries a rifle under his buckboard seat. He's one of the few settlers out here who can shoot like us. Maybe he can hold them off and get to town."

"Be nice if he could get help."

"Even if he makes it, help won't get here until tomorrow. But if we hold them off, we might have some hope."

Reese rolled over on his stomach again near the opening of the door. He looked out but didn't fire. One shot hit the floor right next to his shoulder and he rolled back. All went quiet again.

"They're still watching the openings."

Nate had pulled out his journal and began writing. "Don't give them anything to shoot at."

Now on his back again, Reese asked, "What do you think their next move is goin' to be?"

Nate shrugged. "One of two things. If Jack Flagg gets away, that could force their hand. They could rush us soon or wait until dark and try to sneak up close to get shots through the windows."

"If they rush us, there's no way we could hold them all off. There has to be thirty of them out there."

Nate agreed. "Yes, they would take us, but we would get at least five to ten of them as they came. Maybe that was what they talked about there out in the distance. Might have discussed whether the loss of life was worth it. Seein' as they haven't come *en masse* yet must mean they didn't want to lose those men."

As all was again quiet, Nate settled back down behind his tabletop protection, lifted his journal out of a jacket pocket and grabbed his pencil.

"What you doin' there? Writin' out your will?"

"Nope. Got no one to give this little spread to even assuming someone would be interested in takin' on a two-bit ranch sittin' in the middle of a constant gun battle. Naw, I'm writing a journal. Might be someone reads it and the real story would be told."

"If Frank Canton gets a hold of that journal, he'll burn it."

"Likely. But you never know."

Suddenly, multiple guns erupted. Bullets hit every wall simultaneously. Both Nate and Reese flattened to the ground as best they could. The fusillade struck indiscriminately around the walls, both high and low. There were even shots that hit the roof.

Blinking with every shot that hit near, Reese held his rifle lengthwise on top of his chest. "What in the hell are they doin? Those shots are comin' from everywhere, but seemed to be aimed at no one."

"Agreed," said Nate. "But keep a sharp eye. Somethin' is about to happen."

Bullets then no longer hit the floor, or even the windowsills. They all began to hit high on the walls. Then Nate saw a shadow, and then a second, through the slats on the opposite side of the room. Two men were moving to the window.

Nate knew right away what the plan was. The fire was cover. First hit low and then high so these two could get close to the window and shoot whoever was inside through the opening. Nate did not say anything to Reese. He did not want to give away his position. He waited until the lead man got close to the window and then fired just as he cleared the opening. Nate jacked another round and shot the second man right through the wooden wall. Both hit the dirt.

But then a shot came from right above Nate's head. Reese's legs lifted as his body jackknifed when the shot hit his abdomen. Nate rolled away from his seated position right below the shooter outside, whipping his rifle around to aim and fire at the assailant. The man's body flew backward, away from the wall.

Nate looked for a second man just as there had been on the first wall but saw no others. He quickly scanned the slits in the wooden walls around the house for any other attackers who had run up underneath the bombardment of earlier gunfire. He saw none.

Reese moaned. "Aw, I'm gut shot."

Nate crawled across to Reese. "Here, give me your scarf. I'll put some pressure on the wound."

"Nate, you know what happens if you're gut shot."

"Most times yes, it's not good. But not always. Here, put your hand on this and keep up the pressure."

But Nate saw the strong stream of blood soaking through the scarf. He knew this wound would not be any outlier. Reese would not survive the night.

* * * * *

Darkness had come again in its daily cycle. Later, a bright moon pierced through the fabric of the black nighttime blanket. Moon shadows had given away positions of men moving upright as the night orb rose. Nate took a few shots in the soft white hue and maybe hit one or two more men. While several shots were returned, an uneasy peace ultimately pervaded.

He tried to relax, to get ready for the events of the next day. If Jack Flagg made it to Reno, maybe a posse would get to him by mid-morning. But he knew Frank Canton would be thinking the same thing. They would want to end this before noon so they could all be somewhere else when help arrived. If the group had left before the posse appeared, it would be plausible deniability for any one man to be linked to the massacre.

Reese Striker had died late in the night. Nate was all alone.

In the dusk before night descended, Nate had written his last entry in his journal at a point he did not expect to survive until morning. Well, morning was coming soon. He'd made it that far. He looked at the note and slipped a wry smile. It read:

"Well, they have just got through shelling the house like hail. I heard them splitting wood. I guess they are going to fire the house tonight. I think I will make a break when night comes, if alive. Shooting again. It's not night yet. The house is all fired. Goodbye, boys, if I never see you again."

Nate tried to stay awake as long as he could, but he'd fallen asleep deep into the night. He lay in the middle of the room as far away from each of the walls as he could get.

He awoke when a burning object crashed through what remained of the window to his right. At the same time another came through the window to his left. Torches. Burning torches. Furniture and even the dried wood of the walls quickly burst into flames. In a matter of moments, the smoke and heat began to suck all the oxygen out of the room. If he stayed, he'd fry.

Nate grabbed both his rifle and Reese's. He'd loaded them earlier. He took one last look at his home, his effort at building a new life. It was now in flames. It would be ash shortly.

The sun had not yet risen. But a pale purple-gray light ambled its way across the eastern prairie. The morning preened itself in this budding shade as a color of a new beginning. Or was it?

He ran out the door pulling the triggers of both rifles. He didn't aim, he just pulled the triggers, circled the guns around his wrists to try and jack in new rounds. A hail of shots was fired. Nate Crampion hit the ground face down.

* * * * *

The sun and its yellow warmth breached the eastern horizon rising from the purple womb of the day's birth. Thick smoke the color of old snow billowed from the fourteen-foot by fourteen-foot shack that once housed not only Nate Crampion and Ella Toal, but their plans and dreams. All was now nothing but glimmering coals cooling in the morning air. The sacrificial crucible had purged the reality of Crampion the man, but daybreak brought a nativity of legend.

S.T. Clover looked at the morning sky and then down as he stood over the inert body of Nate Crampion. Clover was here at the request of wealthy ranchers. He'd been asked to report on a pervasive problem facing the American cattle industry : rustling. The project entailed a trip west. Expenses were to be paid. The ranchers said he would observe evidence of this widespread problem and the solution applied to it. It had been explained as a fundamental problem facing a critical form of commerce. Beef processing was big business in his town of Chicago. His editor told him to come. He had looked forward to 'riding the west' as his boss termed it.

A few of the ranchers spent time trying to outline the nature of the problem. He'd learned terminology and issues surrounding the concept of "mavericks", a term he knew nothing about before this trip. But those same wealthy ranchers seemed strangely disconnected from the intimidation and destruction they were imposing on these people out on the range. While some men had circled the premises they called the KC Ranch watching the structure collapse in flames, the politicians and ranchers kept their distance. Only the man named Frank Canton seemed to give the dead body of this man on the ground any attention, Clover thought, and that was only in passing. Probably intended to make sure he was dead. Canton had rolled Crampion's body over face up. Clover watched as Canton scanned the multiple garish rifle wounds. He could detect no emotion whatsoever as Canton walked away.

Clover looked down in fascination. He'd never witnessed another human being killed. The whole attack seemed a bit surreal. Always thinking as a reporter, he wondered how he should set the story. Was it so important for the ranch owners to run people off the range? Was it reasonable that people should be killed over some steers? On the other hand, why would this decent looking young man fight the way he did? He looked around. Not much to his eye to fight over. But Clover had heard the men talking about the fact Crampion and his men had shot and killed six men and wounded three others. There was almost a measure of respect in their comments.

He looked back down at the dead man next to his feet. He heard the others getting ready to leave. His reporter's interest now satisfied, Clover was about to turn to gather his horse and join the group when he saw what looked like a small book protruding from Crampion's jacket. He reached down and lifted the bound pages and opened it. Realizing at once it was a journal, he thumbed to the last entry.

"Won't the people back east be fascinated to read this," he said quietly. As he continued to read the journal, his story came into focus. Clover had just witnessed lives ruined. Who was right? That was his story: *The ranchers are leaving a wake of destruction, all with the belief of righteousness. But here lies a righteous man, his journal tersely describing grass roots efforts to make a new life. That life was cut short. That simple effort should be told. The extinguishing of that life could be made a legend.*

His editor back at the Chicago Herald had a term for something like this: "newspaper gold."

Chapter Twenty-Six

Spring 1878
Reno, Nevada

The wheels of the wagon spun so fast the spokes became invisible. The two horses pulling his rig were lathered white from neck to chest and between their hind legs. The snowy foam started out thick like a custard on a pie, but it thinned as it moved lower on their bodies. As it passed down the flexing muscles shaking under the strain of exertion, the froth thinned to the point it streamed down the equine legs in dark watery rivulets. There was a limit to what a horse could do, a limit as to how long the animal could continue to run at full speed.

But he could not let up. Reno was just ahead. He had to get to the sheriff. The back wheels of the wagon swung extra wide as the team pulled into the last turn before they entered town. The draw and power were all up front generated by the hindquarters of the team hauling the rig. Without any weight in the back of the wagon, it spun back and forth through any turn like a tail being wagged on a dog.

Jack Flagg did not slow as he entered the north side of town. His thick stubby fingers were tight on his reins. The cross over hitch connected the bridles of both horses and left him only two straps of thick leather to hold. He lifted those straps once again and yanked them down slapping the backside of each horse as a message to keep up the speed. The team had slowed out of habit once they entered the town proper. He needed to keep them going at pace. The sheriff's office came up quickly. Flagg yanked back on the reins as he pulled up parallel to the wooden sidewalk in front of Svensson's office.

"Whoa. Whoa, there, Johnny."

The horse on the right stumbled, unable to match the semi-slide of his mate to the left. It pulled both animals jointly tied in the rigging forward a few extra steps until both animals came to a complete stop. It was an awkward end and produced no small amount of dust billowing from behind to engulf the now immobile buckboard. The entrance had also produced no shortage of angry onlookers.

"What are you doing racing that team here in town?" One angry citizen did not hesitate to convey his displeasure.

Flagg did not answer. He did not even turn to look at his accuser. He just bounded out of the rig and jumped down on the boardwalk straight from his wagon's seat. He never touched the dirt roadway. In two large steps he was at the door. Flagg did not bother to knock. Pushing the heavy closure open he announced in anxious tone, "Sheriff, there are thirty guns out there all shooting at Nate Crampion's place. It's the ranchers and their gunmen. There were some shots comin' out of the house back at 'em, but no tellin' how long Nate can last with all them guns shootin' at him."

"How do you know it's the ranchers?" Svensson jumped out of his chair and grabbed the anxious man by both shoulders veritably stopping his progress.

" 'Cause I seen 'em!" Flagg shouted the words. "You gotta come now. And ya need men—lots of 'em."

Flagg could see Svensson still had questions.

"Sheriff, I am not makin' this up. I was just drivin' out to see how Nate was doin' after the loss of Ella. The bastards saw me and started shootin' at me. I turned and hit the team up as fast as I could. They started gettin' close and kept firin'."

Svensson did not let go of the man's shoulders. Flagg slumped into the grasp trying to get enough air into his lungs to finish his story. Svensson waited, but only a moment.

"Go on. Tell me the rest."

Flagg hesitated, let his tongue glide across the outside of thin lips mostly hidden beneath an angry, unkempt moustache. He felt his whole mouth had gone dry. His arms almost trembled. There had been no time to think of fear as he raced into town. The narrow escape with his own life bubbled up from some depth. It left him struggling to find the words.

"They got close, Sheriff. I pulled my rifle from under the buckboard and jacked a round in my repeater with one hand. The team was pullin' like crazy, and I was afraid I'd lose all control. I turned around my right side and fired. No idea if I was even close. Swung the rifle by the lever action to jack a second round in and turned for another shot. This one must'a come close as they backed off a bit. I kept movin' worried they needed me dead."

"Probably exactly what they were thinking, Jack."

"They slowed, but only to a point. Then they pushed their horses forward hard for another effort. Not sure what they were thinkin'. But when they got close enough, they started to fire their handguns again. Bullets kept hittin' the seat and back of the wagon. No idea why they never hit me. They sure seemed to be tryin'. I wrapped the reins around my leg. I jacked another round and turned to my left. Had a-hold of my rifle with both hands this time, and tried to aim careful on the next shot. Think I came close. Either hit the man or his duster, but it was close. They withdrew at that point. I could outdistance them with my rifle, and they knew it."

"I'm sure they were not happy you got away. Must've known you'd come here to town. Jack, you must be absolutely straight with me. You sure there were that many guns?"

"I'm sure. The sound was deafening. Don't know how anyone could survive inside."

"Did you see a man wearing a black duster and a dark hat with fur brim?"

Flagg thought for a moment, then answered. "I didn't spend a lot of time lookin' careful, but there were four men sittin' on their horses up the road from the house. They were talkin'. And now that you mention it, there was one wearin' a black duster. That was just before the two broke off and headed after me."

"Canton." Svensson hissed the word.

Svensson let go of Flagg's shoulders and turned to his deputy. Flagg knew the man only by the single name, Rollie. Svensson looked back one more time at Flagg. His face was painted with hesitation. It was if he knew the next move triggered an avalanche of consequences. Flagg watched as the moment hung in suspension. He was about to say something to push Svensson forward when the sheriff turned back to look at Flagg. A burn flamed from his eyes. Without taking his gaze off Flagg, Svensson spoke to his deputy.

"Rollie, head off and start rounding up the posse we've been talking to. Start with Dell Crandall, and Joe Brimley. But start collecting the whole group. We'll need each and every gun we can get. When we added them up on the list last night, we came up with one hundred and fifty men who agreed to serve. Get them. Get them all."

The words were offered with a steel determination Flagg could not mistake. Resigned that his job had been accomplished, he nodded.

"Sheriff, count me in. Might need a horse as my team is played out. But I'll join. I hope to have a chance to take better aim at those two who came after me."

"Jack, you stay here and keep telling your story to the men as they start arriving at the office. I'm going to ride to the south side and get Dale Paris. He needs to get Will Toal and meet us."

Range War

* * * * *

A hand thudded on his front door. The blasts were heavy. The door had been a special purchase. The house and his miniature lean-to barn were modest, old, and nondescript. Paris bought the door to add a hint of finery to the entrance, the first thing he figured people would see. But as most things fine, it was delicate.

"Quit beating on my door. You'll break it."

"Paris, it's Svensson. Open up! It's important."

Dale Paris woke and dressed this morning earlier than most days. He'd gotten a full good night's sleep and rose before dawn. His normal day did not start until almost nine o'clock. It was about that now. Coffee and breakfast were done. He had planned to get to the sheriff's office first thing. But now the sheriff had come to him. He opened the door.

The Norwegian lawman filled the doorway. His hat remained on his head. His feet were spaced a little further apart than normal. One thumb was tucked inside his gun belt. His shoulders cocked off at an angle to the front opening. The stance conveyed a resolve. But there was something more. Maybe a challenge? Paris could not quite place it.

"Sheriff, come in."

Svensson stepped inside. He still did not remove his hat. This was going to be a short meeting.

The sheriff turned just after fully entering the room.

"The ranchers have attacked Nate Crampion out at his KC Ranch. Jack Flagg drove his buckboard out to see Nate and saw what he claims to be twenty to thirty men all shooting into Nate's place."

Paris did not hesitate. "I'll get my handgun and rifle. I'll meet you back at the jail."

"Dale, I need you to get Will Toal. From what I'm told, he's good with a gun, especially a rifle. I've got plenty of men going to join a posse, but I can't vouch that any of them are that good with a weapon."

A man stood up from a chair in the far corner of the room. Paris could see the surprise on Svensson's face as he turned to assess the movement. He had obviously not seen the man sitting there as he entered. No doubt, he had been pre-occupied with delivering his message.

"No need for Dale to ride and get me. I arrived this morning with an idea. Hoped for Dale's help to try and convince you to gather your posse for another ride out to Ferguson's."

Svensson did not smile. His upper body seemed to lean slightly toward Will. It provided extra emphasis to his words.

"If Angus Ferguson kills Nate Crampion, he will pay. This time, he might not get the benefit of a trial. But I'm going to need all the help I can get. If Ferguson has his Texans, we must figure they are good with their guns. I may have numbers, but I don't want a bunch of my townspeople dying in some gun battle."

Will did not flinch. "If guns go off, people could get killed. Goes with firing the weapons. But if Ferguson wants to start a war, best to beat him quick. He'll only get stronger if he's successful."

"So, you will ride with us?"

Will nodded. "Yep. Brought both my rifles. One for distance and the other a repeater."

Svensson turned back to Paris.

"Then, I'd ask you and Will to head out right now to see if you can get a read on what's happening. I'll gather the men and come as soon as we can. I hope to have the full posse on the road in thirty minutes."

Dale lifted his hand toward Will. "Toal is already saddled and ready. I'll throw my own saddle on, and we'll head out immediately. How many men do you think you can raise?"

Svensson shrugged. "Over a hundred have said they'd come. Lots of folks are upset about the hanging, about the ranchers acting like they're above the law. We may get even more, but you never know who will ride until they actually show up in their saddle holding a gun."

Will then asked a question. "Sheriff, is Canton with them?"

Svensson flipped back to face Will. "Flagg said he saw a man in a black duster just before two henchmen started after him shooting at his rig. He hightailed it and had to shoot his way back to town. They came after him, no doubt attempting to remove any witnesses. But he was sure there was a man in a black duster."

Paris could see Will's face change. He'd seen that look several times before.

Will looked at Svensson. "I will let you take care of Ferguson any way you wish, but Frank Canton and I are going to have a special conversation. Won't be too many words, but there will be some triggers pulled."

Will paused, then continued.

"Men of means cannot just take from others because they have the power to do so. Those folks out in the middle of a prairie are trying to make something out of nothing. They can't steal from the ranchers, but they don't deserve to die trying to make a life for themselves. Killing homesteaders because they staked a proper claim carves into the soul of the country itself. There is a fundamental evil in it. If the ranchers want absolute control over the range, let them buy sections of it like we did to the south. If they don't own it, they should not be allowed to rule over it like some king in the old country."

Paris could not recall hearing Will say that much at one time. He watched as Svensson considered Will's words. To Paris, he thought he could see a smoothness come over the sheriff's face, a form of affirmation. Maybe he had just heard something to bolster his decision to raise the posse. When the man finally spoke in response to Will, it was in a soft, deep tone.

"Then let's go stop them. Let's stop them in a way that they will never again tread on those lawfully breaking ground."

Chapter Twenty-Seven

Spring 1878
KC Ranch, Open Range

"How long do you think it's going to take us to get out to the ranch?"

Dale Paris strained to get the words out as he rode next to Will astride his big gelding, Powder. The gray mustang possessed longer legs than did Paris's mount. Despite traveling at a steady lope, normally a smoother gait, the short legs of his own horse were making travel far more jarring than the ride Will was getting. The supple reach of the mustang seemed to glide forward unlike the hooves of his own mount which slammed on the hard earth with every stride. Usually, his riding took place at a walk. Here, Paris could feel his backside taking a beating. And the jolting nature of his seat made his speech come out in staccato bursts.

Will had not answered. They had used the main road out of Reno riding for at least an hour and then began to cut across country. Will claimed it would get them there sooner. Paris silently noted Will's remarkable sense of direction. He knew from his prior trips out to investigate rustling that Will was right. He was surprised at Will's knowledge of the ground they had to cover.

The pair periodically altered their speed trying to save their horses. Paris knew the distance was close to twenty-five miles, a long trip for a horse being pushed at speed. Interspersed with the steady lope came stretches of a hard trot. That gait was even worse for Paris. His short horse felt like he jumped on stilts with each stride when moving at a trot. Maybe it was time to buy a new horse. He could probably get a good deal from his current riding partner. Will Toal carried a well-earned reputation for breeding and selling excellent saddle horses.

As if he could sense Paris's discomfort, Will pulled up and dismounted.

"Need to give the horses a bit of a blow. We should walk some to cool them down before we finish the trip. We might have to ride even after we get there. Should try to save as much of their energy as we can while still making time."

"Fine by me. My back side needs a blow, too. I can already feel the beginning of saddle sores."

Paris watched for Will's reaction to his attempt at levity. Nothing. New lines of concern and concentration spread across Will's forehead. Paris had never noticed those before. Maybe they were evidence Will had aged with recent events. Losing a last family member would have an effect on anyone. Paris decided to change his tact.

"Thinking about what we're going to find?"

Will strode forward, looking down at his own boots as if to consciously place each foot forward to a circumstance of life he didn't want to confront. Maybe he was trying to avoid thinking about the exact question Paris just posed. He didn't answer at first, but after a pause, he looked up at Paris.

"No tellin' what we're going to find. Right now, it's just the two of us. We're not going to be able to do much except observe what's going on. I can't get past the thought that we might have to watch while Nate gets killed. I've been tryin' to think of some plan to stop the shooting but, so far, I'm having trouble coming up with some way the two of us can stop a group of thirty rifles without getting ourselves killed in the process."

Paris knew of Will's feeling for his sister. That was only natural. But the obvious concern for Nate took Paris aback a bit. He had not been sure of Will's reaction to Nate having lived with his sister, yet not married her.

Then, somewhat to Paris's surprise, Will added, "But if he's there and I have a shot with the Enfield, I'll make sure Frank Canton doesn't live to kill anyone else."

"That could set them out after us for sure."

Will nodded. "And we can lead them right back into the oncoming posse."

"Sounds like you do have a plan."

"It's not much of one, and it probably won't save Nate."

The two started up a slight hill side by side, each with their reins in a hand pulling the horses behind. Both animals were breathing hard and showing no small amount of sweat. They'd been ridden hard, and they still had a lot of ground to cover.

Will looked at Paris. "Nate told me about his run in with Canton out at his range corral. Said he and his hands got the better of him. But I have to figure a man like Canton will be out for blood. He won't let that go without some measure of revenge."

"Oh, there's no doubt about that. I was there at Ferguson's when he rode in with his injured companion. I saw the look on Canton's face when told his man was dead. His face became as dark as his duster."

Will pushed his hands on his thighs to help clamber up a small hill. He moved in a rhythm despite the extra effort involved in the climb. They crested the rise. Both men looked up in the direction of the KC Ranch.

"That's smoke," said Will.

"And that's gotta be in the vicinity of Nate's ranch."

"How far do you think that is?"

Paris instinctively calculated the slope and geography before he answered.

"I'd say we're about ten miles away."

"I figure about the same," said Will. "Let's ride. If that smoke is coming from Nate's place, it's a bad sign. Might be we're already too late."

* * * * *

The smoke had turned from black to white. By the time they got close, there was not much smoke at all. Even at a distance, they could see the reason for the dwindling volume of fumes. Nate's house no longer existed. No walls stood. There had been no chimney. There were no stones left rising from an unhinged fireplace. There was only an iron stove that stood in the middle of a flat bed of black, smoldering ash. Nothing else was left, not even the furniture.

Will knew what he was going to find before he pulled up. The ranchers had smoked any inhabitants out. Nate and his hands were either part of the black char where the house stood, or they would find the bodies scattered around the homestead.

Even at their distance from the house, Will could tell there were no guns. Silence covered the ground as if the smoke had taken with it any living object capable of making noise. Walls of wood had succumbed to the blaze. The flame exhausted all the fuel it could reach, dying its own death from its compulsive consumption. A thin wisp of smoke was the only movement. The ethereal vapor slowly snaked its way into the atmosphere in stealthy, unrepentant retreat.

Will sat on Powder, whose sides heaved to and fro, trying to replace the oxygen in his system lost in the race to KC Ranch. A sigh of deep sadness left his own lungs almost in a mirror image of the exhales exiting his horse. The scene before him told the story, even without any sound. Nate was dead. Will had not been able to save either Ella or Nate. The connection to his past, to his family, now stood completely cut.

Paris broke the silence.

"Best we circle around to make sure no one else is out there waiting to take a shot."

Will scanned the horizon again. "We'd see their horses. Don't see any."

Not dissuaded, Paris said, "Still, I'll ride around slowly and check the creek beyond the house. About the only place anyone could keep out of sight would be down the banks of that creek. You stay here and watch my progress. If you see anything that looks like a gun barrel, shoot it."

Will reached down and pulled his Winchester out of its scabbard. He also carried his old Enfield long range sniper rifle which he'd used during the war. But he didn't see anything that would require a shot of some distance.

"Go. I'll watch for any movement."

Paris turned his horse off at a slow walk holding his own rifle across his lap. Will watched as he traveled toward the creek bed, moved down to water level where Will could see only Paris and not his horse, and then rise again. He raised his gun in a motion as if to say "come on in."

Will walked Powder toward the bed of black ash. Paris moved toward the corral focused on something nearby. The corral itself was empty. Will remembered Nate told him of his plan to bring his stock off of the range and close to the house. But the stock that had been here just days before was now gone. There were no animals near, not cattle and not horses. Nothing but stillness.

Paris stopped next to the corral gate. There, reclined with his head propped against a fencepost, was the bullet riddled body of Nate Crampion. Will did not count, but there had to be at least a dozen bloodied sections on his jacket and legs. A note hung from a rope strung around his neck. Will did not have to dismount to read the large letters.

"Cattle thieves beware." A red sash circled his waist.

Will stepped down and squatted next to Nate. Gently, he lifted the sign off his neck and looped it around the top of the fencepost.

Will spoke to Paris without taking his eyes from Nate's body. "You ever see Nate wear any red sash?"

"I never saw him wear a sash of any sort," commented Paris.

"Neither did I. This must be the rancher's sorry attempt to justify something they knew was wrong."

"Yeah," said Paris. "Paint a favorable picture."

"We might as well wait for the posse here. But we should be careful what we tell Svensson about the sash. He has to know there is a story about this beyond first sight."

"Agreed."

Will stood. "I'll start digging a grave out next to the tree where we buried Ella. Why don't you take a look to see if you can find any tracks?" Will's voice lacked any passion, but his mind seared hot in a deep anger.

"No need, already seen them. Not difficult. Looks almost like a herd of buffalo went rushing through. They must have had some cattle with them 'cause the tracks are fresh and wide as a small river. Won't be hard to follow them."

"Nate had some stock here when we found Ella. We saw his hands bring another batch before you headed to Reno, and I went to Ferguson's. The ranchers must have driven the cattle out when they left."

Paris dismounted and wrapped a rein around the uppermost rail of the corral. He turned to lean his back up against the structure.

"Murder. Simple as that. Murder."

Will nodded. "They must think they are truly above the law. They are mistaken, sorely mistaken."

Will pulled off his jacket and walked along the corral. The shovel Nate and he had used to bury Ella lay on the ground next to the lean-to for the horses. He lifted the tool, staring at it in his hands. What a strange instrument to bring closure to a life. Ella was blood. Family needs to bury family. He had only known Nate a very short while. But he'd been close to his sister. There was an obvious affection. Despite his initial misgivings, Will had seen Nate's reaction to the loss of Ella. Only fitting they rest next to each other. They were a family, part of *his* family. He carried the spade and stood next to Ella's grave. His boot jammed the blade into the dirt.

* * * * *

In the distance to the west, Frank Canton lay flat on the windward side of a slight mound. He and his horse were out of sight to anyone back at KC Ranch. He had a telescoping long-range lens pressed against his eye.

"Will Toal rides a gray horse, does he not?"

Liam Witherspoon knelt on the ground to the rear holding the reins of both his horse and Canton's.

"He rode a big gray into Ferguson's place according to the hands there when they arrested Ferguson. They said he always rides a gray."

"Well, that's got to be him, then."

Witherspoon stood. "If so, then the guy with the wagon must've made it to Reno."

Canton collapsed the lens. He still looked out over the distance.

"I don't see any dust to indicate there's more than two of them. But if that guy with the wagon made it to town, we better figure a group may be coming. We can hit the two nesters Ferguson wants next and then move on to the T.A. Ranch. Best to hunker down until we know if anyone follows. We can get one of the homesteaders tonight, camp, and hit the other tomorrow morning. But we should convince Ferguson and the group that we should head to the T.A. after that, just to be safe."

Witherspoon mounted and looked at Canton.

"You really think they'll come?"

"Oh, they'll come. But I think we have enough firepower to scare off any normal posse or collection of town folk."

"Could be a battle if they bring numbers."

"Could be. Let it come. One way or the other, the issue of rustling must get resolved. Maybe these townspeople and their sheriff need to come face to face with the consequences of cattle rustlers."

Chapter Twenty-Eight

Spring 1878
Open Range, North of Reno

A pale blue-gray horizon began to rise from the desert to the east fighting to lift the darkness hanging overhead. Will sat on the ground with a cup of terrible coffee in his hands. *Beth makes a great cup of coffee,* he thought. This pot contained a miserable trail mix of water and dark beans.

As he looked east, he wondered if the sun could lift the darkness that had settled in the ranchers. He found it hard to comprehend how a group could just ride out and start killing people. Over losing cattle? Maybe. But there was more to it, and he couldn't get his mind to grasp the core justification. All he could see was a taking. He saw the Union Army's killing his mother and father as the same: another taking. It left his family and farm in ruins. And he'd lost the war on top of it. Those combined losses had driven both him and Ella west. He had been able to leave the defeat behind. Beth and the kids had a lot to do with that. But here again there was a darkness, a gray confederate pall of taking that covered this range.

Leif Svensson strode to the campfire, picked up the coffee pot, and poured some of the brew into his tin cup.

"Nice to have warm coffee ready."

Will dumped the remnants of his own cup on the ground. "Best take a sip before you start with the compliments. One taste and you might change your mind."

"That good, eh?"

Will shook his head. "Definitely not home cooked."

Svensson sat adjacent to Will. "Jack Flagg drove in late last night."

Adjusting his stare back to the low burning camp flame, Will said, "Thought I saw a group of the men greeting someone after we had camped."

"Yes, it was Flagg. Jack went straight to his own ranch when we left Reno. He was afraid he'd been seen by the ranchers. Worried they would take it out on his ranch and family. Sure enough, when he arrived, his house had been burned just like Nate's."

"They didn't hang his wife, did they?"

"No, they told his wife to take their two boys and start walking. Drove off all the stock and incinerated the home. Jack found them wandering not too far from the burned-out remnants."

"Were they able to save anything from the house?"

"No. According to Jack, his wife was told to start walking. They didn't let her back into the home to even get a jacket or shawl. They'd have frozen last night if Jack had not found them."

Will shifted his legs. "So, we now have three families all scorched out and left with nothing. Nate and Ella, Jack Flagg's family, and the Millers, the spread we are camped at. By the time we buried Nate and tracked the ranchers here, the Millers had met the same fate as Flagg's family."

Svensson took another sip and winced at the bitter taste of the brew.

"I've had whiskey that packed less of a bite than this coffee."

"Told you."

Dale Paris walked up. "Had to go relieve myself. Looking forward to a cup of my coffee."

Will looked up. "Figures."

Dale looked puzzled. "Figures what?"

"You made that swill. Neither me nor the sheriff could even finish one small cup. Not fit for human consumption."

Range War

"I make great trail coffee."

Will shook his head. "Only if your trailin' swine. The only beings on this planet who could stomach that stuff would be pigs."

Svensson smiled and decided to join in the exchange. "Half of the posse is over yonder puking their guts out and each one's been blamin' the coffee."

Paris looked devastated. "Really?"

Will grinned. The first grin in days. "Rightly so, too. You could start a fire with the burn that fluid starts in your throat."

Noticing the grins spreading on both Will and Svensson's faces, Paris looked relieved. "Okay, so it may not be the best coffee, but no one's sick, right?"

"Not yet, we warned them off. Why do you think the pot's full?" Will did not let up.

"Well, what are we going to do with this giant pot, give it to the horses?"

Will scoffed. "Won't be giving any of that stuff to Powder. I need to ride the animal, not bury him. Done enough of that in the last couple of days."

As if body punched, all levity ended. Will had let himself get carried too far. His last comment yanked him back to the reality of the moment. Silence followed.

Svensson waited, and then ended the lull. "We have close to one hundred and fifty men here in camp. It may even be as high as two hundred."

Will looked surprised. "That many?"

Svensson nodded. "Yes, that many. All are armed, but not sure if any of them can hit what they're aimin' at."

Paris finished pouring coffee into his cup. "If we have that many shooting, probably don't have to worry if they aim at all. The volley alone could cover an entire corral." He took a sip from the tin receptacle. "This isn't bad."

Svensson stood as he responded. "Your standards need to be adjusted."

Will rose too. "I don't think the standards could be adjusted enough. I think we should make sure Paris is not allowed to have anything to do with making the coffee in the future."

Svensson turned to Will. "Flagg brought with him some interesting information. Says his wife heard a pair of men who seemed to be the leaders of the group talking about heading to the T.A. Ranch."

"What's that, another homesteader?" Will expected to hear of another target.

"No, that's what makes it interesting. The T.A. Ranch is owned by Ronald Tisdale and a Dr. William Harris of Laramie. But it's run by his manager, Charles Ford. It's one of the first ranches established here on the range. It's old, big, and well run."

Paris added, "And Ford is a big supporter of the Stockgrowers Association."

Will was taken aback. "So, these owners let their entire operation be run by some hired manager?"

"Sure," said Paris. "Happens all over the place. There are probably five or six of the Stockgrowers' ranches that are owned by investors back East and even in England, which are run by managers who file written reports to their owners."

Will shook his head. "I suppose it's not that strange. Now that I think about it, my business partner, Henry Millard, owns ranches all over California and Nevada that he has run by managers. But here with these men acting as they are, it sure seems responsibility gets removed further and further from those who sink the money into the operation."

"It doesn't matter who owns the property, I intend to bring those who are doing the raiding to justice." The comment came uttered simply as a matter of fact by Svensson.

"I was at the T.A. Ranch once," said Paris. "It's out in the middle of nowhere. This group would be seen for miles before you even got close."

"Probably the reason they're headed there. They can see us coming and be ready to defend," responded Will.

Svensson looked over to the burned-out Miller house. "Based on what we've seen here, I'll bet they have already arrived and set up their defenses."

Will agreed. "They probably had scouts out watching to see if any posse followed them. Once they reported the size of this group, a decision was made to retreat to a place they could defend. Smart strategy."

Svensson raised his hand to his chin where his thumb and forefinger straddled the sides of his lower jaw. "If they've seen us, then they'll get good and ready for our arrival. Could be a serious battle."

Paris dumped the rest of his own coffee which drew knowing smiles from Will and Svensson, but did not draw any additional comments.

"I think Angus Ferguson knew all along this is where things would end up. That's why he hired those men from Texas. He thinks he can beat anything sent against him."

Svensson answered. "Agreed. But that don't mean he's right. Let's get this army saddled up. I would ask you and Dale to start out first like yesterday. Ride ahead and scout the T.A. See what we're up against. Then retreat a bit and report. We'll then come up with a plan and set our men."

In a quiet and almost detached tone, Will offered while staring at the coals as if a sacrifice to the flames. "With all these armed men, we should give them all the battle we can."

Chapter Twenty-Nine

Spring 1878
T.A. Ranch, North of Reno

Frank Canton peeled off his duster. Then he removed his black vest, outer shirt, and string tie. Muscled arms of colorless skin now met the warming rays of the sun uncovered. A line of men stretched twenty yards each to his right and left. All were digging a pair of trenches. Despite a small gap wide enough for one wagon, the trenches were set at a right angle and were positioned directly in front of the main roadway gate to the T.A. Ranch. Canton picked up a shovel and began to dig.

"Any sign of Witherspoon?" Angus Ferguson moved up behind Canton just as he drove his spade with his boot into the softer than expected turf. Angus had not yet deigned to help dig.

"No, not yet," responded Canton.

Angus persisted. "And who was it that claims they saw a posse of two hundred men?"

Canton lifted the spade-full of dirt and threw it forward continuing the effort to build up a set of breastworks to the outside of the trench.

"Liam Witherspoon was out scouting as rear guard. He reported seeing the posse and gave me the estimate as to its size."

"Do you think he's right? I can't believe there would be two hundred men who would join a posse out of Reno against us." Canton had no trouble detecting a strong hint of concern in Ferguson's voice.

"Mr. Ferguson, Liam would have no reason, no reason whatsoever, to exaggerate the size of the group trailing us. He saw them heading from the KC Ranch to that Miller place we hit yesterday early. They

Range War

were obviously following our tracks, which would not be difficult to do."

Canton continued his digging. Ferguson did not move.

"Maybe we should send out a delegation to discuss things."

Exasperated, Canton stopped and turned.

"Exactly what would you consider a good argument? We burned three homes, ran off two families, and killed all the occupants of a third."

Angus leaned down to be closer to Canton's face as he bent forward to drive the spade home again. To an uninterested onlooker, Angus appeared to be chasing Canton. To some degree, he was chasing for justification.

"We argue that the law is on our side. We argue that each and every one of these people were both trespassing and stealing."

"Mr. Ferguson, you know, and *I* know, that is all true. But you must admit that other than a collection of beef cattle bearing brands we dispute, we have no evidence. And we even dispersed those cattle. They're gone. That crowd following us knows only that we've run off three families and killed four people."

"So, you don't think we should even try to talk?"

Canton stopped again. The tone of his response left little doubt as to his waning patience.

"Angus, if I may call you that, you had no hesitation starting this push to remove the nesters. Not only did you know what we were going to do, but you also insisted. Did you think the town would simply roll over and ignore what we were doing? You knew this was going to be a fight, and now, we're going to get it."

"But I didn't think I'd have to kill half of the men living in Reno. If there are truly two hundred men out there, it has to be almost half of the able-bodied men in town."

"It sounds like you're worried. Don't be. With the fortifications we're building, and with the twenty men from Texas I've hired, we should be able to hold off even a force of two hundred untrained men."

Ferguson raised up to his full height. "Maybe you're right. Let 'em come. What better way to make a statement than to show the sheriff what laws should be enforced?"

Canton relaxed. His arguments seemed to have prevailed. He returned to his digging, his body warming to the exertion. The group had to finish the breastworks within the hour. He'd place his men around the perimeter, in the barn and in the main house. He should have the entire field covered. Barring a collective rush in which dozens of oncoming men would be killed, his guns should be able to hold them off. They had brought wagons of ammunition and supplies. They could hole up here for two weeks if they rationed. No posse would last two weeks. Especially if they were dodging well-placed return fire.

* * * * *

Will and Paris crawled forward. Their horses were hobbled behind them. With only the slightest of rises in the topography, they had left the animals far behind. Dust covered both from chin to boot. While only a small rise, it was enough to block any view of their position. Paris pulled out his hand-held telescope.

"Looks like they are digging trenches. Several trenches out front across the entrance."

Paris handed the glass to Will so he could see.

"Looks like there are buildings to both sides. They'll have men in those. Probably digging the same trenches on the opposite side to protect the road through the ranch as it exits the compound. Between the barn and what looks like the main home and bunk house, they have the field covered."

"Yes, but we have so many guns we can spread all the way around and still bring hell to bear with a vicious series of volleys."

"Probably so," said Will. "We'll have to coordinate the shooting, but it might loosen up the ranchers if we blast their positions for a couple of hours or so. Might be like what they did to Nate. Sounds like Jack Flagg described a similar ring of multiple guns all aimed at Nate's home. Only just that the favor is returned."

Paris started to reverse his crawl. "Let's get back and tell Svensson what's in store."

Will turned to follow Paris when he saw a rider several hundred yards off riding fast toward the T.A. The rider looked to his right and saw the horses, and now, both Paris and Will.

"Should we take a shot at him?"

Will shook his head. "No. He's got a good head of steam. By the time I could get my Enfield set up, he'll be too far off and still moving fast."

Paris looked out at the rider. "They now know we're here."

Will sighed. "They knew a long time ago. The reason they have retreated to this ranch and started building defenses is because they knew not only that we're here, but how large a group we have."

"We have our work cut out for us," said Paris.

Standing at full height, Will looked back at the T.A. "No sense in trying to avoid being seen now. I think we'll be fine. We have so many guns and they have twenty to fifty. If nothing else, it will be a war of attrition."

* * * * *

Angus Ferguson returned to the main house. The home was elegantly furnished without being overstated. Nothing seemed jammed. There was a pleasant space throughout. A piano stood in the drawing room. Paintings hung on every wall. Mirrors made the rooms seem even larger than they were. His own home had a rustic almost medieval feel. This home had an open, airy feel.

He found Carter McKinnon and motioned him over.

"Carter, word is there are two hundred guns coming after us. This could get out of hand. I'm thinking we need some back-up plan."

"What kind of plan?"

"Who here has the best relationship with the governor? We know he supports us. Hell, half of the money he gets for his campaigns comes from men sitting in this house. He'll be sympathetic."

McKinnon nodded. "True. But what will he be able to do? He's in Carson City, and no one down there is going to come to our aid."

"He can call out the military."

"Angus, no, he can't. There are no state troops, only U.S. Army out at Fort Churchill."

"Then our good governor might have to wire the president. So, I'll ask again. Who has the best relationship with the governor to push him to wire the president? My idea is to have this person leave now, wait, and watch to see what happens. If all two hundred of these townspeople start shooting, he can go contact the governor. He can ride to Carson City if he has to."

McKinnon gave the question some thought, then answered. "Mike Shonsey. He has family who is related to the governor. He sees him regularly. He also contributes large sums to the governor's campaign."

"Good. Find him, and without anyone else knowing, tell him what to do. Tell him to leave now. He should travel far enough to avoid becoming involved, but close enough to watch."

Range War

"I'll tell him. He's not much of a gunman so he'll probably relish having a valid excuse to get away before the shooting starts."

* * * * *

Will and Dale Paris trotted up to Svensson at the head of his huge posse. Dale looked at Will. "You tell him."

Will settled in his saddle and leaned forward.

"They're ready for us. The ranch compound has a road through the middle of it, the main house on one end, a barn and bunkhouse on either side. They have dug trenches and built breastworks at the entrance and exit. They will position men in all the trenches, the house, barn, and bunkhouse. That done, they can cover any approach."

Svensson exhaled. "They had this planned. Probably a back-up plan, but figured on it, nonetheless. The arrogance of these men is boundless. To plan a raid as they did to this extent moves beyond pre-meditation."

Several of the townspeople rode up close. "What's the report."

Svensson turned. "They are digging in getting ready for us to arrive. I was just about to ask Will what he'd recommend. He's been in major battles during the war. This could just be the biggest battle that's ever taken place in Nevada. So, Will, what would you do?"

"I'd love to have a cannon. We could make short work of this with a cannon. Without that, then I'd recommend we surround the place to make sure no one leaves. Then, I'd ask if we have any shovels?"

"We do," said Sam Thurgood, one of the men who had just ridden up. "Plenty."

Will nodded. "Then, I'd suggest we form a few groups of excellent shooters with good rifles. We have that group make its way around the circle. They lay down a barrage of fire while men dig trenches toward the compound. When they get close enough, they dig trenches branching off to the right and left where men can lie flat and shoot without being hit. They must get close enough to be well within rifle range, but out of range for any handgun."

Svensson lifted his hand palm up. "But they'll have rifles, too."

"Yes, but if these men are dug in, they can pepper the buildings with a constant fire. Sooner or later, they'll start hitting men, even if it's through the walls."

Paris now spoke. "That just might work. Protect our people while we lay into them with constant fire."

Will continued. "Like I said before, our strategy should be a battle of attrition. We can resupply both food and ammo. They can't. We can call for more men. They can't. If we have trenches in which we can crawl in close, our people should be protected. Only a matter of time until we see how committed the ranchers are."

Sam Thurgood then spoke again. "We can do the shovels and ditches. But what if we got Joe Connelly back at his blacksmith shop to try and make a cannon?"

Will smiled. "A cannon would be wonderful. But they aren't easy to make. Wouldn't say no. But I'll tell you what a blacksmith could build that would be even more useful."

"What?" asked Thurgood.

"Have him modify a wagon by adding metal shields. We'd have to be able to push it by hand. Couldn't have any horse pull it. They'd only shoot the horse. But if we could get a group of men to push it forward, we could get close to the compound."

"Why do that?" The question came from Svensson.

"Because if we could get close to the compound, a man with a good arm could throw dynamite at the barn or the bunkhouse. After all the guns are flushed out of those structures, we then move on to the main house."

"Now, there's an idea I really like." Svensson looked back at Thurgood. "Sam, can you head back to town and get Joe working on that?"

"Sure."

"Then we go with Will's plan. Sam, you head to town. Will, you and Dale start collecting the riflemen and tell them what we want them to do. I'll get groups together to circle the place. I'll also instruct those who will dig forward and set up close how they should do it along with the rifles. Let's go to work."

Chapter Thirty

Spring 1878
T.A. Ranch, North of Reno

    The fusillade of gunfire was deafening. Gun smoke hovered over the entire scene like low lying storm clouds or smoke from a prairie fire. It blocked all vision other than the sharp outlines of the ranch buildings. But that was all the posse needed. They had been told to aim low and shoot even at the sides of the structures. Bullets could strike a victim through the wooden walls. Just keep on firing. And they did.

    Will waited for the smoke to clear. He sat in the bed of a supply wagon using the side to support his Enfield '53. His father had given the rifle to him just before Will went off to fight for the Confederacy at the age of sixteen. The rifle was the only good thing about the war. Other than his own survival, the rifle was the only other object in his life to make it through all the battles with him. It was deadly if used by a trained marksman up to seven hundred yards. It was deadly in Will's hands up to a thousand yards. But he had to see what he was shooting at. The cloud of smoke prevented any such view here at the onset of gunfire.

    The posse had encircled the T.A. Ranch compound. Upon the instructed signal, the entire field of almost two hundred guns opened fire. The initial salvo brought back bad memories of Will battling with Johnson trying to prevent Sherman from getting to the sea. They had failed. Frank Canton had killed Ella. Will had no intention of failing here. He shook off thoughts of the battles with endless retreats. He waited. All snipers had a strong sense of patience. The Enfield was a muzzle loader. The Winchester at his side was a repeater. But if he wanted to pick off Canton or Angus Ferguson, he'd have to wait and be patient. He could do that. There were plenty of other guns leveling a spread of bullets.

Initially, there had been some return fire. But now, all was quiet on the opposing side. To Will, it showed the mark of disciplined men. No sense in shooting if you couldn't see anyone. Wait until the first barrage ended. Then, pick your spots. Will had a good view of almost the entire compound. He'd seen one or two men in the rancher group get hit, but that was all. At least those inside knew there was no escape. Anyone who showed their face would be struck by multiple shots immediately.

* * * * *

Mike Shonsey watched, horrified at the sheer volume of gunfire. He knew right away what he had to do. His instructions were clear. If the posse brought its full weaponry to bear and it looked like the ranchers might not prevail, he was to head for the governor's office and plead, insist, intimidate him into calling the President of the United States to have the army put an end to the hostilities. It did not take long after the gunfire started for him to make his decision. No one could survive that onslaught; at least, not for long.

There were almost sixty ranchers and hired guns inside that compound. Probably thirty were wealthy men, large property owners. All those men had contributed to the governor's campaigns. The Nevada Stock Grower's Association was a huge supporter too. The governor was aware of the rustling problem. He'd tried to have legislation passed like Wyoming where all mavericks were deemed the property of the Stock Growers. The legislation had not passed, but not for lack of effort by the governor.

He would have to ride through the night to get to Carson City. If he was lucky, he might get access to the governor early tomorrow. How long it would take to communicate a message off to Washington and back to Fort Churchill was anyone's guess. Shonsey just knew every minute counted. That hail of bullets was otherworldly.

* * * * *

The smoke had cleared. Gunshots were only sporadic. Svensson had communicated around the circle to hold fire unless one of the enemy was actually exposed. Will had seen one man rise and walk across a room in the main house. He fired through a window and the victim was thrown back and down. He had no idea as to the identity of the man. But he knew there would be one less gun shooting back.

Darkness approached. The men of the posse held their positions. Svensson sent word that he wanted to talk to Will. Grabbing both his rifles, Will moved away from the wagon, heading to the rear. A campsite with a fire signaled a headquarters of sorts. A cook wagon had been set up and there were waves of men arriving to eat. Svensson stood nearby, asking for reports from each group.

"Will, come. We need to talk."

Both men moved away from the fire to be alone.

Will started. "How many men have we lost?"

Svensson shrugged. "So far, I don't think we've lost a single man."

"How goes it with the trenches?"

"We have trenches to shooting posts in two positions. One opposite the main house and one opposite the barn. We will continue working into the night. Under the cover of darkness, the men think they can dig the last two trenches before morning."

"That's good," said Will. "If all the trenches get completed, we'll have the entire compound surrounded by guns close enough to cause real damage if anyone shows themself."

"Agreed. But we can't really flush them out. It's basically a stand-off."

"True, but we don't want to lose any men. The trenches are the best way to do that. Tell the men to keep low unless they fire, and then only raise up enough to take aim."

"But Will, do we just sit here for days taking sporadic shots?"

"No. I'd recommend we tell the men that at certain hours of the day, we lay out another barrage. Don't make it predictable. Keep them off balance. But have one sometime in the morning when you'd expect men to eat, and the same at sunset, for the same reason. We should make it as uncomfortable as we can. Keep them from moving. Keep them from eating. We have to test their resolve."

"This could go on forever. Some might try to escape. There are almost a hundred head of horses in the corral. Might try to slip away in the dark." Svensson could not contain his concern.

Paris was quick with a thought. "Shoot them."

"What?" Svensson did not hide his shock.

Will was a bit shocked at Dale's suggestion, too, but decided to listen.

Paris tried to explain what he was thinking. "You can't risk having anyone get that close to the corral and release the horses. They would be killed for sure. So, shoot them. Can you imagine the psychological impact that will have for those inside when they know they don't have a horse to even think about escaping? They'd be trapped, and they'd know it."

Will had seen leaders in several battles. All had concerns at some point. But the trick was to let his men see nothing but resolve. All leaders had to make hard decisions, often multiple decisions each day in each battle. Svensson had the capacity to do that. So far, he'd done a remarkable job of leading a large force for someone without military training. However, shooting one hundred horses was a significant decision. Will decided to offer an alternative.

"Might be another way."

Svensson turned. "I'm listening."

Will shifted his stance to look out toward the corral. "We could stampede them."

Paris objected. "Too dangerous. The corral is right next to the main barn. How are you going to get that close without getting shot?"

Will smiled. "Crawl."

Still skeptical, Dale questioned. "In broad daylight?"

"Not that stupid. I'll do it in the dark, real late at night. You can cover me. I'll get to the furthest end of one of the trenches and then crawl to the gate. All I have to do is to open the gate and then crawl back. We might have to figure out a way to scare the bunch towards the open gate, but if we can spook them, they will all bolt."

Will watched to see Paris's reaction. He did not look convinced. "I still think it's too risky."

Will pushed the idea. "We can take two or three other men who are good with rifles. They can spread out in the trench close to you and pick off anyone who looks like they might take a shot at me. I looked earlier today and there was no one positioned near the corral to protect it."

Dale scoffed. "That's because it's a short shot from either the house or barn. They don't need to expose anyone. If you are seen, there are probably multiple men with instructions to cover that corral."

Will answered. "With you and a couple more men we'll have just as much firepower as those covering the corral."

"In the dark?"

With a smile, Will answered. "I'm hoping you have good night vision."

Paris shook his head. "The moon will provide some light, but Will, it's a big risk."

"I'll go out between two and three in the morning. Most will be asleep. Trick will be not to wake anyone until I'm back in the trench."

"And how are you going to spook the horses into a stampede?"

Will had to think a moment. "I'll crawl out with a bucket. Maybe I'll put it in a sack and tie it to my belt. That way, it won't make any noise until I'm inside the corral. Once I get there, I can walk among the horses to the far side of the fence. The horses will be a shield when I'm in the corral. Then, I'll put the bucket on one of the fence posts."

Svensson then asked, "Why a bucket?"

"Because after I get back into the trench, I'll shoot the bucket off the fence post and keep shooting it after it hits the ground to spook the horses. All we need is a few leaders to run, and the whole herd will follow."

Dale shook his head. "I don't like it."

Will pointed at Dale's chest. "But you're the one who argued that removing the ranchers' chance for escape will have a devastating effect on their morale. I agree with that. I just don't want to be fighting while there are some one hundred dead horses rotting here for days."

Paris was silent. Will could tell he didn't like it. But Will didn't wait for any further discussion. "I'll do it tonight."

Hesitant at first, Svensson seemed to come around to the idea. "If those ranchers knew their horses were gone, it would have a huge effect. Maybe enough of those inside would push Angus to start negotiating. Will, do you think you can do it?"

"I do."

Svensson paused, then decided. "If you think you can stampede those horses without getting killed, then do it. But I need you here, Will. Don't go getting shot."

"I'll do my best to avoid it."

Paris swiveled in his stance then came back to face Will. "I suppose if you're bound and determined, then I'll have to get some decent shooters to help protect you. I just know who is going to have to go out there and get you if someone drops you on the dirt. That's going to be me."

Will shook his head. "You won't have to come get me."

Svensson then asked, "Is there anything else we can do to bring this to a head?"

Will changed focus. "Removing the horses is a good idea, but if we really want to bring this standoff to an end, the best way would be some kind of siege wagon."

Svensson looked interested. "You said something about this before. What do you have in mind?"

"If the blacksmith can create a shielded wagon, then we send it in with armed men and, more importantly, men with a few sticks of dynamite. The combination could definitely bring this to an end."

"I like that idea, Will. I like it a lot. But will it work?"

Will nodded. "It should if we can get the wagon close enough to the barn and house. We destroy their cover, this will end quick."

Svensson looked down to the ground and then back at Will. "I hope you're right, Will. I hope you're right."

* * * * *

A sharp-edged moon cut a small hole in the encompassing dark void of night. Sporadic shooting had ended long ago that day. Silence pervaded. Stillness spread. Night was a tonic in each man, soothing the ragged emotions of an apprehensive day. Men had died. Everyone knew more would face the same fate. The darkness was like a blanket on each man's bed, a cover to crawl beneath until tomorrow's return to the churning grind of fear.

Will lifted up and over the edges of the trench. Tied to his belt was a burlap sack which held the critical bucket. The metal bucket was wrapped inside the sack to further prevent any noise as Will dragged it behind him. The first few feet would be the most dangerous. If anyone was watching, he'd be hit just as he came up out of the trench.

Once on top, he stretched out flat and held still, waiting for the shot to ring out. More silence. A good sign. Will waited before he moved again. While still flat, he looked down his side back to the trench. Paris watched anxiously. Both nodded. Will moved forward, one slow arm and leg movement at a time.

After each segment of the motion forward, Will stopped. To rush would be to risk discovery. Patience was the key.

A hoof banged against a wooden fence rail. Will froze. One of the animals must sense something approaching. Horses in a wild herd naturally had some which remained awake while others slept. They would then trade off the guard duty and let the original sentinels sleep. Predators were everywhere, and vigilance meant survival. But the equine guard might be his downfall. He hadn't thought about the horses giving away his approach. A large object crawling toward them would be noticed. He should have thought of that before he'd started. Too late now.

He made it halfway to the corral. Again, he stopped. He listened. A horse stomped with his back leg, a sure example of consternation. The stomp of a back hoof was a demand for Will to state his intentions. Will held still. He could only hope his slow pace would allay any fear in the equine sentry.

The door to the main house opened slowly. About fifty yards away from his position, the hinge made just enough noise to let Will know there was a human guard, too. He kept his head to the ground. The man probably heard the horses and despite the risk opened the door for a better look. The room behind him was dark, so there was no silhouette. The man held still, silent. The barn was on the other side of the corral from Will's position. The group of horses blocked any view of his approach for anyone in the barn. But the field of view from the ranch house was only partially blocked by the corral. Will hoped it was enough. He tried to hold his breath, exhaling only with shallow, subdued movement. If Paris thought the risk too high, he'd shoot at the man at the door. But then, Will would be laying flat underneath an exchange of gunfire. Not where he wanted to be.

The door closed. Will waited a few more seconds and moved forward again. Painstaking progress interrupted by regular stops continued as a pattern. He reached the corral. Will slowly rolled underneath a rail and came to a knee. Again, he stopped. Horses actually seemed more relaxed now that he was partially upright. They were used to humans, but not crawling versions. The more upright he got, the more relaxed those in the immediate vicinity became. Hunching down, he moved with determined steps through the herd to the other side of the corral. He lifted the bucket out of the sack and placed it atop a fence post. He waited. No sound. No movement.

Next, Will moved slowly to the corral gate. Before he could get there, a space opened in the collection of the herd. In between animals, he could not be seen by anyone either in the barn or house. But out in the open, he was a stark figure to which an eye of a guard would be drawn to. He hesitated.

Just then, one of the horses sprang across the opening in front of the gate. The gelding bucked, flaying his rear legs and hooves in Will's direction. This, too, was another equine statement of anxiety, of distress at something out of the ordinary…an unknown human in the midst of the herd. Obviously, this animal didn't like it. He snorted as he kicked. It was loud. Will knelt and held still. The door to the house opened again. Will did not turn to look, almost afraid to do so. Down low in the midst of the herd, he should not be visible. But if they all moved away from him following their kicking compatriot, Will would be completely exposed as a piece of fruit in a frozen block that had begun to melt away. If he moved, he'd be seen. Will had to hope the horses stayed around him.

The horses around him settled. The door closed. Maybe the man watching just thought some mare had rebuffed the nocturnal attentions of a suitor. Will waited until all was again still. He moved to the gate and unlatched it.

A round, flat-back sorrel moved up to him. The animal must have been aware that the gate led to open ground. It made sense. Each of these horses would have daily been in corrals similar to this and known what a gate meant. While a horse's brain was not known to be the most robust of animals on the planet, Will knew that their capacity for memory could be very long standing—even better than humans, in some instances. Once abused, a horse would not forget the offending movement for a lifetime. Freedom was obviously a long-standing instinct in any horse. The sorrel nuzzled up against Will as if to ask what he was doing. Will had the gate almost completely open. On the spur of the moment, Will had a thought. The plan had been for Will to crawl back to the trench and then shoot the bucket. But he was about to change that. Will hoped Paris would see what he was doing and run with the new developments.

Will grabbed a handful of the sorrel's mane. He swung up onto the animal's back. Without a saddle there could have been an adverse reaction. The sorrel could have started to buck. The lack of bridle or even a halter would put Will at a loss to keep a hold of a horse out of control. But the sorrel held. The horse was facing open ground; Will gently squeezed its sides. The big animal needed little encouragement. It began to trot through the open gate and then broke into a canter. Several other horses began to follow.

Then, a shot rang out. Will flinched. Riding bareback, he hesitated to lean too far forward or to the side. Without stirrups or a saddle horn there was nothing to hold on to except the handful of mane. But the shot did not come from the house. Will heard the bucket crash back off the fence post clanging as it fell. Paris had watched and figured it out. Dale had been the one to fire the shot. The bucket banged and rolled, spooking the horses toward the gate. Soon, the entire herd was following Will's mount. Now at a gallop, Will rode out of range of any rancher rifle much quicker than had he crawled away from the corral. And the herd readily followed a leader. The changed plan had worked even better than the original.

Chapter Thirty-One

Spring 1878
Governor's Mansion, Carson City

The legs of his horse trembled from exhaustion. When Mike Shonsey stepped off his mount his own legs buckled. Only a strong grip of his saddle horn kept him from falling. His right knee had given way as the boot hit the ground. Nothing in his lower extremities felt stable. Veins now burned as blood began to flow into stretches that had not been supplied for hours.

Looking at his horse, he was surprised the animal remained upright. He had ridden most of the night. Thin wisps of smoke floated from the horse's body as its internal heat dissipated in the sharp morning air. His own seat was wet with sweat, yet everything that had not been touching the horse was cold as ice.

Still holding on to the saddle horn now with both hands, Shonsey looked at the residence before him. Set in draping sycamore trees, the white columned home had only recently been built for use by the sitting governor. Placed on a rise from street level, a pebbled walk rose from the hitching rail splitting manicured lawns on either side. It was not a large residence or even a large plot of property. But the front double doored entrance framed by two story columns gave suppliants a sense of importance. Obviously, he noted his own impression was exactly what the builder's intended.

Shonsey gingerly let go of the saddle horn. As a child taking its first steps, he still held on just a bit, making sure he had his balance. Convinced he would not collapse; he felt no small amount of accomplishment having ridden this far. The distance from the T.A. Ranch to Carson

City must have been close to fifty-five miles. Shonsey had stopped in Reno to change horses, but this mount had been ridden hard for almost forty miles. As soon as he finished talking to the governor, he would take his poor animal to the livery and make sure he got proper care. Time enough for that later.

Shonsey stepped to the walkway and looked up at the columns. Governor Amos W. Barber knew Shonsey, but that didn't guarantee an audience. He dusted off his clothes as best he could and walked over the graveled path. He knocked on the door. A Chinese servant answered asking him to state his business. Shonsey had spent hours in the saddle thinking of how this initial exchange should go. He'd spun imaginary conversations one after another trying to refine the approach. But no matter how many times he practiced his lines, they still sounded outlandish, unbelievable. He decided to be brutally blunt.

"I must see the governor immediately. He needs to take action right away, or fifty of his most ardent supporters and most of the largest landowners north of Reno are going to be massacred."

The Asian attendant did not react. Shonsey could not tell if the man was impressed or disbelieved every word. His facial expression gave no clue. He decided he had to press forward.

"Please tell the governor that Gentry MacDonald, the Nevada Attorney General, Reiker Johnson, the Nevada State Water Commissioner, Ron Tisdale, State Senator, Angus Ferguson and Carter McKinnon along with the majority of the Nevada Stock Growers Association are holed up at a ranch while two hundred men with rifles are laying siege. Do you have that? Almost sixty men are going to be murdered if the governor does not react right now!"

Shonsey's voice rose to the level of a shout by the time he had finished.

"Pi, who is that bellowing at the door?"

Shonsey recognized the voice. It was the governor himself. He walked up to the entrance standing at the side of the attendant to assess the minor commotion.

Barber was a short man, far less than six feet tall. Dressed informally due to the early hour, the governor wore a thick sweater with nothing around the collar. White Burnside whiskers rimmed a broad face with ruddy reddish skin peeking out in the spaces between nose and beard. It was not the face of an intellectual. Though his impression might be rooted in his prior interaction with the man, Shonsey saw this face as an image of someone who got things done. He had witnessed Barber carve through arguments and opinions amid the myriad of offerings set before him each day, and make decisions. Quick decisions. The man did not have trouble making a call. Probably a good trait for a politician in his position. You could not dwell on judgements you made. Shonsey thought it must be a required personality trait for any successful leader to arrive at an informed determination and not worry about future assessment. Barber looked at Shonsey, then place a hand on his attendant's shoulder.

"Pi, I'll take care of this. Please bring some coffee into my office. Mr. Shonsey, here, looks like he could use some."

Shonsey did not miss the fact that the governor had used his name.

"Thank you, Governor. You are absolutely right. A warm cup of coffee would be welcome. It has been a long night."

"Come, let's get closer to the fire. I thought I heard you say that Gentry MacDonald is involved in a siege. Did I hear that right?"

The pair walked into the home, moving into a room covered with carpets reaching almost to each wall. The space had an immediate sense of warmth, of confidence. A desk sat in one corner with two chairs opposite. But there were two other distinct sections to the room. A series of four high-backed chairs faced each other close to the fire, and there was a round table with low chairs circling it. Shonsey had the thought that in this one room the governor could preside at his desk, look at drawings on a conference table, or have a comfortable chat in front of the fire. He wondered where the governor would direct this conversation. The politician then moved to sit in one of the high-backed chairs closest to the fire and directed Shonsey to sit across from him. Shonsey welcomed what he took to be the more informal location of the three, also the warmest.

"Governor, I've ridden all night from the T.A. Ranch, north of Reno. I believe it's owned by Dr. William Harris who lives in Laramie, Wyoming."

"I know that ranch, it's run by Charles Ford is it not?"

"Yes, absolutely right. Charles is a member of the Stockgrowers Association."

"I've talked to Charlie many times. That ranch is one of the originals out on our range. It's an old established operation. And you said Reiker Johnson, along with Tisdale, are there, too?"

"That's not all. About fifteen ranchers led by Angus Ferguson and Carter McKinnon are there. Also pinned down with them are a collection of Texas men the Stockgrowers hired to police the range and put a stop to cattle rustling."

"I received word from MacDonald that the Stockgrowers had hired essentially gunmen to get after the rustlers. I am aware of the losses the ranchers have sustained from people stealing their cattle. You might know that I tried to have a law passed making it clear that unbranded calves belong to the ranch of the heifer who bore them. I had hoped to put a stop to the endless argument of who owns the unbranded cattle out on our open ranges."

"I know you tried, Governor. But it didn't pass. The Stockgrowers kept losing portions of their herds. So, they hired the range detectives."

Range War

Barber lifted his hand thumbs up off his lap and above his head.

"And I agree with the action they took. So, what's the problem? How in the hell did these men end up in some siege? If I understood your comments to Pi, you said there were two hundred guns shooting at them. How did this reach such a point?"

Shonsey hesitated. He instinctively knew his next comments would be critical. Either his words would convince the governor to call the President, or the siege would continue to whatever conclusion might be in store.

"Governor, the range detectives spent time scouting and came back with a report that there were several small, alleged homesteaders who were taking unbranded cattle. Investigation also was done which found that there were no formalized homesteads on land with existing grazing permits."

"So, the Stockgrowers took the position that these alleged homesteaders were there illegally, correct?"

"Exactly."

"Well, if the status of those homestead claims is accurate, then I'd agree. Go on."

Shonsey continued. "There were also reports that a gang called the Red Sash Group tried to steal stock. Members of that gang were caught in the act, chased, and one man hung on the spot."

"Cattle rustlers run that risk," said the governor.

"That, they do, but the range detectives also said that some of these nesters had been working with the Red Sash ring. The Stockgrowers met and decided that they finally had to take action. So, a group rode out to two of these minor spreads, released the stock which included unbranded mavericks, and ran off the people."

Barber leaned forward resting his elbows on his knees. "What do you mean 'ran them off'?"

"We gave them a chance to walk away and then set their homes on fire."

Barber sat back into his chair. He did not respond immediately. Then he looked at the blaze in the hearth to his right and returned his gaze to Shonsey.

"Don't like to hear about citizens having their homes burned."

"But, Governor, we checked on each of these folks. None had valid finalized homesteads. They had just arrived on the range, set up a shack, and started collecting cattle. They didn't have any stock when they arrived, but they had stock in their pens when we confronted them. How did that happen? They took that stock from the herds on the range. They stole them."

"I know the argument. I've had an earful from Angus Ferguson about how all the Stockgrowers are losing money. Between the drought last couple of years and the stealing of mavericks, he has pestered me several times about how many of the ranch owners might go under."

"And he's right, sir."

"But there has to be more to the story. How did two hundred guns collect to lay siege to the ranch owners?"

Shonsey tried not to look stunned at the governor's acumen to deduce the whole story had yet to be conveyed.

"Yes, you are right. As best as I can describe it, the range detectives had discovered a nester named Nate Crampion working unbranded stock about a week ago. They tried to stop him and there was a shootout. One of the detectives was killed. Ferguson ordered them back to Crampion's house for convincing evidence of rustling. When they arrived, the report was that there were unbranded cattle in a corral next to the home. A woman was present. They accused her of rustling and hung her."

"They hung a woman?"

Range War

"There had been reports that this lady who lived with Crampion had been involved both with rustling and prostitution which she was conducting from the abode."

"What about the man Crampion? Was he there?"

"No, but his was the first spread the group of detectives and ranch owners rode to. Ferguson said the real problem was Crampion. He's the one who had been working with the Red Sash Gang and enlisting other nesters to work with them, too. He had to be stopped."

"If there was evidence of wholesale rustling, then I agree something had to be done. The ranch owners have a right to protect their herds."

"Well, there was a gunfight at the Crampion house. Four or five men from the ranch owner's group were killed. Three occupants of the house were killed, including Crampion. But during the fight, another neighboring homesteader drove up in a wagon, saw the gunfight and hightailed it for Reno."

"And now, we've hit the crux. Leif Svensson collected a posse and lit out after the ranch owners."

"Right. And it's an amazing posse. At least two hundred men, and they've circled the T.A. Ranch and opened fire. It's a shootin' gallery. The ranch owners can't survive for long."

Barber stood and walked over toward his desk. Before he reached his seat, he stopped, turned, and moved back to the fire. He reached one hand across the hearth to the mantel. He stood motionless their absorbing the warmth coming from the blaze inside.

"I can't have citizens fighting citizens in large groups like this. The numbers you describe could almost form battalions in an army. Both of these battalions, as I've dubbed them, will undoubtedly claim the law is on their side. But this sounds like a military engagement in the war. Two hundred guns against fifty. Can't have fifty ranch owners gunned down."

Shonsey felt he was winning the argument.

"But I have no access to the army. I am a state governor. We have no state militia here in Nevada."

He felt the moment had arrived. It was time to make the final pitch.

"But, Governor, you could wire the president and ask him to call out the military from Fort Churchill."

"I could wire the president. He is a close personal friend. Harrison came to Nevada. He's one of the few presidents who have ever come west of the Mississippi. But Mike, if I do, I'll have to appease the townsfolk from Reno. The ranch owners might not like it, but if I get the president to intervene, I'm going to insist that the order include that the ranch owners along with their detectives stand trial for any killings or destruction of property. You tell me that the nesters did not have finalized homestead claims. But there will have to be more evidence to support any such allegation. If those homesteads were valid and the Stockgrowers ran those folks off, then they'll have to stand trial."

This caught Shonsey off guard. The ranch owners were undoubtedly still hunkered down under a hail of bullets. He had been charged to convince the governor to wire the president and call out the military. But no one talked about a cessation that included an arrest. Barber watched no doubt assessing his reaction. If he asked for the military intervention without consequence, it might look like the ranch owners were guilty. That might cause the governor to let events play out on the current path. Shonsey had seen the gunfire. He knew continued hostilities would only mean the death of all who remained in the T.A. compound.

"Where would they be tried?"

"State, court of course," answered the governor.

Shonsey knew the owners held strong influence with the judges throughout northern Nevada. Several were even members of the Stockgrowers Association themselves. In agreeing to legal oversight, Shonsey and his brethren would look like they believed in the righteousness of their cause. Trial would be a decent risk. A better risk than avoiding two hundred rifles.

"Agreed. Stop the battle. Let them stand trial. If their cause is just, they have nothing to worry about."

"Then, I'll wire President Harrison immediately."

Chapter Thirty-Two

Spring 1878
T.A. Ranch

Will's eyes burned. Despite the pre-dawn lack of sun, the lining around his eyes felt dry as a desert bone. It hurt to move his eyes in their sockets. The same thing used to happen during the war. It came from lack of sleep. He'd been up a good part of the previous night working to stampede the ranchers' horses. He closed his lids and forced his muscles to move the orbs underneath attempting to generate enough fluid for reasonable function. The exercise was only mildly successful.

"Can't sleep either?" The words came from Leif Svensson.

"Morning's coming."

Svensson scoffed. "Not a very good excuse. We all need sleep, even under these conditions."

Will moved closer to the fire. "Same could be said about you."

"That, it could."

"Anybody try to escape last night?"

Svensson shook his head in the negative.

"Not that I know about. I will have to talk to the men of the last watch when they get replaced and come in. But I did not hear any gunshots in the middle of the night. Not like the night before."

"The men on the north side did a good job staying awake and spotting those two trying to crawl their way out. Those men from the ranchers' group tried to leave even before we released the horses. If Dale is right, more might be inclined to try now that their horses are gone, and they've decided things have turned for the worse."

"Yes, their men did try to escape, but I still think our folks could have tried harder to apprehend them rather than simply shoot them down."

"The escapees were armed. Hard to question their actions when dealing with armed adversaries who have been shooting at you for two days."

"That's right. This will be the third day of this little adventure, won't it?"

Will took another sip of his coffee. "Not sure I'd call this an adventure. Too many have died."

"Suppose you're right. We've lost three, and we know that the other side has lost at least five, counting the two from the other night." Svensson stooped to pick up the coffee pot and started to fill his own cup.

"Please tell me Paris did not make the coffee."

Will smiled. "Nope. I did. Haven't see Paris yet. We'd probably have a mutiny if we let him make another pot of coffee. The men would revolt."

"All I know is that my throat gives thanks Paris is not the chef."

A serious mask descended on Will's face.

"More are going to die today if the boys are right, and the wagon shield gets delivered this morning."

"True," said Svensson. "But the hope is that most if not all of those men will be in the T.A. compound and not ours."

"If it's built the way the men described, and if we have enough dynamite, then it should bring things to a head."

"We should give the other side a chance to surrender."

"We probably should," agreed Will. "But we shouldn't give them much time to decide. Give them ten minutes at the most. Don't want them to have a chance to think of some special defense."

"Oh, I won't give them much time. I was thinking five minutes. And I'm not going to tell them what's coming."

"Be tough to hide the wagon. It's flat all the way to the horizon. Once they see the metal shielding, they'll know a push to the front door is coming. What they won't know is that the dynamite will lead the way."

"So be it. Let them know about the metal. But the dynamite will remain a secret until the first stick gets lofted over the sides. The metal is three sheets thick. Boys said the total is over one inch all the way around. They shot a buffalo rifle at the thing, and it barely dented the shield."

"Hope you're right. Also hope it's not too heavy to push."

Dale Paris strode up to the small gathering. "Early risers, are we?"

"Could say that," answered Svensson. "Might be the day should hold some special developments."

"Coffee made?"

"Yes, the coffee is made. Will put it together, so there is little likelihood of consumption."

As before, Will joined in poking a little fun at Paris. "That coffee could have caused more casualties than those Texans over on the other side."

"I think it did," added Svensson.

"You two can't get over one pot of coffee. Just can't let it go, can you?"

Both men smiled knowingly at each other.

Will refilled his cup. "We should talk about who should man the siege wagon."

"Agreed," said Svensson.

* * * * *

Soft morning rays had given way to relative warmth as the sun rose. A positive buzz circulated among the men who gathered around the siege wagon which had just arrived.

Working with what had originally been a simple buckboard wagon, the Reno blacksmith had erected four-foot metal walls inside the bed. A door on the rear panel allowed entry. Then came the most ingenious part of the quick design. There were a pair of folding panels attached to the front of the wagon that would swing out forward. Cutouts allowed the folding panels to cross over the tongue normally used to hitch the horses. As the concept was explained to Will: the idea was for the rig to be reversed, and men would grab hold of the tongue and push the wagon, its back end first, toward the intended target. The bullet-proof folding panels locked when extended out along to the side of the tongue, thus protecting those men pushing. The design was simple. Quick anchors had been used to erect the panels inside the bed. A series of leather hinges held the folding panels which would lock in the open position to protect the men pushing. There were additional small panels that slid down over the cut outs once the folding panels were extended. Once in place, those panels provided complete protection for those pushing the wagon.

Men experienced in the use of dynamite had been identified. Men who had the strongest and most accurate throws of rocks had been tested. The dynamite men would light the short fuses, and two throwers would heave the sticks at the targets.

The first set of objectives would be to the front where the ranch group had dug a pair of trenches. Those had to be cleared out. Men with the ranch owners had been stuck in those trenches unable to move back to the house for three days. If anyone stood in one of those trenches, they were immediately blasted by multiple guns. The men who had remained had to be cold, hungry, and miserable. But the worst was yet to come when the sticks of dynamite started to fly in their direction.

There was a single gap in the center of the front trench. The siege wagon would have to enter the compound, crossing over that gap. With only men to push it, the weighted rig would get stuck if they tried to maneuver it through one of the trenches. Once the guns were removed from the front trench, then sticks would be thrown out either side, taking out the barn and bunkhouse. After those buildings had been destroyed, the rig would push forward one last time toward the main home where most of the opposition was housed.

Instructions were given to those manning the perimeter. As soon as the explosions started, they were to be ready to fire at anyone who tried to exit away from the source of the dynamite. Everyone was to hold their positions until all the men in the compound were apprehended, or all three of the structures were demolished.

Noon was set as the time the siege wagon would begin to move forward. Men throughout the posse had reloaded their weapons and were beginning to fill the gaps of the perimeter. The early morning watch would normally be replaced at noon. But no one in the posse wanted to miss the fireworks. All two hundred guns were manned and ready.

* * * * *

"Captain, do we know what kind of situation we are going to find?"

Captain James Fisher did not verbally respond. He just shook his head in the negative.

Lieutenant Martin Connelly had ridden up from the rear of the column after being told by his captain to check on the soldiers trailing behind. After reporting that the column looked as fresh as could be expected after their ten-mile ride, he'd asked his additional question.

Without much of a response from his commanding officer, Connelly did not know if he should pursue the topic further. Just then, Fisher raised his gloved hand signaling a halt. His visual signal was followed by a verbal order.

"Troop, halt!" Lieutenant Connelly repeated the verbal order and the troop of one hundred mounted soldiers from the 6th Cavalry came to a stop.

"Lieutenant, order a dismount and have the men collect in a circle around my position."

The order was relayed, and the Lieutenant trotted back to the captain's side. Fisher had not taken his eyes off the prairie ahead. "Lieutenant, does that look like a ranch compound in the distance?"

Connelly took out his telescoping glass for a better look. "You are right, Captain. It is a compound. There looks like a series of wagons to the left, maybe a cook wagon and others for supplies. I also see some contraption that looks like a fortified wagon with metal sides."

The captain inquired, "Can you see men with weapons?"

"Hard to tell. I think there are signs of trenches on the near side, but I cannot see men down inside them," the lieutenant replied.

"We have to assume those trenches are manned with men who are armed. The good thing is that they will be looking at the compound."

"What are they doing?" the lieutenant questioned.

"We've been told that a posse of some two hundred men have surrounded that ranch compound full of wealthy landowners who apparently went on a raid to kill and run off some homesteaders they thought were rustling their cattle."

"What are we supposed to do?" the lieutenant questioned again.

"Stop the battle and take custody of the ranch owners."

"What are we to do with them?" Another question from the lieutenant.

"Escort them back to the fort and secure their persons until they can be brought to trial or obtain bail, whichever occurs first."

"How many men are we talking about?"

Captain Fisher looked at Connelly for the first time and did not attempt to hide his displeasure. He sighed heavily as he answered, "Our information is that there are at least fifty and maybe even as many as sixty men in that compound we will be responsible for."

"Begging your pardon sir, but our barracks brig holds no more than five prisoners. What are we going to do with fifty or sixty men?"

"I don't know, Lieutenant. That'll be something the major will have to figure out. I have orders to stop the siege and return with the prisoners."

"What if this posse decides to shoot at us?"

"Then, Lieutenant, we shoot back. Are the men collected?"

Connelly spun his horse and saw that the troop had formed a large u-shaped group behind its captain.

"Yes, sir. The men are in attendance."

Captain Fisher walked his horse to the center of the partial loop of men. When the captain arrived, troopers filled in around him to complete a full ring. Fisher began to move his mount in a small circle of his own as he spoke.

"Men, we are approaching a ranch compound which apparently has some two hundred members of a Reno posse laying siege to it. Inside that compound are some fifty men or more. We are charged with the duty to stop the siege and take custody of those fifty men, returning with all of them to the fort. Those are my orders, and I am here to see that they are carried out. I want the troop to ride at speed and fall into two lines, taking mounted positions outside the perimeter now set by the posse. I want you to draw your carbines out, place them at the rest with aim upward, but ready for use. I want us to look intimidating. But I do not want anyone, and I mean *anyone*, to open fire until I give the order, or I am shot. My intention is to ride into the middle of the compound between the opposing forces. There, I will tell all concerned that this troop is to take control of the situation by order of the President of the United States. If the opposing sides agree, then we collect the prisoners and start back. If either side shoots me, fire at will. Until then, remain ready for further orders. Any questions?"

No questions were posed.

"Mount up."

The troop mounted and returned to their dual side-by-side columns.

The captain motioned toward the compound.

"Forward, ho, at the gallop."

* * * * *

Men had climbed into the siege wagon. Six men had volunteered to push the rig into the compound grabbing the hitching tongue. Will stood next to Sheriff Svensson watching the preparations. He noticed movement off in the distance out of the corner of his eye. He turned to look and saw the flag, the United States flag. He'd seen that enough during the war. It was a cavalry unit. From his quick glance, it looked like an entire troop. That would be one hundred trained cavalry soldiers.

"Leif, we have company."

Svensson looked up in the direction of Will's gaze.

"What in blazes are they doing here?"

Just as he uttered the words, the two columns of soldiers split and started to encircle the posse's perimeter. Two riders came right at the compound. Both looked like officers. One stopped. The second slowed to a walk, pulled a handkerchief out, and stuck his saber through it. He held the obvious sign of truce as he walked his horse straight into the compound. The scene held everyone spellbound.

"I guess we are about to find out," said Will. "Appears to be a captain. That is a full complement of cavalry by the way. You are looking at one hundred trained soldiers now positioned around us."

In a loud commanding voice, the officer faced the main body of the posse standing around the siege wagon.

"My name is Captain James Fisher. I have orders from the President of the United States, Mr. Benjamin Harrison, to take control of this situation. All shooting will now cease. My orders further charge me to take custody of all those within this compound and deliver them to Fort Churchill."

Svensson walked forward to the front of the siege wagon.

"Deliver them for what?"

The captain spun his horse around to face the sheriff.

"Are you in charge here?"

"I am. My name is Leif Svensson, Sheriff of Reno. I have warrants for men in that compound, and this is a duly constituted posse charged to bring them to justice for murder."

"Sheriff, these men will be tried, but as an officer of the United States, I will be taking them into custody."

"What if we don't agree to come?" a man called from the house.

Will recognized the voice. The tinge of Scottish brogue gave the identification away. It was Angus Ferguson.

The captain spun his horse around to face Angus, standing in the doorway of the main house.

"Sir, that will not be an option. If need be, I am authorized to utilize this posse to secure the group into my custody. If you shoot at any of my soldiers, they will shoot back. From the looks of it, your opposition has something of a siege wagon and is preparing to press in for close combat."

"And that wagon will bring dynamite, Angus."

The captain was the next to speak. He started his comments looking in the direction of Svensson, who had just uttered the threat of dynamite. But he began turning, and when done, ended up facing Ferguson.

"I am charged to take custody. If these men submit to my authority, they will come out without any weapons. All men who submit will be under my protection. If any of the posse fires upon them, that person will be met with force from my troops."

There was a silence. Dale Paris arrived next to Will. He tapped Will on the arm.

"Was that a good idea to tell them about the dynamite? I thought we were going to let them find out about that with the first explosion."

Will shrugged. "Figure Svensson sees the army has surrounded us, same as our men who've surrounded Angus. If the army does take them into custody, maybe he thinks our mission is accomplished without any further loss of our men."

The captain then issued an invitation in his same resonant voice.

"Gentlemen, why don't the two of you approach me here, in this position, and I will give you more information. Maybe we can end this without any further bloodshed."

Svensson and Ferguson walked warily toward the captain. A conversation was held as they met. No one outside of the three leaders could hear what was taking place. It did not last long. Svensson began to walk back to Will and Paris.

Svensson took off his hat and wiped his brow with a forearm. Despite the modest spring temperature, Svensson had broken a sweat. Will had the thought that the circumstances were finally getting to him. He looked at Will.

"Captain Fisher says he is to transport the prisoners to Fort Churchill. That's the word he used—*prisoners*. They will be held there for trial."

"How are they going to get there? We've run off all their horses."

"I told him that. He says they'll have to walk."

"Oh, that'll be nice. All those high booted ranchers walking ten miles will give their feet sores, for sure." Paris could not contain his laughter at the image.

But for Will, there was more important considerations.

"Where are they going to be tried? Who will hold them until that is set?"

"I asked the same question. The captain says they will be held at the fort. The whole group will be bound and held until either they make bail—if that is offered—or trial takes place."

"The owners will make bail right away. Angus has already shown how that will happen."

"Not so sure," responded Svensson. "This time, we have evidence of their destruction and their murder of Nate Crampion. Jack Flagg saw their operation. That should be enough to deny bail and have them held in jail until trial."

Will was not altogether convinced. "Maybe. But are we talking a federal court or state court? If trial is to be held in state courts, those men have a lot of influence."

"I don't know the answer. I don't think the captain knows the answer either. He's just been charged with taking the group into custody."

Paris then interjected, "Where do things stand at this point?"

Svensson replaced his hat and looked at Paris.

"He's given Angus five minutes to make his decision."

Range War

Will shifted his feet. "Might be just as well that the cavalry takes custody Leif. Where were you going to house all those men anyway? Your jail can hold only about four or five, right?"

"Never thought I'd have to jail that many. Up to now, I thought it would be decided out here with bullets. But standing there talking to the captain, I had the same thought. Might be better for the army to take them. I sure don't have the facility or the manpower to hold a group that large."

At that point, the voice of Angus Ferguson rang out.

"We'll go with you, Captain. We are coming out unarmed."

Chapter Thirty-Three

Spring 1878
Carson City, Nevada

Will Toal stepped up from the road after looping his rein around the hitching rail. The leather sole of his dust covered boot landed on the dry wooden planks of the boardwalk. He took a deep breath. He was not looking forward to the conversation coming next. Four days had passed since the end of the siege at the T.A. Ranch. Those days were spent home with Beth and the children. A bed, home cooking, and family provided a wonderful salve to his emotional wounds. He'd plunged into work around the ranch catching up on things put on hold while he was up north. But all the work, all the time alone, only heightened thoughts of loss. These same thoughts plagued him as he left Georgia following the war. Ella's death dropped a bucket down a well of emotions he'd thought had been dry some time ago. The bottom of that well still carried fluid scars born with the loss of family, of his father's link to the clans of his grandfather's Scottish roots, and the loss of his mother and sibling. The thoughts would not cease. And now, word had reached Will that his dear friend, Samuel Grande, was representing one or more of the ranchers.

Will moved to the door. Every time he pulled on the swinging entrance in days passed, Will would play with the small bell Grande hung to announce anyone entering. But Will did not feel like games today. His mood was much darker. A man he considered one of his closest friends was representing ranchers who, as members of the Stockgrowers, were the originating cause of Ella's death. If so, it could be another loss, the loss of a good friend. He jerked the door open and stood in the doorway.

The bell sounded, but Will did not move fully into the small lobby. The door closed behind him, and he stood with his back in contact. Further movement led to a realm of unappealing unknowns. Beth had pushed Will to come see Sam. Will had not wanted to come. The combination of anger and betrayal hit hard. But Will and Sam Grande had been friends for a long time, and he knew the only way to get the real story was to confront Sam about what he'd heard. Further, Beth insisted that he should speak directly with Sam, as things might not be as they looked on the surface. Will knew she could be right. So, he rode into town to talk to Sam.

Grande's Asian law clerk was the first to respond. He came to the doorway of his own small cubicle space to see who had come in.

"Mr. Toal, I don't believe we have you on today's calendar of meetings."

"Warren, I need to see Sam. Is he in?"

"I'm here, but I'm busy. I've got a hearing tomorrow and need to prep for it."

"Is it a hearing to get one of those ranchers out of jail to avoid responsibility for the murder of my sister?"

Will knew his words were harsh. But the tenor with which they were uttered carried a hostile tone that could not be mistaken. Grande appeared in his door.

"Okay, we obviously need to talk. Come in. Do I need to ask you to leave your gun at the door?"

"Gun's not coming off."

Warren Fujimoto, Grande's clerk, visibly flinched at those words. He backed into his room slowly. Sam Grande moved toward Will. Will could see concern on Grande's face. Normally full of confidence, Grande conveyed non-verbal apprehension. But Will could not tell if the concern was for Will or Grande's own personal safety in the face of a clearly upset man carrying a gun.

"Will, we've known each other for a long time. I know what happened to Ella. I know what the arrival of a long-lost sister meant to you. I cannot come close to putting myself into your shoes to appreciate the sense of loss that you must feel because of her death. But I can tell you this, and I need to be clear. I would never represent any of those men who were involved with taking Ella's life. I rarely practice criminal law, and lately, it's only been to make sure you are clear from legal burdens arising out of your skirmishes in Virginia City, Glenbrook, and Tahoe City. But even if I was actively taking on criminal clients, I would not represent any of those men. I would not do that to you."

"I heard you were representing some of those ranchers."

"You know I do. You know I represent ranchers regarding business interests. And, yes, some of those clients belong to the Nevada Stockgrowers Association. I've told you about my efforts to clarify ownership interests in stock for some of these owners. And to make sure the whole truth is on the table, I have spoken with two of my clients who are now incarcerated at Fort Churchill. However—and you need to hear this clearly—while my representation of any client is privileged and confidential, I can tell you that my advice and representation has nothing to do with the criminal charges that have been set against them. My representation has to do solely with the transfer of their property interests should they be convicted and sent to prison for any period."

"I'm not sure I feel a whole lot better."

"Yes, you do. I've known you too long. You're upset about Ella. I understand that. But I'm not involved with that situation. Come, sit."

Will followed Grande into his office. Sam moved all the books away from his desktop. Will had never seen him do that before. Grande's office was a disorganized library of book stacks. Everything, including the floor, was covered with books. They were always more important to him than the conversation at hand. He took the clearing of his desk as a measure of Grande's concern with Will's issues.

"You need to hear some things. And while I might hesitate to do this in your present mood, there are things that need to be said. Please understand that I do this out of concern for you. I am worried about the outcome of any criminal proceedings and how you are going to react."

"How so?"

Grande slipped further into his high-backed chair. He stared at Will.

"Are you going to listen with that small part of your rational brain? Are you ready to hear some hard truths?"

"All truths are hard. I was on the losing side of the Civil War. Hard truth. I lost my family, hard truth. I've dealt with truth before. But I was also a Texas Ranger and rode down criminals who had shot people to make sure they faced the justice they deserved. That was hard truth. These men murdered my sister. So, what is it that you are concerned about when it comes to the hard truth? I'd say her death is another hard truth in my life. It was certainly a hard truth for Ella."

Grande waited to reply until Will was finished. As an experienced trial attorney, he had developed acute sensitivities to moods and emotions of witnesses at trial. And Will was, himself, on trial of sorts here. He just didn't know it.

"You are going to be disappointed. All those men now at Fort Churchill are not going to be convicted. I feel an obligation to tell you that because I don't want you to go off half-cocked and get yourself in trouble."

"I can't remember the last time I went off *half-cocked* as you call it." Will stared at him without blinking. "When I use a gun, I am usually forced."

"That may be true. But this is going to be different. I'm worried that the majority of those who have been arrested are going to walk. If you're this mad now, that reality will only make things worse. While I don't want to be the one to tell you, I figure I am the best one to do it. I'm the only one who might be able to keep you from infusing yourself in something I can't get you out of. I don't want to see you go to jail when it's some of those at Fort Churchill who should be there."

Puzzled, Will asked, "Why are you saying this? What is it you know that leads you to think these men will be set free?"

Grande sighed. He collected his thoughts. Will could tell he was weighing how to say what he thought he should.

"Sam, okay, I forgive you. I'm no longer mad at you. You have a practice to run and some of your clients run cattle on the open range north of Reno. I understand. But you're sittin' there trying to figure how to tell me something. Just spit it out."

"Based on my experience in the trial courts here in town and Reno, I had some doubts about how this whole arrest was going to work out, what the outcome was going to look like. After my trip to Fort Churchill, I think my concerns have been confirmed."

"And what are those concerns?"

"There are two aspects to what I'm going to say. There are two aspects to why I think most, if not all, those men are going to be set free. So that you hear it from me and not someone else, here are those reasons."

Will waited.

"One, all the defendants are to be tried in state court, not federal. The state courts in Reno are notoriously corrupt. The main defendants have significant—even undue—influence in those courts. Frankly, I'll be surprised if the majority of those at the fort are even prosecuted."

Will did his best to control his emotions and remained quiet. Grande took his silence as a cue and continued.

"Second, even if there is a trial, the law in this area is not black and white. It is completely gray. You and I have discussed the whole legal mess when talking about the grazing rights versus homestead claims. And sitting right in the middle of that inconclusive legal web is the additional lack of clarity when it comes to establishing ownership of unbranded cattle versus rustling."

"If you walk into a saloon anywhere in the West, every man inside could tell you exactly what rustling is. There is no real dispute."

"We are not dealing with saloon justice. We have progressed, for better or worse, to courtrooms and legal trials. A legal trial first begins with the law and then moves to evidence. Here, those ranch owners have a right to protect what's theirs. You would react much like they have if someone were stealing your horses or cattle. But in this state, you and I have discussed how the law itself is unclear when it comes to rustling versus taking mavericks. You and I have further discussed the law and how it poorly distinguishes between grazing rights and homestead rights. That will give any decent criminal attorney lots to work with. To make matters worse, there is very little evidence when it comes to the death of your sister. There were no witnesses. They have more when it comes to the death of Nate Crampion and his workers, but even there, the only eyewitness is Jack Flagg, and his view of things took place from a mile away. Anything he saw occurred in his haste to flee. While understandable, there is little likelihood his recollections are very specific such that he can identify the actual perpetrators."

"So, you think they will be found not guilty. Sam, they are guilty."

"*I* may know it. *You* may know it. But we are talking about a criminal trial where the standard of proof to convict is *beyond a reasonable doubt*. I have no hesitation saying that if I were to cross examine Jack

Flagg, I'd have him turned around in circles and I'd make his recollections look like the stuff of dreams. By the time I finished, Flagg's testimony would not come close to qualifying as beyond a reasonable doubt. And I'm not even a criminal lawyer. The jury will be hog tied by their instructions from the judge. There is just too much gray, Will."

"Gray. It's the shade of all things bad that have followed me since I donned a uniform of that color during the war. Sam, the law may be gray, but right and wrong are simple black and white."

This time, it was Sam who held his counsel.

"So, you and Sandra coming to dinner this Sunday?"

"When we started our little talk today, I wasn't so sure I'd live to see her tonight, much less come to dinner. But, yes, we will definitely come to dinner."

* * * * *

Will stepped off the boardwalk in front of Grande's office. He looked up. The sky was covered with thick, low-hanging clouds. A damp cold did its best to pierce his jacket and scarf. He stood looking at the billowed shroud blocking the clarity of the sun's rays.

Gray.

The color matched his mood. The color matched the demons that never ceased to nip at his history's heels.

Chapter Thirty-Four

Spring 1878
Reno, Nevada

The afternoon winds had long since started their daily blow down the Sierras heading east. The gusts would die in the desert when the cool air finally warmed to settle with like temperatures amid the cactus. Small whirlwinds spun off the edges of buildings along the boardwalk lifting dust and light particles skyward only to drop everything raised when the power of the twister petered out. No one was out on the street. Reno looked like a ghost town. Shops were closed. Even the saloons were closed. Will sat outside the city jail, resting on the boardwalk with the back of his chair leaned against the jail's front wall. He was alone.

Everyone had moved to the outskirts of town attending the first and only open aired courtroom. There was not a building in town that could house a hearing with fifty-eight defendants. No other alternative could be identified, so outside it was. The hearing was set to decide whether any of those fifty-eight men would be bound over on the charges in the indictment.

After arriving in the late afternoon of the day before the trial, Will and Beth stayed at Dale Paris's home overnight. Beth had said she wanted to accompany Will. Back home, she had voiced her concerns for her husband. She pointed out his history of confrontations.

"Maybe this time," Beth said, "I can keep you from getting shot at if I come along."

Will was not enthusiastic about the idea of Beth coming, but there were times she would not be deterred. This was one of them. He told himself he must come and see the hearing. But after he got here, his motivation waned. Sam Grande had veritably killed his hopes for proper justice. At dinner last night with Svensson and Paris, Will mentioned he was having second thoughts about attending the hearing. Svensson asked that if Will was not going to go, would he keep an eye on the jail as Svensson testified? Though the original plan was for Beth and him to attend the hearing, Will agreed. However, he'd asked Beth to stay at Dale's house out of fear there might be trouble.

Will reveled in the quiet. A peace blanketed the town. It wouldn't last. No matter which way the judge ruled on the indictment, the city's normal chaos would return. In fact, if the judge ruled in favor of the ranch owners, there might be trouble. Svensson expressed his unease of such a possibility the night before. Multiple groups of citizens had voiced outrage at the killing of Ella. People wanted simple justice. But Will had heard Grande explain the reality of the legal technicalities. As a result, the only surprise Will anticipated would be if the ranch owners were bound for trial. Though Will was prepared for the judge to set them free, the townspeople might not take kindly to any nuanced result of the legal process.

Dale Paris walked up Will's side of the street. He stopped next to Will's leaning chair.

"Not going well."

"I told you what Grande said would happen last night at dinner. I didn't like to hear his prediction, either. But the more I thought about it, the fewer arguments I could come up with to dispute it. That's why I didn't want to go. I didn't want to see it. Somehow, I hope to keep a more distanced appraisal, one that rests on simpler concepts of right and wrong."

"Understood. It was disgusting the way the defendant's attorney treated the sheriff. Pointed out one critical missing point after the next. By the time the attorney finished with Leif, the sheriff looked like he had pulled his indictment and arrests out of the air for no reason and without any support at all."

"Grande said it would be easy. Same would happen with Jack Flagg if they ever got to trial."

At that moment, several boys came running up the road as youthful heralds screaming news, oblivious to the fact there was no one to hear.

"Judge let them go! The ranchers are free!"

The line was repeated time after time as they ran beyond the jail. A large crowd could be seen forming to Will's right coming from the direction of the trial's location. Sheriff Svensson strode down the middle of the street a good distance in front of the crowd. He looked up at Paris and Will. Concern written all over his face, he hurried away from the group following.

"Svensson, looking to run away from what you've done?"

It was Angus Ferguson. He was at the head of the large group coming up the street. There was a line of men on either side of him. Carter McKinnon was there, too. Beside those two were a collection of men Will did not recognize. A flash thought hit that after the shootouts at Nate Crampion's and the T.A. Ranch, they were probably what was left of the Texas gunmen. Will could not see any of the other wealthy ranchers. But Frank Canton was on the other side of Ferguson.

"Your time is done, Svensson. You've bungled your last arrest. This town cannot continue to ignore your incompetence."

The arrogance with which Angus made the comment rankled Will.

Svensson twisted his upper body left to face his accuser. As he did, his right arm swung upward from behind his back over the top of his holstered gun. His hand came close to the gun itself, but to anyone watching it was clear the sheriff turned without intent to take hold of the grip. Svensson was about to speak when a shot echoed up the street. Smoke rose from a six shooter in the hand of Frank Canton.

"He was going to draw. You saw it."

Svensson spun, dropped, and hit the dirt hard. He rolled at least once. In another of those battlefield instant judgments, Will knew the man was not dead. At least, not yet.

Paris had his gun out, aimed and fired at Canton. But the round hit one of Canton's men standing next to him. Canton had backed up and headed for an alley on the opposite side of the street from Will and Paris. Will drew just as five of the Texans were doing the same. Will got off two quick shots and both men he'd aimed at clutched their midsections and sank to the ground. One of the men struck dropped his gun, which went off as it hit the dirt. The released weapon discharged and hit Angus. Ferguson screamed and grabbed his lower leg, then collapsed after being hit by the wayward shot.

People who had been following the leaders in the crowd started scattering. Screams and shouts came from all sorts in that group. Two of the Texans fired at Dale. But they were moving at the same time to avoid shots coming from both Will and Paris. For some reason, both men missed Dale with their initial shots. One ran to a store to the right of Paris's position, kicked the door open and leaped inside. Paris pulled his hammer back and sent two more shots in the man's direction as he disappeared through the door.

Will had jumped down into the street heading across toward the alley to follow Canton. The only Texan left in the street had aimed to fire at Dale, but hesitated as Will started across the dirt roadway. The man turned away from Paris to look back at this second opposing assailant just as Will strode straight at him. It was if he could not determine whether to shoot at Dale or Will. Will already had his gun arm extended and aimed directly at the Texan. The Texan's hesitation was fatal. Before the man could thumb his hammer, Will fired and hit him right in

Range War

the middle of his forehead. The man dropped in a heap with a small red dot marking his demise.

"Dale, you take care of the man who went into the shop. I'll go after Canton."

"Agreed."

Will stooped down to check on Svensson as he got to the center of the street. The sheriff was on his side, and Will gently rolled him onto his back. Svensson was alive and conscious. Blood oozed from his upper right shoulder.

"Hold on, Sheriff. I'll get help."

"I'm okay, go do what you have to do. Don't worry about me."

Will looked down the street in the direction of where the main crowd had been. People were pinned against store walls and lying flat, anything to avoid flying bullets. Will could not let Canton get away. But Svensson needed help.

"Someone get a doctor. The sheriff is alive. Help him to a doc."

One or two men sheepishly began walking toward the scene.

"Sheriff, there are people coming to help you. I'm going after Canton. He started this, but he won't be alive to see the end if I can get him."

"Go, Will. Get him."

Will moved out of his crouch starting to run in the direction of the alley. His route took him by the writhing body of Ferguson. As he rolled around in the dirt Angus saw Will approach. The rancher fumbled to reach for his holstered gun. Will got to his side first and kicked the gun out of his hand. He then quickly knelt next to the fellow Scot. He stuck his gun right at Angus's forehead.

"Ferguson, I have one bullet left in this magazine. It's got your name on it. Say one more word, and you will pay for the death of my sister right here in the middle of a dirt road."

Angus winced, but then snarled, his face twisted by both anger and pain.

"You haven't got the right to be a ranch owner. You haven't got the guts to do what's needed."

"Angus, you may have guts, but your lack of values has warped your brain. Despite what happened outside of town at that hearing, you are not the law. *You are not the law.* This is for my sister."

"Will, no! Don't do it!"

Will looked up and saw Beth running toward Angus and him.

"Will, you can't just kill him in cold blood," she said as she neared.

"That's exactly what he deserves."

Beth reached Will's side and held his arm at the elbow. It was not a touch of resistance, it was a touch of understanding. That contact brought him back from the brink of an action he'd later regret. Angry though he was, he leaned forward toward the prone Ferguson.

"You're lucky my wife is here. But you cannot escape the day without consequence."

In a lightning movement, Will stretched his right hand across his body and swung it as it to backhand Angus. But Will had hold of his gun in the same hand. He made sure it crashed into the right side of the prone man's skull. Will heard bones crack. Angus moaned and rolled completely on his back. Will stood motionless for a moment as if to make sure Ferguson would not move.

"He won't die, but that might last long enough to keep him from doing anything shameful for a while."

Will looked at Beth with a softened gaze. "I don't think I'd have shot him, but having you arrive here brought me out of the depths just in time to make sure. But this is not done. Beth, you have to be careful. Here, take Angus's gun and keep an eye on him."

People had begun to congregate around the stricken Svensson who lay not far from Ferguson. Will waved his hand at the approaching people as he spoke to Beth.

"Let those folks help you get the sheriff and Ferguson off the street. I have to find Canton. He can't get away."

With that, Will jumped forward, heading to the alley.

As he ran, Will lifted his gun upright, opened the magazine and spun it around to empty the spent casings. He began to fill the empty spaces with new cartridges pulled from his belt. He finished reloading as he reached the back of the buildings at the end of the alley. He stopped. Without knowing which way Canton had taken, he had to be careful. He took off his hat and put it on the end of a stick lying close at hand on the ground. Still standing inside the spread of the alley's end, Will extended his hand slowly beyond the back edge of the building. A shot immediately blew the hat off the stick. It came from the left. Direction determined.

Will reached around the corner angling his gun a bit downward. From the way his hat flew off, lifting upward, Will guessed Canton positioned himself down low behind something. Just a guess. He pulled off one shot to get Canton's attention and raced around the back of the building heading toward the direction of Canton's shot. He was now exposed. However, he hoped the first shot around the corner had forced Canton to take cover and give Will time to get a view. He fired another shot again, simply to try and keep Canton on the defensive, if only for a moment. A hand rose above a low-lying wooden bin attached to the back of the building. Canton fired blindly from the other side. *Two shots from a full magazine in Canton's hand,* thought Will. *Each had four shots left.*

A small porch with covered overhang had been built leading out of the back of the same structure. Canton was behind a low bin several feet to the other side of this same porch. Thick supports lined the side of the opening running from the floor to roof. Will flattened his body against the wall using the supports as cover. He was higher than Canton, who he could see lying prone behind the wooden bin. Will could not see the man's head, but as he was standing above the prone Canton, he could see his boots.

Will aimed and fired, hitting the backside of Canton's right foot. He screamed in pain and rolled away from the building, then spun over, but remained prone. Now out in the open, his angle at Will was no longer blocked by the porch supports. Canton ended his roll and spin coming to a stop on his stomach. His right arm was extended as he held his gun aimed at Will. Will dove to his right in a controlled tumble over his right shoulder. He, too, was now fully exposed. Canton fired, hitting the wall where Will had just been standing. Canton fired a second time, anticipating that Will would roll only once. But Will rolled twice, coming up to his knee. He lifted his gun and fired right at Canton's face.

It took only a matter of seconds for both sets of fire to be exchanged. Will's bullet must have passed through the man's jaw as Canton did not drop his gun but tried to get off another round. The shot missed Will, who stood and fired two more rounds at Canton in quick succession. The gun dropped out of the man's hand and his body went limp.

Will walked over to the inert form. He had one shot left and kept his aim focused on Canton. Still no movement. Will used his foot to lift Canton over on to his back. The man's face was a mass of blood and exposed bone. His eyes were closed. Will bent down to touch his neck checking for a pulse. There was none.

"Did you get him?" Paris rounded the back of the building from the alley Will had used.

"He's dead," said Will.

Paris came forward until he was standing next to Will. "Good riddance. Won't need any trial for this murderer. Right and wrong came down simple for him." The tone did not carry a sound of satisfaction, but it definitely carried a subdued, but distinct, sound of righteousness.

Will then asked, "What happened to the Texan that ran into the building."

"He ran straight through the building and in a stroke of luck found a saddled horse on the other side. He took off before I could get a shot."

"So, one of the gunmen got away."

"But five of the six men who walked up the street with Ferguson are dead. Canton's dead. Not sure Angus has much of his Range Detective force left."

"They'll just hire more men, Dale. If people keep taking cattle, then the battle will continue until the law catches up with the reality out there on the range."

"Probably right. Not a pleasant picture for the future."

Will shifted the topic. "How's the sheriff doing?"

"People said they took him off to the doc. Let's go see."

* * * * *

Will and Paris walked into the saloon. Sheriff Svensson had been stretched out on a faro table. His shoulder was wrapped in white bandages. The hand on his uninjured arm was held by Beth. Both turned to look at Will and Paris as they entered through the bat-winged doors.

"Toal, you have a wonderful woman, here. She has filled me in as to what happened before you two left the street. So, tell me, where do things stand now?"

Paris looked at Will. Will took it to mean he should do the talking.

"Five Texas gunmen are dead. One got lucky and ran off with a stolen horse. Angus is hurt, and last I saw him he was out in the street. He'd been hit in the leg. He tried to pull a gun on me, and I was about to fill him with what he deserved. Beth, here, arrived and convinced me not to do it. But I'll confess that I struck him in the face."

"Should have shot him," said the sheriff.

"He's in pretty bad shape, but I would guess he's alive," said Will.

"Oh, he's alive," replied Svensson. "Beth has given me an update on our wonderful Mr. Ferguson. She was with the folks who lifted Angus from the street. The doc did what he could for me and then some of the ranch owners came and took him over to the Stockgrowers building to look at Angus. That old miscreant won't die."

"Lot went on here, Sheriff. Based on how things go, I suppose they will want to see me arrested and a date set for arraignment." Will sat on the side of the table as he spoke.

Svensson smiled.

"You're in luck. I survived, and I'm still sheriff. I am going to sign an affidavit to the effect that Canton started all this and that you bear no fault. I will not be filing any warrants or indictments for either you or Dale."

"What if Angus pushes for one?"

"Still has to come through me. As far as I'm concerned, there is no issue. Take your lovely bride and go home."

Will reached out to shake Svensson's good hand.

"Sheriff, wish all lawmen hereabouts would have the heart and soul you do."

* * * * *

Outside the saloon, Paris turned to Will.

"Have to say thanks for backing me there when Canton opened fire."

"You backed the sheriff. I just came in late."

"Either way, glad you were there."

"Dale, I'm going home just like the sheriff ordered. You take care of yourself. And next time you think of getting me involved in one of your investigations, think twice." Will smiled and grabbed Beth's hand as he turned to go.

Chapter Thirty-Five

Spring 1878
Toal Ranch, Jack's Valley, Nevada

Both hosts and guests sat facing each other, having pushed back from the dinner table. Cloth napkins sat on top of the empty plates as evidence the meal was done.

"Beth, once again you have outdone yourself. That was a wonderful dinner. It is a true joy to come here every Sunday for your outstanding cooking. You are a most gracious hostess."

"And the host?" inquired Will. "I note that you completely omitted any reference to the host."

"That was absolutely intentional. The last time I saw you, I thought I was going to be shot."

Will smirked. "Maybe I should have."

"And you would have lost the only rational brain other than your lovely bride to have the most minimal hope of reaching you with logical advice."

"I took your advice to heart. I didn't even go to the arraignment hearing for those fifty-eight defendants."

"Based on the commotion you got involved in after the hearing concluded, I would say it was a Godsend you were not present. No telling what havoc you could have wreaked had you been at the hearing itself."

"I did everything I could to stay out of the fray. Only stepped in when they shot the sheriff in cold blood."

Grande waved his hand across the table in front of him as an overly dramatic move in keeping with the lighthearted banter.

"And I understand only five people died once they sought your opinion." Playful sarcasm left no doubt that the verbal jousting was not serious.

"Opinion with bullets. Be difficult to hold a rational discussion with someone shooting at you." Beth now entered the verbal fray wagging a maternal finger at Grande.

"Thank you, dear. Nice to have my wife cover my back. Our guest never seems to appreciate the nature of the danger presented. I have been cleared by local authorities of any wrongdoing. But there still may be a hearing. I was going to ask our guest to represent me, but he never seems to have my interests foremost."

"Oh, when you entered my office last week ready to gun me down, you didn't want me to practice any criminal law. Now that you might be in trouble again, you need a good lawyer."

"Who said you were a good lawyer?" Will made sure a wide grin spread across his face.

"And you would put yourself at risk of prison with a bad lawyer?"

"I just figured I'd have to take my chances with some local small-time counsel from here in Carson City, as all those high-priced lawyers in Reno are probably connected to the Stockgrowers Association."

"High-priced lawyers. Shoot. There isn't a lawyer in Reno who could keep up with me in a courtroom."

"Okay, you two—time to quit." Sandra Grande reached out to touch the elbow of her husband.

Grande glanced at Sandra, who gave him a stern look.

"My wife is right. I should be much more sensitive to your loss Will. The men who perpetrated the killings probably got their just due. While the legal system was unable to handle the situation satisfactorily, the common man with community support finds a way to handle things we in the legal society could not. And Will, again, I offer my condolences for the loss of your sister."

Will smiled. "I told you, life has its right and wrong. It just takes someone of much more simple means to apply them. And by the way, you have beaten those Reno lawyers time and time again. You will always be my first and only stop for advice."

"Remind me never to take you to court. If you apply your simple methodology to most of the judges sitting in our local courtrooms, you might feel obligated to use your method resulting in gun smoke."

"I will make it a point to avoid courtrooms at all costs. I leave them to you."

"Speaking of courtrooms, we should be heading home. I have appearances lined up all morning tomorrow to do battle with our learned bench of jurists. Thanks to both of you again for dinner. We really relish coming out to relax and enjoy."

Sandra added, "I would offer my thanks too, Beth. It is such a pleasure to not have to cook one night."

* * * * *

Beth held Will's elbow as the pair stood in their doorway to wave goodbye to their guests.

"They are a perfect pair. And despite your banter, he's your best conscience—and you know it."

"Oh, I do. But I'm not sure I'll ever admit it to him. Keeps him on his toes to think I have doubts."

"The system he works in often seems a legal morass."

"Yep, as he called it 'one big gray area'. But as I told Sam, in life and outside of courtrooms, it is much simpler. There is right and wrong. It's not hard to figure it, either. The ranch owners should hold more frequent roundups and include all those with valid homestead claims. Then, they could establish a positive communal effort that would work for all. The government should have sections for grazing and sections for homesteading. Having both on the same ground is just asking for trouble. But shooting folks and running them off their land is not right. Still, if someone is caught with a straight iron changing brands, then I have no problem with justice being administered."

Beth leaned her head into Will's shoulder. "I like things that are simple."

"Where are the kids?"

"Off with Juan and Maria over at their place where they always are on Sunday evenings."

Will swept Beth up in his arms. "Well, how about some simple contact and communication here at home?"

"Be careful, cowboy. You might get more than you bargained for."

"Not possible, darlin'. Not possible."

Fact From Fiction

If you have read any of the other books in this series, you'll know of my admiration of author Steve Berry. His stories usually have an interesting foundation in some historical mystery or unsolved question. He then weaves his own story around that history. But at the end, he includes a section outlining the history which undoubtedly drew him to the story in the first place. So, here is another of my humble attempts to emulate Mr. Berry. Below I try to identify some of the historical facts that drew me to my story.

Chapter 2

The informed westerner will quickly notice that my fictional story draws heavily from real historical events and participants of the Johnson County Range War. That war between established large ranchers and small homesteading stock growing operations took place in Wyoming from 1889-1893. The character Nate "Crampion" is a short-change from one of the main victims in the real events named Nate "Champion". Ella Toal is a stand in for the historical lady named Ella Watson. Essentially, I have lifted several historical events that occurred in Wyoming and transferred both those and some of the people involved to Nevada for purposes of my story here. I will identify more of the historical facts and personages below to follow along in the chapters where the story develops.

The Open Range was a fact of western life and the raising of stock to feed the eastern population. From Texas to California, the western states were all confronted by rampant cattle rustling. For a thorough and extremely well-researched book on the impact and legal consequences of rustling activity, see the book *Calling the Brands— Stock Detectives in the Wild West* by Monty McCord. Twodot Publishers, 2018. Mr. McCord does a wonderful job of describing the various methods of altering brands, rampant mavericking, and thievery of stock. He also includes several chapters identifying the lawmen, detectives, regulators, and gunmen who became involved. Not all the activity undertaken by the stock growers fits glowingly into the romantic image of the West.

In 1830, original residents of Mexico had abandoned an estimated three hundred thousand head of cattle in Texas alone. By 1860, that number had risen to three million head. The Republic of Texas declared any unbranded stock on open land as "public property", subject to be taken by anyone for branding. It doesn't take much to foresee the problems that ultimately became known as "range wars". See *Calling the Brands*, p. 11-13.

The term "maverick" refers to unbranded cattle, normally newborns still suckling and attended by heifers. While there is some dispute as to the origin of the term, general consensus finds the term originating with Samuel Augustus Maverick, a Texas land baron who was one of the original signers of the Texas Declaration of Independence. While a successful lawyer and owner of vast tracks of land, he was a terrible rancher. While other ranchers branded their stock, Maverick refused to do so with his. Cattle roamed across land near and far from his ranch, but he claimed them often with some success as they were 'unbranded and thus Maverick's'. The term stuck in Texas ranching circles and beyond. Ultimately the term found its way into legal jargon and even legislation. See Marks, Paula Mitchell *Turn Your Eyes Toward Texas: Pioneer Sam and Mary Maverick*, Centennial Series of the Association of Former Students, Texas A&M University Press (1889), p. 81.

There was, indeed, a Wyoming Stock Growers Association, originally headed by the governor of Wyoming. It was formed in 1871. See *Calling the Brands*, p. 47-49. There was no such group as the Nevada

Stock Growers Association at the time of our story here. However, the Nevada Cattlemen's Association was formed in 1935. See *Calling the Brands* p. 41.

For a biographical description of some of the "lawmen" hired by the Wyoming Stock Growers Association to "root out" grangers and nesters that participated in the Johnson County War, again see Mr. McCord's description of W.C. "Billy" Lykens, Nathaniel K. Boswell, and Ben N. Morrison. *Calling the Brands* p. 74-81.

Chapter 4

If you have read the previous books in this series, you know that I have already used the name Millard Luce as a thinly disguised play on the Miller Lux Cattle Company. Henry Miller was a meat processor by trade from Germany who traveled over the Panama Isthmus from New York, to land in San Francisco. He started as a butcher's apprentice. He ended up quickly buying the business. He noticed the need for beef in the growing San Francisco city and began buying up cattle property within easy reach. The interests expanded, and by the end of his life, Henry Miller and the Miller Lux Cattle Co. owned over a million acres of ranch land and was responsible for quality land management, reservoir construction, and administration of extensive ranch operations from Oregon to Bakersfield. See *"The Cattle King"* by Edward F. Treadwell. The Carson Valley Cattlemen's Association and their collective to sell beef through the Millard Luce "network" is complete fiction of my own creation.

Ella Toal is a thin disguise for Ella (Ellen Liddy) Watson sometimes known as "Cattle Kate". Ms. Watson and James Averell moved west into Johnson County, Wyoming, much as did the Ella Toal and Nate Crampion of the story here. They tried to start a general store and small ranching operation but met with serious confrontation with the larger ranch owners. It is questionable whether Ella and Averell were married. Some accounts say they were, some not. Averell had a checkered history that some said included minor rustling. But that history was written mostly from the large ranch owner's vantage. Later accounts of another historian document the fact that Averell ran a dry goods store along the Sweetwater River and doubled as a postmaster, justice of the peace, and notary public. Ella joined him to run cattle after leaving an abusive husband back east while still in her 20's.

The real Ella Watson and her dress with bonnet.

Chapter 5

The Red Sash Gang is an interesting historical question. Some say that they were real. Some say they were only an imaginary figment of the powerful Wyoming Stock Growers Association germinated solely to spark justification for the employment of "range detectives" to run off small ranchers. The red sash was also said to have been worn by the "Cowboys" of Tombstone fame and confrontation with the Earp brothers. However, some even question whether they wore the sash. I will leave the decision on this historical reality to those more experienced in this nuance of the old west. However, I have chosen to fit their alleged existence into my story—one of the benefits in writing novels rather than non-fiction.

The wearing of a sash instead of a belt began with the Mexican vaquero. It was part of the vaquero's standard outfit. Often a sash was worn not only to hold up one's trousers, but to carry multiple different items. In fact, some references say that Wild Bill Hickock wore a sash instead of a gun belt for part of his storied history as a gunfighter. He set up his guns for a cross-handed draw out of the sash, not holsters. However, there are many pictures of William Hickock and none of them that I've ever seen show him in a sash.

Chapter 10

Frank Canton was real. Ultimately, he was the leader if not the instigator of the most aggressive steps taken against homesteaders in the Johnson County War. See more on his history below under Chapter 12.

During the Johnson County Range War, ranch owners, journalists, and state legislators such as Ronald Tisdale and Attorney General Gentry MacDonald did ride with those who pursued the homesteaders. While more on that below, both Tisdale and MacDonald were true historical figures who, both as ranchers and formal officials, played a part in what eventually took place.

Chapter 11

There was an open range in Nevada generally placed as in the story. Washoe County runs north from the Truckee River along the eastern base of the Sierras all the way to Oregon. Some have estimated that, in the late 1800's, there could have been as much as four million acres of open range.

Grande's law clerk, Warren Fujimoto, says that he is American because he was born in a US Territory. However, Hawaii was independently ruled by the royal lineage of King Kamehameha until it became a US "Protectorate" under suspect authority in 1893. Formal "annexation" did not occur until 1897 and full statehood did not happen until 1959. The "real" Warren Fujimoto, who rose from law clerk to partner in my old law firm, was definitely born into a Japanese family but a full American citizen.

The status of conflict between a rancher's range right and a Homestead Claim as of 1862-1890 was fairly described by Sam Grande in the story. In a fascinating, tremendously well researched Law Review Article entitled *Private Provision of Law* from the Texas A & M School of Law, a writer described the problem of identifying maverick cattle during that era as:

". . . the most confused, embittered, explosive question ever to bedevil the cattle range."

That same article confirms that the Wyoming Maverick Act defined a maverick as "all neat cattle, regardless of age, found running at large in this territory without a mother, and upon which there is no brand." The article goes on to confirm the Texas custom that a maverick was "public property." However, according to the author, the underlying reason for the conflict between rancher and homesteader stemmed from the fundamental disparity of property rights. It was indisputable that the ranchers "had no means to secure property rights in the range." It was public land. Whereas, if a homesteader perfected his or her claim, they owned the property in fee. Yet, the large ranch owners had money and political clout which also led to an aberration of jury verdicts which routinely failed to hold overly aggressive ranch owners accountable. See *Miners,*

Vigilantes & Cattlemen: Overcoming Free Rider Problems in the Private Provision of Law. Texas A & M School of Law 33 Land & Water L. Rev 581, pp. 638-676, by Andrew P. Morris.

Ranchers could only secure a license to use the range. But cattle needed a wide-open area upon which to feed. However, the Homestead Act gave any random individual the right to claim a quarter-section of that land, even if it fell within a grazing area. The conflict was not fully resolved until the Taylor Grazing Act was passed by the Federal Government during the Roosevelt Administration in 1934. It took that long to address the problem. In the Act, some 59 districts made up of one hundred sixty-eight million acres of land was set aside for grazing and exempt from homestead rights. The Taylor Grazing Act would later be completely superseded by Subchapter IV of the Federal Lands Policy and Management Act of 1976. In that legislation, the Homestead Act was officially terminated. See *The Old West in Fact and Film: History Versus Hollywood*. McFarland: 1st edition (2012) p. 40, by Jeremy Agnew.

However, the conflict between rancher, rustler and homesteader continued until then. In fact, many have pointed to a rebirth of rustling, even in the present day.

Chapter 12

As mentioned above, Frank Canton was a real range detective. His history is as described in the chapter. Canton was a significant player in the Johnson County Range War. Hired by the Wyoming Stock Growers Association, he brought 23 men from Texas to carry out marching orders to clear the range. He was ruthless in how he discharged that duty. He negotiated an insurance policy in the amount of three thousand dollars per man be taken out on each of his hired attendants. As in the story, there was also a "bonus" to be paid of fifty dollars for every rustler killed. This bonus led to several suspicious accusations of malfeasance stemming from executions for which compensation was sought. See *Johnson County War*, Wyoming Tales and Trails.

As for assessment of the man himself, Frank Canton was said to be a "merciless, congenital, emotionless killer" who had killed 8-10 men. *Wyoming's Wild Past,* Occidental Wyoming. Retrieved April 3, 2015. More on Frank Canton's activities in the Johnson County War below.

Picture of Frank Canton

Chapter 17

As mentioned above, Ella Toal is a name thinly disguised from the true historical person, Ella Watson. While many might find the storyline in the book overly gruesome, this unfortunate act of Ella's death is historical. Though there is some question as to whether Ella Watson was married to James Averell, they lived together in Johnson County, Wyoming, during the range war. Averell did not own cattle, but Ella 'dabbled' with ranching. A range detective working for the Wyoming Stock Growers Association accused Ella of rustling. In retaliation, cattlemen from the area were sent out and they captured both Ella and Jim Averell on their homestead. Both were hung in front of their house on or about July 20, 1889. See *The Old West in Fact and Film: History Versus Hollywood* by Jeremy Agnew. McFarland; 1st edition (2012), p. 40.

After the event, and maybe in response to the general groundswell of local disapproval, claims were made that Ella was a prostitute. However, later investigation showed otherwise. Averell had held himself out to be something of a journalist and went to some lengths to document the harassment and questionable legal tactics of the Wyoming Stockgrowers Association. As a result, he became a target to be removed.

As mentioned, local townsfolk and especially the small ranchers and growers were outraged at Ella's death. This just did not happen to women. Her death became one of the lightning rods leading to the formation of the Northern Wyoming Farmers and Stock Growers Association. This group was created as direct competition to the far more powerful Wyoming Stock Growers Association. The Northern Association would soon elect a leader: Nate Champion. That election put Nate in the cross hairs of the WSGA and their hired Texas gunmen. More on that below. See *Wyoming* by Nathaniel Burt. Compass American Guides Press, (1991) p. 159.

Chapter 21

Albert John Bothwell, a Wyoming ranch owner, had hired a range detective named George Henderson to patrol the range nearest his land. It was George Henderson who accused Ella Watson of rustling. Bothwell then directed Henderson and five others to go out and deal with the rustlers. It was as a result of this directive that Ella Watson and her residential mate, James Averell, were both hung. The lynching according to a historian was purely the result of cattlemen of the day being upset with a woman who claimed ownership to land, especially cattle land. The right of a woman to own land in the Wyoming Territory had only been granted in 1840 and still did not sit well with most males of the day and age in Wyoming's open range. See *The Tragedy of Cattle Kate* by Eliza McGraw, Smithsonian Magazine (March 2012).

Chapter 22

As in the story here, following the historical death of Ella Watson, arrests were made. Johnson Wyoming County Sheriff, Frank Hadsell, arrested six men after the lynching. A trial date was set. However, before the trial, threats were made to witnesses who were slated to testify against the accused. Several mysteriously disappeared, others left town. The jury foreman was involved in a shootout and disappeared. Averell's nephew, Ralph Cole, who was set to testify about Averell's lack of ranching, died on the first day of trial, apparently poisoned. The accused were never convicted.

Frank Canton did carry a gripsack during the Johnson County War. According to one source, the list contained some seventy names of homesteaders who were to ultimately be assassinated or run off. This startling fact found its way to the east coast newspapers. See *The New York Times* "To Kill Seventy Rustlers", April 23, 1892.

Gentry MacDonald was the actual Wyoming State Attorney General at the time, and State Senator Ronald Tisdale, State Water Commissioner W.J. Clarke, and ranchers William C. Irvine and Hubert Teshemacher were also real people. Each would become further involved in the actual historical war even while ostensibly carrying out their official elected or appointed duties.

Chapter 24

A total of fifty men rode out into Johnson County Wyoming to rid the open range of nesters. They were initially led by cattleman Frank Wolcott. However, later during the expedition, leadership was assumed by Frank Canton. The group consisted of 23 gunmen from Paris, Texas, who had been recruited by Canton. It also included Senator Tisdale, Commissioner Clarke, William C. Irvine, and Hubert Teshemacher, themselves large land holders. There were also a surgeon and two reporters, as mentioned here in the story. Ed Towse worked for the Cheyenne Sun and Sam T. Clover worked for the Chicago Herald. It was Clover who reported first-hand accounts in the eastern press of the grisly results of the excursion. See *"To Kill Seventy Rustlers"* The New York Times. April 23, 1892.

The Wolcott Regulators ("Invaders") who set out to remove nesters.

Chapter 25

The "Wolcott Regulators" as the rancher group called themselves, camped near the Kaycee Ranch owned by Nate Champion on the evening of April 8, 1892. They surrounded the ranch buildings before daybreak the next day. Nate Champion and his two hands apparently had two random travelers who stopped for the evening looking for shelter. Champion allowed them to stay in the house also. Those travelers did leave at the direction of the invaders just before the shooting started. The battle actually lasted for seven hours. Champion and his hands, Nick Ray, along with Reese Striker, held off a group of over fifty rifles far longer than the Regulators anticipated.

Jack Flagg was a neighboring settler. He drove up in a wagon during the attack, saw what was happening, and turned to flee. He was pursued by several of the invaders, but made his way to Buffalo, Wyoming, to alert the sheriff just as in the book. A large posse was raised and headed out after the invaders.

Nate Champion did keep a journal which was discovered by one of the newspaper reporters after his death. In that journal, Nate speaks of the two 'guests' who had stayed the night but rode off before the shooting started. Nate's actual journal had been started earlier in time than depicted in the story. The last entry as written in the story was published in the national papers. Sam T. Clover wrote a series of sensational articles describing the entire Johnson County escapade. Copies of Champion's journal made their way to several of the eastern newspapers. See Texas A & M Cushing Memorial Library collection on the Johnson County War. The final entry of Nate Campion's journal read exactly as indicated in the story.

Chapter 26

Upon hearing Jack Flagg's story, Buffalo Sheriff William "Red" Angus gathered a posse of over two hundred men to stop the invaders. Angus had regularly sided with the homesteaders. The numbers are hard to believe, but they have been confirmed from several sources over the years. See New York Times, *Trouble in Wyoming*. April 14, 1892.

Chapter 27

History is not clear on how many homesteaders were ousted by the invaders. But there were far more pushed out around Johnson County than the two or three mentioned here in the story.

Nate Champion was killed much like it is described in the story. His body was left with the sign as indicated. He had been a leader of the local homesteaders. All had looked up to him. The original accounts were all locally written at the direction or influence of the ranchers, and Nate was painted in a less than favorable light. But when the events broke as written by the eastern journalists, the story line changed dramatically. Nate became a veritable hero. Today, a larger-than-life statue stands in Buffalo, Wyoming, extolling the courage of the man who took a stand against the ranchers.

Photo of Nate Champion

Range War

Photo of Nate Champion Statue in Buffalo, WY

Chapter 28

Fort Churchill in Nevada had been deactivated before the dates of the story here. The actual fort that was involved in the Johnson County War was Fort McKinney. I have changed that reference to an actual Nevada fort, even if it was no longer in service at the time.

Chapter 29

The siege at the T.A. Ranch in Wyoming did take place. The ranch still survives to this day. Trenches were dug as described. The actual siege lasted four days until the military arrived.

Mike Shonsey was a real person. He was a member of the invaders and designated to contact the governor of Wyoming, Amos W. Barber. He had a history with Nate Champion such that Champion had accused Shonsey of being part of a group of cowhands that had raided his house some time before the shootout. Shonsey was said to have held a grudge against Champion because of the accusation.

Shonsey's exit from the T.A. Ranch was much more exciting than the path described in the book. He had remained with the group until after the shooting started. He had to slip "through the lines" in the dead of night before the horses had been shot (something that was done). He could have easily been shot at any point. But he made it through the posse's perimeter and got word to the governor.

Chapter 30

In the story, Dale Paris suggests that they shoot all the horses corralled by the ranchers. Will convinces Svensson and Paris to stampede them instead. At the true-life siege, the townspeople and posse did, in fact, shoot the entire herd of horses ridden by the ranchers and the Texas gunmen. It must have been a truly gruesome sight.

Chapter 31

The governor of Nevada in 1878 was Lewis R. Bradley who served until Jan. 6, 1879. Amos W. Barber of the story was the governor of Wyoming in 1892 which is the year the events of the siege at the T.A. Ranch took place. I have obviously moved Gov. Barber from the state of Wyoming to Nevada. It was Amos Barber that Mike Shonsey met, and it was Barber who, in turn, wired President Harrison. It should also be mentioned that the actual U.S. President at the time this story takes place was Rutherford B. Hayes. But it was Harrison who actually took the wire from Gov. Barber in 1892, so I have transposed the presidential line to fit the story.

It is unknown what arguments Mike Shonsey used to convince Barber to wire the president. But Barber did send the wire. Copies have survived. It read:

About sixty-one owners of livestock are reported to have made an armed expedition into Johnson County for the purpose of protecting their livestock and preventing unlawful roundups by rustlers. They are at 'T.A.' Ranch, thirteen miles from Fort McKinney, and are besieged by Sheriff and posse and by rustlers from that section of the country, said to

Range War

be two or three hundred in number. The wagons of stockmen were captured and taken away from them and it is reported a battle took place yesterday, during which a number of men were killed. Great excitement prevails. Both parties are very determined and it is feared that if successful will show no mercy to the persons captured. The civil authorities are unable to prevent violence. The situation is serious and immediate assistance will probably prevent great loss of life.

Harrison wired instructions the next day to Fort McKinney for the commander to end the standoff and bloodshed. The order was issued by U.S. Secretary of War, Stephen B. Elkins, pursuant to Article IV, Section 4, Clause 2 of the U.S. Constitution allowing for use of U.S. forces on domestic ground for "protections from invasion and domestic violence." The Sixth Cavalry was dispatched. See the *N.Y. Times* article of "No Title" dated April 14, 1892. More on that below.

A picture reputed to be of the 6th Cavalry at the T.A. Ranch

Chapter 32

The posse sent out after the Wyoming Stockgrowers did have a bullet-proof siege wagon built on short notice by a blacksmith in a nearby town. I was not able to uncover any specific description or specifications. The "design" of the siege wagon in the story is a creation of my own imagination.

Chapter 34

The men who had ridden out as part of the invaders were incarcerated at Fort D.A. Russell. Originally, the captives were to be kept at Fort McKinney. The prisoners were allowed to roam around Fort Russell without direct supervision as long as they did not get in the way. Johnson County folks did not like the soft treatment. They were under the impression the group was to be held at Fort McKinney, which would have been closer. The army wanted to keep the prisoners as far away as possible to do what they could to cool tempers. But the army also knew they did not have the resources nor the finances to feed and house such a large group for any extended period of time.

Ultimately, all the well-to-do landowners were set free. They were not even indicted. Charges were never even filed. This was despite an investigation by Johnson County officials that uncovered documents from Frank Canton's gripsack containing a list of seventy "rustlers" who were to be shot or hanged. The gripsack documents also contained a menu of payments that were to be made to Canton and his men for their daily fees as well as a fifty-dollar bounty for each person killed. See *Johnson County War* Wyoming Tails and Trails, January 6, 2004.

The Texas gunmen were also set free. That included Frank Canton. Despite his past, which included cattle rustling, bank robbery, and the shooting of a U.S. soldier, Frank Canton left Wyoming following his release from Fort Russell and headed to Oklahoma where he became a U.S. marshal. In his new life in Oklahoma, he is reputed to have assisted the legendary lawman Bill Tilghman track down Bill and John Shelly.

Born Josiah Horner, Canton confessed later in life to his previous years as an outlaw, but was pardoned by the Governor of Texas, which is where the crimes were committed. See Joe Horner (aka Frank Canton) *The Encyclopedia of Lawmen, Outlaws, and Gunfighters*, by Leon Claire Metz. Infobase Publishing. 2003, p. 122.

Canton died in 1927, obviously not shot by Will Toal. While Frank Canton appears to have devoted his later life to a proper administration of justice, and though he was pardoned for the crimes he had committed early in his life while in Texas, he never paid for the events which took place in Johnson County, Wyoming.

About the Author

J.L. Crafts was raised on the outskirts of a very large city in Southern California. Thankfully, back in those days the very distant outskirts of that city still included open spaces and small ranches. As a young boy he worked wrangling horses on one of those ranches learning to rope, ride and train one of the most magnificent animals our planet has to offer. Those early years created a lifelong connection with, not only horses, but with the west of the 1800's. College led to law school followed by over thirty years of trying cases to juries up and down the state of California. Speaking to juries in a simple directness, he did what he could to elicit facts and arguments wherever possible through stories of life in the saddle and open spaces. He now spends his days creating those stories on the page and enjoys every minute of it.

Coming Soon!

J.L. CRAFTS

TAHOE DESTINY
WILL TOAL SERIES

Will Toal's cattle are dying of thirst. A prolonged drought has put not only his herd, but the herds of the entire Carson Valley in jeopardy. He decides to move his stock and the herds of his fellow southern ranchers to his northern ranch where mountain grasses are still succored by the flow of the Truckee River. The Truckee flows from beautiful Lake Tahoe leaving the lake in the confines of California but then flowing east into Nevada.

The move north to save his herd lands Will right in the middle of a brewing battle over the Tahoe's water. The building feud originated with John C. Freemont's mistaken decision to split Tahoe in half with the state line running almost down the middle. California and Nevada don't see eye to eye on the use of the Lady of the Lakes' waters . . .

For more information
visit: www.SpeakingVolumes.us

Now Available!

J.L. CRAFTS
WILL TOAL SERIES

**For more information
visit: www.SpeakingVolumes.us**

Now Available!

W.R. PARK
THE SHADOW MASTER SERIES

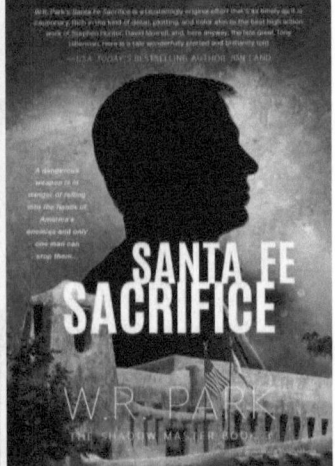

**For more information
visit: www.SpeakingVolumes.us**

Now Available!

AWARD-WINNING AUTHOR
R.G. YOHO
ACTION/ADVENTURE WESTERNS

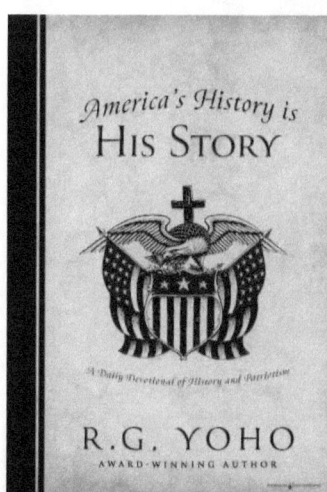
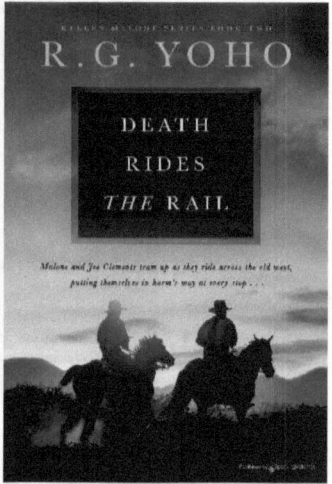
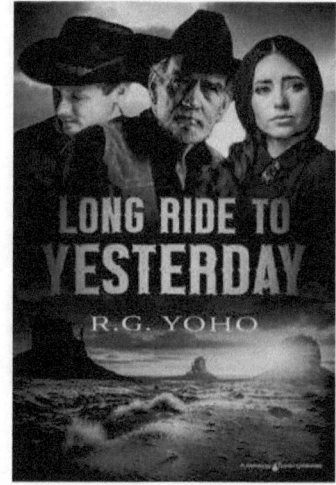
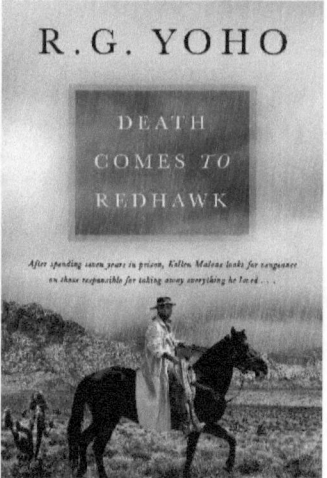

**For more information
visit:** www.SpeakingVolumes.us

Now Available!

AWARD-WINNING AUTHOR
GEORGE T. ARNOLD

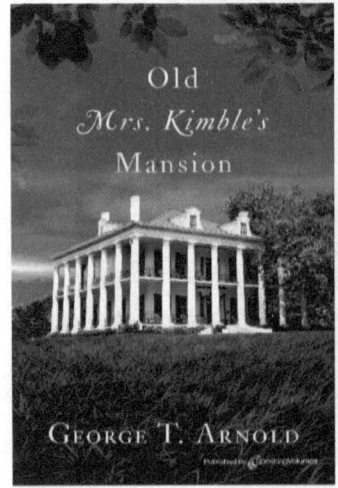

**For more information
visit: www.SpeakingVolumes.us**

www.ingramcontent.com/pod-product-compliance
Lightning Source LLC
LaVergne TN
LVHW091623070526
838199LV00044B/917